Greenside

Glenn Burwell

Published by arrangement with Somewhat Grumpy Press Inc. Halifax, Nova Scotia, Canada. SomewhatGrumpyPress.com
The Somewhat Grumpy Press name and Pallas' cat logo are registered trademarks.

ISBN 978-1-7387998-7-9 (paperback)

ISBN 978-1-7387998-8-6 (eBook)

November 2023 v3

Acknowledgements

M any thanks are due to my editors, Dorothyanne Brown and Tim Covell, and my unofficial editor, Susan McKenzie. Dorothyanne and Tim have been very patient while I try to figure out the ins and outs of writing and I owe them a great deal. Susan has a special talent for spotting missing things that no one else seems to notice. Thanks also go to friends for their continued support, particularly in the early days. Lastly, I want to thank my wife, Corrine, whose mastery of food makes our life very happy indeed.

Cast of Characters

Team
Robert Lui.....Private Investigator
Sophie and Robin Lui.....children of Robert
Ethan and Mary Lui.....Robert's parents
Rose Esmeraldo.....Sophie's friend

Politicians, Project Team & Others
Stanley Dunbar.....Mayor of Vancouver (Eco Party)
Kristian Axness.....Mayor of Oslo
Nile Gecko...Councillor (Eco Party)
Mamie...Accounts Senior Administrator, City of Vancouver
Arby Knutson...Site Superintendent at Greenside
Jean Kwok...Planner, City of Vancouver
George Ascot...Lawyer, City of Vancouver
Dan Prudence...BC Coastal Insurance Co. Claims Manager
Ken Jalla...Sun Energy (hydrogen suppliers)
Chopper...Ken Jalla's lawyer
Chas / Charles Burrows...Liquid Metal pipefitter at Greenside
Roy...arms supplier
Bernard Lily...reporter

Gilberto...Cafe Paulo owner

Carmelita...barrista

Siegfried Damler...trainer & free agent

Chip Diamond...Assistant Deputy Minister, Municipal Affairs
and Housing

Vancouver Police Department

Thomas Harrow...Head of Investigations, Ex Taskforce Lead

Caleb Woo...Chief Constable

David McKnight...Deputy Chief - Investigation Division

Steve Christie...Superintendent - Investigative Services

Ranit...Assistant to the Chiefs

Camille Laurent...Detective

Rodney Fister...Sergeant Detective

Tony Bortolo...Detective Constable

Vito Cotoni...Detective Constable

Finn Black...Detective Constable

Norma van Kleet...Admin for Tom Harrow

Two Tigers Gang

Manny Dhillon...leader

Bobbi Atwal

Safa Atwal...sister of Bobbi (not in gang)

Paneet

Ho Li-Fan...former Wide Bay Boy

Edward Su...leader of The Wide Bay Boys (Vancouver)

Sometimes organized crime
isn't that organized.

CHAPTER 1

The conference facilities were huge, and far from central Oslo. Nile Gecko, senior ranking councillor for the Eco Party representing Vancouver, British Columbia, stood outside the main hall in Stokke, Norway. He shook his head at this major gaffe in siting. How were visitors to the famous Norwegian capital supposed to sample the pleasures of downtown Oslo when it was so far away? At least his city had the good sense to develop their newest convention centre smack in the middle of downtown Vancouver, right on the water's edge with the million-dollar view of the North Shore mountains. Not that the city really had much to say about the matter. More senior levels of government were the ones ponying up the money, with a national railroad company owning the land.

Standing next to Nile was Vancouver's mayor, Stanley Dunbar. Stanley looked bookish, greying hair kept short, eyes close together behind blue-framed spectacles, with a thin set of lips. He gathered his small group of city councillors close before entering the large lobby, searching for more coffee to help keep them all sharpish in anticipation of the day to come.

Groups from across the world were in attendance, and for many of the delegates, their first time in Norway. The conference topic centred on municipalities, not countries, explaining the number of mayors in attendance. The focus was on sustainability for cities in the twenty-first century. Only world-class city delegations had been invited. Cities such as Pocatello, Idaho, or even Minsk in Belarus were still looking for their invitations in the mail, email, or wherever people looked for acknowledgement of their existence.

Urban centres are mostly at the mercy of higher levels of government, their levers of influence usually few and feeble. The conference was trying to be positive; focusing on what cities could manipulate, handwringing absent about what they couldn't affect. The lead-off subject for the morning's session would be energy use in cities, and the first speaker was Stanley Dunbar. Five senior civic representatives lounged on couches around centre stage, looking very casual, as though the group were visiting a fishing lodge and on top of the world. A moderator sat at one end, also on a couch, a low table covered with water bottles and snacks within easy reach. A few of the delegates thought all the plastic water bottles a little rich, considering the supposed theme of the conference. The remainder either didn't notice or didn't care.

Nile Gecko and his fellow councillors from Vancouver were in the large audience. Only those who were a member of the City of Vancouver's governing Eco Party were on the trip to Norway, helping the stated aspirations of the mayor to make his town the greenest city in the world, as if a hundred other world cities weren't trying to claim the same thing. Nile found the hubris hard to take, although the all-expense paid trip to Oslo funded by Vancouver taxpayers soothed his feelings very nicely thank you.

He supposed that Stanley would be his usual self once on stage. He had a big mouth, and it was about to go on full display.

The moderator started with introductions in front of the crowd of some three thousand delegates and onlookers, then looked at Stanley to kick off the proceedings. Stanley started with his 'greenest city in the world' malarkey for about five minutes before launching in on his pet baby, Vancouver's latest residential project, called GreenSide. Large screens on either side of the stage showed Stanley's face with translations for those not conversant with English.

"Our flagship project stands at some eighty thousand square metres and is located adjacent to Vancouver's beautiful Queen Elizabeth Park. I am talking about this today because of the novel power generation system that I brokered specifically for the project. And that system is based on hydrogen."

Several hundred of the younger delegates were listening intently, eyes glistening. It was as if they were witness to a miracle being harnessed for the good of Mother Earth. Some were making notes on their tablets.

What a yutz, Nile thought to himself. As if the mayor could have brokered anything remotely important.

A few nearby delegates were talking quietly amongst themselves. "Did he say hydrogen?" They were puzzled. A couple were shaking their heads, knowing how energy intensive it was just to come up with a supply of hydrogen. How would that work economically? Does he realize how unstable that system could be with improper handling?

Meanwhile, Stanley was just getting warmed up. "Our city has been mandating district energy systems that larger residential and commercial projects can build for themselves, reducing reliance on traditional energy sources, thus lowering our greenhouse emissions as a city. If the energy systems are robust enough, other adjacent developments can tap into them, for a price, of course. Despite the traditional developer's objections, we no longer permit the use of natural gas in their new developments within the City of Vancouver."

"Did he say no natural gas? Chefs aren't going to like that." Some delegates seemed to have trouble following the mayor's logic. The younger ones weren't troubled. A few of them were yelling out, encouraging the mayor, like he was some kind of nerdy rock star. All they could see was an immediate future, absent fossil fuels, with little understanding or care for how they were clothed and fed and how the world's economy functioned.

"Our modest project is well under construction, with a couple of the rental buildings geared to lower-income families about to receive their occupancy permits. This fulfills our promise to the people of Vancouver that we can build affordable housing that is sustainable as well." Some cheers came from the back of the hall.

'More like a putz,' thought Nile. As if the distinction was even important. He had no respect for his mayor, and this conference wasn't changing his opinion. Cities couldn't afford to build affordable housing by themselves. Again, higher levels of government were needed.

Stanley continued, his eyes sparkling, "As you know, when hydrogen is combined with oxygen, electricity and heat is generated, with water as a by-product. And hydrogen is inexhaustible in the universe." The mayor was giving the assembly a basic chemistry lesson, whether they wanted one or not. Younger delegates were all ears. The older ones knew that chemistry wasn't the issue, economics was, as in, could one use hydrogen as a fuel source and not bankrupt someone, or something, like a city?

"We expect GreenSide to be a model for the world to follow as we save our small planet. I will be happy to discuss the project with anyone interested after this round table is concluded."

Nile's eyes were rolling around so much it was hurting his head. However, in the company of the other Eco Party delegates, he kept his thoughts to himself. He smiled as he clapped politely with the rest of the audience. After Stanley had been all he could be, the moderator let the other mayors have their turn. Each mayor had a different tale to relate as to their cities' energy sources and infrastructure, but no one else was touting hydrogen. Stanley Dunbar's story was unique at this conference.

One of the participants on stage was the mayor of Oslo, so really, the host politician. After the round table concluded, he walked over and introduced himself. "Welcome to Norway. That was an inspiring presentation, Stanley. My name is Kristian Axness of the Blue Party." Kristian tended to portly, but with a thin, long face sporting horn-rimmed glasses, looked more like a plump, well-dressed goat than a politician.

"Thank you, Kristian, you are too kind."

"What are you doing after the conference today?"

"Trying out the pleasures of Stokke again, I believe."

Kristian laughed at the thought of this. "I think it might be better if you accompanied me back to Oslo for the evening. I can show you around, if it is possible for you to get away from your group?"

"I'd like that. Stokke's offerings are frankly getting slightly old."

"They were never very new to begin with. We shall see what kind of trouble we can get into this evening. We'll leave here in about an hour. My assistant will come to find you."

Stanley dropped down to the floor where the lowly delegates sat, meandering over to his group of councillors, accepting plaudits along the way. While some of the Eco Party faithful congratulated the mayor, Nile remained silent, knowing that Stanley would end up at his side. He didn't do much without Nile's advice. He finally came up to Nile and let slip his plans for the evening. Nile shook his head. "Think I'll tag along if it's all the same to you."

Stanley looked flummoxed, not sure if Kristan's invite was inclusive of others. For a politician, he had very little knowledge of proper etiquette, which Nile was aware of, often using it to his advantage.

An hour later, Kristian and his assistant made their way over to fetch Stanley for the ride back to Oslo. "Ready to go?"

"Can I bring along my friend Nile? He is a councillor." Stanley answered. Nile chuckled inwardly as he waited for the response. He knew that Kristian could hardly refuse this little *faux pas*.

Kristian smiled, "Sure. More the merrier." Inwardly he was now regretting the invite, but who knew how awkward these North Americans were. He needed better briefings from his staff next time, that was certain.

"Follow me." He strode off towards the rear of the stage area, threading his way through the back of the house, eventually exiting outside to a parking lot where a driver was waiting in a Mercedes SUV. All four piled in. "We're going to a restaurant named Fjord. Don't worry, it's not in a fjord, ha ha. Hope you enjoy seafood."

Nile looked up at Kristian in the front seat, wondering what he was getting himself into. Was this guy as big a goof as Stanley? Seeing as how Kristian had gravitated towards Stanley told Nile everything he probably needed to know. After an hour of driving and some idle chatting, they entered the centre of Oslo.

"Here we are." The SUV had pulled up in front of the restaurant on Kristian Augusts Gate.

"Hey Kristian, is this your street?" Stanley trying to be the comedian.

"Sadly, no. Named after some old Danish prince, I think. Let's go people." They exited the car and walked into the restaurant, Kristian leading the way to the bar. The first thing Nile noticed were the wonky light fixtures fashioned out of antler horns over the bar. The second were the shots of aquavit that miraculously appeared in front of the group. If this was how they were starting the evening, then he could only pray for survival. They sat in a line at the bar and sampled the aquavit. After the second flight appeared, Kristian started in on telling jokes, Stanley laughing too loudly. Nile remained mystified by the Norwegian humour, watching as Stanley worked hard at being a good guest. After a half hour of this, a host led the four to their table, where they perused the menu. Monkfish and hake dinners were ordered, with some oysters to begin.

"So, Nile, how did you come to meet up with Stanley?" Kristian led off the dinner conversation as they waited for the starters.

"I was tired of the direction the governing party was taking Vancouver, and thought I'd give civic politics a try. Previously, I had dabbled in development. The mayor graciously took me under his wing. We met at a community action weekend."

"Ah yes, community action—where fires are kindled, no?"

"I guess." Nile was already feeling rocky, hoping his words weren't being slurred.

"And the hydrogen thing? Very unusual for a city to pursue, yes?"

This was the last thing Nile wanted to talk about. "Stanley brokered a great deal for the city, so we should be in excellent shape moving forward." It was unusual for Nile to lie so blatantly, but he could tell that Stanley was already losing the thread of the conversation, so he felt on safe ground.

The food was excellent, helped down by several white Burgundies hailing from Meursault. After the remains were cleared off, dessert in the form of a Norwegian cheese plate was brought to the table. Naturally, some more aquavit accompanied the offering and after further talk about Kristian possibly visiting Vancouver, Kristian changed gears.

"Let us go to a club I know. It's not very far away. We can walk." His assistant seemed to perk up at this idea. She had been quiet throughout the dinner, letting Kristian take the stage. Short auburn hair with sharp spikes framed a young, eager face.

Nile's antennae immediately came awake. He sensed both danger, and just perhaps, an opportunity. Stanley was grinning stupidly and having a grand time, the liquor having done its job.

Kristian's assistant paid the bill for the table, then excused herself to go to the ladies room. Nile had a suspicion she knew what was coming but stayed quiet. After she returned, the four sauntered down the street as daylight dimmed, streetlights coming alive. It was early spring, tourists scarce, but there seemed to be a fair number of local citizens enjoying the temperate air. They came upon a small lineup of younger people on the sidewalk waiting beside an entry. A couple of largish blond-haired minders dressed entirely in black watched over the line. Kristian walked up to one of them, produced a card, and was pointed to the door. On the wall beside the door was a small oval sign, *Club Otta*. Nile would try his best to remember the name.

After negotiating a long hallway, they opened a second door and walked into a wall of techno music of distinctly Nordic origin; the thud thud thud of the bass grinding a hole through Nile's brain. Flashing lights synched to the sounds reinforced the out-of-body experience. On reflection, Nile also blamed the aquavit. The place looked to be full, mostly people younger than their small group. As they were led to some seats, the music changed to something that ABBA might have had something to do with, the pounding beat relentless. Unsurprisingly, another round of aquavit appeared on the low table. Nile was starting to relax again. Perhaps he had been hasty in his judgment about the evening. Kristian and Stanley were yapping happily to each other, although Nile didn't know how they could hear anything the other was saying. Because of the music, Nile didn't try to converse with anyone. He also didn't want to let on how drunk he was feeling.

A half hour went by, then another tall, blond gentleman in a tight olive coloured suit worked his way over to Kristian, bent down and whispered in his ear. Kristian grinned, struggled to his feet, and beckoned for Stanley and Nile to follow. Nile knew the evening had just changed. They walked down a short corridor and entered a smaller room where the light was dimmer, but the sounds of techno music still pounded in. Furniture consisted of three low leather couches with some coffee tables, as well as side tables against the wall with more booze and what looked suspiciously like lines of some drug. The four hadn't been sitting drinking beer for more than five minutes when the door opened again, and four young women entered. Or, as Nile reckoned, more like teenagers. Mr. Olive Suit had left the room. The girls didn't look much older than sixteen, as if they had just arrived from some sassy private school dressed in very short skirts. They wandered over to the table by the wall and leaned over to put their miniature purses against the back of the table, revealing in the process that they were wearing no underwear. Nile nearly spit up his beer at the sight.

Geez, thought Nile, talk about a honey trap; they were already halfway stuck in it, as he tried to tear his eyes away from what he was seeing. He was kicking himself for not acting sooner on his suspicions. Kristian's assistant seemed to have a laser focus on one of the girls, like a lioness readying for the kill. He didn't know why he had assumed that this wouldn't happen because she had joined them. Actually, even in his haze, he did know. It was called pre-judging, and now his mistake had stuck him in this potential mess. He knew damned well that photos were probably already being taken of the group. There was no evidence—he just felt in his bones that this was happening because politicians were involved. No way was he going to stay. He still had a family back in Vancouver, which he kind of wanted to keep if he could. One of the girls had already unbuttoned her top, breasts on full display, and was sitting down beside Stanley, who still had an idiotic grin plastered on his face. Nile looked at the faces of the girls. No one was smiling. He sensed they were not in the room of their own volition.

"I have to visit the men's room." was Nile's best gambit to extricate himself. He stood up and wobbled slightly.

"Don't be long, or I'll entertain your girl as well." Stanley at least could talk. What else he could do would be left in the hands of experts. As Nile left the room, he looked back. The blond sitting next to the mayor already had his pants open and down around his ankles, wasting no time in preparations for the incriminating photos to come.

Nile looked at Mr. Olive, who was standing guard outside the door. "Men's room?"

He followed the pointing finger, looking for a way out of the club as he went. Since he had no clue about the back of house layout, he decided his best route was the way they had entered. Once on the street, he quickly hailed a cab, stumbling as he pried himself into the rear seat and asked to be driven back to Stokke.

The next morning was a struggle for Nile to even get out of bed, let alone walk to the shower. God damn aquavit was all he could think. After showering and fortifying himself with some pills, he dressed and went down to the cafe in the hotel to get something to line his stomach. With some strong coffee and feeling slightly more human, he went back upstairs to see if his highness, Stanley, had returned from his night in Oslo. After hammering on the mayor's door for a minute, he heard a croaking sound, but that was it, nothing else. He decided to leave the mayor and head out back to the conference. As far as Nile was concerned, it turned out to be another boring day, but the interesting part was seeing Kristian Axness looking sharp, as though he had spent the evening in bed at home. There were obviously degrees of alcoholism that Nile was unfamiliar with.

After lunch, Kristian came up to Nile to check on him. "Last night too much for you, Nile? You really missed a treat. Those women had special skills that I think you would have enjoyed."

I bet, thought Nile. And calling them women was a laugh, more like young teenagers. "Too much aquavit Kristian. I'm impressed with your tolerance for it."

"Perhaps another time then, Nile. Enjoy the remainder of your stay in Norway."

"Thanks, maybe we'll see you in Vancouver."

There was no sign of Vancouver's mayor for the rest of the day at the conference. Nile didn't see Stanley until the next morning when the Eco Party entourage was checking out for their long journey home. When pressed, Stanley admitted that he couldn't remember very much from their evening out. To his credit, he still had a faintly amused grin on his face. Nile shook his head, pretty sure that at some point in the future, a reminder would make its way into Stanley's life.

Chapter 2

M anny Dhillon had been a busy man the last few months. He had taken over a criminal organization based in the City of Surrey called the Gupils. As a suburb of Vancouver and British Columbia's second largest city, it had been taking on big city characteristics and problems—gangs being a very public example of this. After the Gupil's leader had been unexpectedly killed during an altercation with police officers, the gang was left headless. As the most intelligent member, as well as being the largest and scariest looking, Manny naturally gravitated to the top of a short ladder to take charge. He sported dreadlocks atop a body of some three hundred and thirty pounds. Manny had done some horrific things as a gang member; some at the bidding of his late boss, some on his own initiative, all part of the process that kept people in line and money filling the coffers. To date, not a single police force in the Lower Mainland had managed to attach any specific crime to his name, and it was a record Manny wished to continue.

His study of the situation the Gupils were left in indicated that changes needed to be made. He had taken his time with this review, something the other gang members found disconcerting.

After finding some ledgers in the locked desk of his former leader, Manny unwrapped the location of the group's funds and holdings and was surprised at first at how extensive they were. The previous head man had been hiding some things from the rank and file. After further thought, he understood why that would be, and knew he'd be doing much the same. It meant he could draw on these funds for a time while the re-make was underway. Included in the stash were deeds to a few properties around the Lower Mainland that the former leader had purchased to clean money.

The first thing to go would be the gang's name. One meaning of the word Gupil was 'secret'. Manny was certain that the secret was out after the death of its leader. He called one of the members into his office. "Bobbi, we need to change our name. Got any ideas? I want something menacing."

Bobbi Atwal had always disliked the gang's previous name and had already been mulling options. "I have a few ideas, but how about Two Tigers? It'll reference some Sikh warrior history."

Manny stared at Bobbi. "You know about stuff like that?"

"Yes."

"Okay, Two Tigers it is. I like it."

After looking at his roster, the next thing he worked on was a personnel overhaul. He cut loose a couple of dim-witted members, deciding that some minimum standards should apply, not unlike any corporation doing business in the Lower Mainland. He didn't have these people killed, figuring that their stupidity would eventually do that for him. Next, he struck off the members who were recently deceased, incarcerated, or who were unlikely to walk again due to gunplay gone wrong. This whittled the list down some more. A member named Maccha Sunner had not come out of his coma prior to passing away a few weeks earlier. Manny had sort of forgotten that he was the man responsible for the coma in the first place. He shrugged. One less piece of deadwood to deal with. After the honing down process, he decided he now needed a few new members to round out his team.

First, though, a promotion was in order for Bobbi Atwal, a long-time member. Bobbi had been the only other Gupil member at that last fateful meeting in Steveston where the previous leader had met his demise, and he had come out unscathed. Not that he hadn't been tagged and charged, but after a few months, the charges were dropped, and Bobbi released from remand. Manny thought this to be an indication of leadership material. For once, Manny didn't consider other alternatives, such as whether Bobbi had made some kind of deal with the authorities to dodge possible jail time.

After Bobbi had come up with the new gang name, Manny decided the time was ripe. "I'm promoting you. You'll be my assistant—second in command."

Bobbi was speechless. He lamely smiled, not wanting to offend Manny.

"Sounds great. Thanks!"

"We need some more people. Any ideas?"

"What about your younger brother?"

"No."

"Why? Doesn't your older brother get us guns from Seattle?"

"Different. My younger brother has a few problems. He's nuts."

"Oh. How about the remains of the Wide Bay Boys?" Bobbi suggested.

The triad had been decimated by the events of the previous spring. Based in Richmond, an adjacent suburb to Surrey, they had hired the Gupils to do some of their dirty work. Their Vancouver leader, Edward Su, sat in remand awaiting charges of attempted murder and kidnapping, so his prospects looked dim. Edward's second in command had managed to get himself drowned in the Fraser River, leaving only a few triad men who had not participated in that final meeting in Steveston.

"Okay. Try that Ho Li-Fan. He just came over from Hong Kong. You'll have to find him first. Maybe he could lead you to a couple of the others." Bobbi nodded and left to check his contacts about where Li-Fan might be hiding.

After proclaiming his tourist status, Li-Fan somehow had managed to get free on bail and promptly gone underground, forfeiting the bail surety. After Bobbi found him, it didn't take long for an affirmative answer to come back. Li-Fan was enchanted by Vancouver, and thrilled to stay even if he had to keep his head low. Whether he would also be enamoured with Surrey remained to be seen. Manny didn't know how long the honeymoon would last, but he snapped him up. The Gupil's crew had originally been primarily from the Punjab, but Manny was diversifying things. As long as communications were clear and everyone knew who was running things, he didn't care where his gang members hailed from.

Manny's next area of concern was economic diversification, sometimes associated with money laundering. It was definitely that, but also more. He wanted his fingers in different pies, much like any normal company, so that if one aspect wasn't doing well, the other parts could pick up the slack. Their core business to this point had been running drugs, like most of the other gangs. He knew that the Wide Bay Boys had done something the Gupils had no clue how to do, that is, plant moles into the government apparatus. He found out that they had someone on the inside of the Gaming and Enforcement portfolio over in Victoria, but he didn't know who that was until recently. The person in government had actually contacted Manny, asking if he could be of help. Manny was surprised and initially couldn't believe his good luck. After some thinking, he realized that with Edward out of action, the money flow to Victoria had stopped. The government mole was so used to the extra money that his lifestyle was impacted by the lack of it. Manny also made overtures to a young constable working out of the Surrey Police detachment.

In addition to the drug business his gang was built upon, Manny's expansion ideas included gun running, dabbling in construction, and procuring boys and girls for those whose sexual tastes ran to this. He decided to call these avenues departments, liking the sound of it. One other avenue he wanted to explore was computer crime, but he really had no idea how to go about this. So, for the time being, he'd concentrate on the other areas while keeping his eyes open for a computer whiz who wouldn't mind getting his fingers dirty.

His last expansion target was the development industry. It was a perfect way to launder money, as well as get some legal business going, which was his real end goal: becoming legitimate. Manny had an acquaintance who ran a sizable outfit called the Bamboo Construction Company, so he contacted him to see how he could be of assistance. The president of Bamboo wasn't all that keen to have Manny involved in anything, but Manny's assistance in ironing out some problems with a stubborn subcontractor left him feeling indebted. Development in Vancouver had generally been on a tear ever since 1986's World's Fair except for a couple of down years, so it seemed like a good place to invest some money. Manny didn't know much about the development industry, so couldn't appreciate the risk and hazards involved for even the best developers, nor did he really care. From his outsider's perspective, it looked like a lot of people were making gobs of money, so why shouldn't he?

While Manny was busy changing and building things, Robert Lui was tearing things down. Not so actively busy, more like decomposing from disinterest. Robert had been a senior detective with the Vancouver Police Department, then joined the anti-gang task force set up to combat gang activity in Vancouver and its adjacent suburbs. While he was regarded as a top detective, his work on the task force had been sometimes outside the general officer's rulebook. The Gupils kidnapped his son a year earlier at the bidding of the Wide Bay Boys. Robert hadn't been allowed to be near the case, but that didn't stop him from tapping his friends in the investigation to keep abreast of what was happening. Robert felt justified in his subsequent actions, and he wouldn't have changed anything that he had done to successfully retrieve his son. However, senior management held a differing view. It was the Deputy Chief of Police, David McKnight, who made the decision for Thomas Harrow, head of the task force.

Thomas made the call, "Hello, Robert, it's Thomas. I have some news. Not the good type, I am afraid. I've been told to let you go. I'm sorry about this, Robert."

"Oh. Not unexpected, I guess, but it's taken a while."

"Nothing happens quickly around here. You know that. I did my best for a decent severance package, which should be heading your way shortly. I don't know what else to say, Robert. Best of luck with your next endeavours."

"It was good working with you, Thomas."

"Forget that crap about luck. If you need anything from me, anything at all, just call, okay?"

"Roger." He hung up. Depression set in.

After the decision was rendered, Robert promptly invested some of his newfound wealth in whisky bottles from several countries. What had become a general attachment to alcohol born from the pressures of his work evolved into a genuine love for it. As he spent more time thinking about the last couple of years, self-pity was becoming ever-present, particularly when he was drinking. First his wife had passed away, then his son had been kidnapped, now he had lost his job, which, to be frank, he kind of liked. Were the gods frowning on him for some unknown transgression? He could not come up with any reasonable explanation for this run of bad luck, but he knew what smoothed things out—whisky.

Robert's live-in girlfriend, Detective Camille Laurent, quickly tired of Robert's malaise. She had kept her job while Robert had been let go. But just because she kept her job did not mean she was enjoying it. The senior detective in her office, Rodney Fister, marginally more proficient than a traffic cop, was making her work life miserable. When life at work is not going well, one can usually rely on home life to provide some counterbalance. Camille made a decision that she wouldn't have dreamed about six months earlier.

She was going to leave Robert and head back to Montreal, where she hailed from, leaving *les maudit anglais* to their own devices. She was done with Vancouver. The attachment she had for Robert couldn't be labelled love for the last few months, and she finally admitted to herself that trying to be a mother to his two teenage children was beyond her skills. She was no longer even sure that she wanted her own children.

After being discharged, Robert made little attempt to acquire other employment. He instead felt that his real job was to protect his daughter and son from the predations of gangs. It didn't occur to him that his lack of employment by any law enforcement agency rendered this need debatable. His children started to consider his concern extremely overbearing. They also noticed the drop-off in domestic bliss. The house seemed to be dirtier than it had ever been, and Robert's cooking had tailed off. Instead, he was relying on frozen items and ordering in food that formerly, Robert would never have touched, or fed to his children. The kids felt like they were living in some kind of bad television drama where the parents hated each other, and the household falls apart. Robert's daughter, Sophie, was able to confide in her close friend Rose, but even Rose had no real answers for her.

Chapter 3

Robert tried to keep an eye on his children as they walked home from school for a few days running. These antics were brought up at that evening's dinner by Sophie, who, at seventeen, was starting to feel quite grown up. Camille was nowhere to be seen, apparently working late on a case, an increasingly used excuse of late. Robert had no idea if Camille was really working or avoiding home life.

"We are not little children any longer, Dad. What you are doing is embarrassing us." Sophie opened with the obvious, Robin holding back for now, waiting to see where this would lead. She had recently expressed an interest in becoming a city planner, a career that her deceased mother had been very good at, so Robert knew beyond a doubt that his daughter was spreading her wings. His son had also started some kind of life direction, first signing up for, then excelling at a welding program that his high school offered.

"I know, I know," Robert responded, as they dug into a previously frozen chicken dinner. He was half blitzed from the wine consumed during the food preparation, so he vaguely realized he should choose his words carefully. "It's just that there are a lot of bad people out there."

"Isn't that kind of cynical?"

Where did his kids learn these words? Robert thought. The sentiment probably was cynical, but this seemed to be where his last employment as a detective had left him. "It may be cynical, but it is also true. I'm just trying to protect you both. I didn't do a very good job last time."

"Past is past, Dad. No one at school is pestering us about gangs anymore. Leave us alone. We're fine." She looked over at Robin while continuing to eat, her eyes daring him to say anything different. Robin wisely decided not to add anything to the conversation, concentrating instead on finding some enjoyment in the chicken left on his plate.

Robert didn't respond, instead pouring himself the remains of the white wine that had come from the Naramata Bench in the Okanagan Valley. Perhaps his children really didn't need him anymore. He was having a hard time wrapping his head around that one. Maybe Camille could help him out. Where was she, anyway? The kids excused themselves, leaving the mess on the table for Robert to attend to. He sat for a bit before heading to the whisky cabinet, pouring himself a decent shot of a twelve-year-old from Speyside in Scotland. The cabinet was full, Robert feeling it was only appropriate to spread out a bit; whiskies from Scotland, Ireland, Japan, Wales, and one regretfully from Canada made up his collection. He went to the fridge and added a small cube of ice, stumbling back to the couch in the area beside the dining table. He had fallen for Camille partly because she was somewhat of an outsider on a police force that was still dominated by white

English-speaking men. Being half-Chinese himself didn't endear him to some of the officers, so apart from the physical attraction he felt for Camille, a communal bond had developed between the two as they waged their war against prejudice and stupidity. The bond had snapped when Robert was let go, and the physical lovemaking didn't seem to be rescuing the relationship, particularly when Robert would prematurely pass out from whichever mix of alcohols had been fuelling the evening.

After half past nine, Camille walked through the door to see the dinner remains still firmly in place on the table and kitchen counter. She had not been working, but had been at a small cafe, having a few drinks to help fortify her decision to leave. Robert had poured himself a second larger shot, trying to make sense of why his life had come so unravelled. At some point, he had lapsed into unconsciousness.

Camille stood looking at the mess. "Robert, I'm home. But I have some news. My mother is ill, and I am flying back to Montreal tomorrow to be with her."

Robert roused himself. "What did you say?" He tried to focus his eyes on Camille.

"I am going back to Montreal tomorrow." No further mention of her mother.

Even in his haze, Robert knew the lie for what it was, a way to bring an end to their relationship. He waved his hand at nothing in particular, watching as Camille turned and went upstairs.

Half an hour later, she came down the stairs with two suitcases. "My flight is early in the morning, so I am going to stay at the airport hotel tonight. I've just called a cab." She stood there, waiting.

"I can drive you at least," Robert managed lamely, from his prone position on the couch.

"No. You are in no shape to be driving anything. Goodbye Robert. I'll call." She bent over and kissed him quickly on the forehead. A tear fell on his face, and with that, she was gone. He hadn't even managed to stand up. As she stood outside on the curb in the dark with her bags, Camille started crying openly, waiting, either for Robert to come get her, or for the taxicab to take her away. The taxi won, Robert being too stupid and drunk to even try to call her back.

Somehow, eventually Robert struggled to his feet and, after peering hopelessly out the window into the darkness, went over to the whisky cabinet and poured an even larger shot than the previous two. He went back to the couch and felt very sorry for himself. It appeared no one else would tonight. There was no thought as to what Camille might be feeling.

Camille's flight wasn't that early the next day, but there was no way she was staying the evening after telling Robert they were done as a couple. While in the cab, she sent a text to her sister, who was probably asleep in Montreal, telling her to expect Camille's arrival the next evening. With that, her Vancouver odyssey was at an end. Somehow, she had expected more of a reaction from Robert. His drunkenness and lack of care for their relationship confirmed her decision, but it did not make things any easier.

The next morning, Sophie left her room to take a shower and noticed that her father's bedroom door was wide open. She looked in, but the bed looked un-slept in. Worry set in quickly. She called out as she descended the stairs, "Dad, where are you?" As she entered the family room, she saw the dinner remains still sitting on the table. Robert was moving, but slowly, from his position on the couch. "Where is Camille?" She added, not understanding what had happened. Her dad didn't look sparkly.

"Gone, Sophie." He croaked. "She's gone back to Montreal."

Sophie stood quietly, analyzing this piece of news. It didn't bode well for her father's state of mind, this much she knew. She headed back upstairs to get ready for school while she thought this through. She had gotten along better with Camille the last few months, but she wasn't her mother, and never would be. So maybe this departure was a good thing. Maybe good for her and Robin, but definitely bad for her dad. One would have to be blind not to notice all the alcohol her dad went through, but she wasn't sure how to handle it yet. She was needing to mature much quicker than her friends.

After she had showered and gotten dressed, she came down to clean up. Robert had headed up to his bed, so she was by herself as she shovelled the dinner remains into the garbage, then loaded the dishwasher. Robin came down, and they looked at each other while searching for some breakfast.

After they had finished eating, she said, "I'll explain on the way to school." And with that, they both walked out the door, heading to some semblance of normality, while trying to not think too much about the mess their father had become.

A couple of hours later, Robert woke up for the second time, looked around, the events of the previous evening reappearing slowly in his fogged brain. He shook his head and went to take a long, hot shower. After getting some workout clothes on, he headed down to the kitchen, surprised to see that someone had cleaned up. He put the kettle on for coffee and looked for some juice. His head hurt, so he added some pills to the juice. Breakfast of champions, he told himself. He pulled out the ledger book where he kept track of his bank account. Rent was coming due and after that, things were going to be dire if he didn't do something to get some money coming in.

After a couple of cups of very strong coffee, he spent a while reflecting on his life. Robert hadn't descended to drinking during the morning yet, but he stared at the whisky cabinet, thinking about it. He really didn't want to sink any further, and his drinking apparently hadn't made his life better, so he decided to do something positive — go for a run. He had been in the best shape of his life a year earlier but had sadly slipped the habit of regular workouts. A couple of months had passed since he had run anywhere. He felt like shit most of the time. After losing Camille, and he didn't kid himself, she wasn't coming back — he needed to take a hard look at Robert Lui. He recalled that running always gave him time to think. and evaluate things. He prayed that this was still true, even as he knew the run would definitely hurt.

As he was about to go out the door, the phone rang. He hesitated. Nothing good usually came from landline calls, but succumbed. "Hello?"

"Robert?" The accent was unmistakable.

"Yes, Tony?"

"Yup. I've been thinking about you. Got some news. I passed my detective's exams." His voice was jubilant. Just hearing Tony made Robert immediately feel better.

"I have you to thank for all your help, Robert. Couldn't have done it without you."

"Are you going to stick with the VPD, then?"

"Yes. Thomas has been promoted to be our new head. Don't know what happened to Steve."

"Sounds promising Tony. Thomas is a good one. Pay attention to him."

"I will. We need to do coffee someday soon, okay?"

"Roger, Tony, take care." He hung up, considered this piece of news, then went out for a punishing run.

CHAPTER 4

The location for GreenSide was one of Vancouver's most valuable building sites. As the site had been owned by the city, and giving up land was one way for the city to jump-start housing projects for financially strapped citizens, it seemed to be a natural fit. The area, near recently built community facilities, as well as one of the city's best-known parks, made it also extremely attractive to developers looking to build condominium towers for profit. Little Mountain, as the area is also called, is the remnant of an ancient volcano, and the highest point in the City of Vancouver. Views from the top floors of any building erected in the area would be endless.

Most people wouldn't guess it, but only one hundred and forty years earlier, the land around Little Mountain had been covered in old growth forest providing a home for copious numbers of deer, elk, bears and even salmon. Local native groups hunted and fished to support their families; the area's bounty seemingly inexhaustible. The spawning fish travelled up the streams from the Burrard inlet to lay their eggs before dying. All those waterways had since been covered over. Early European settlers did what settlers do, dealing efficiently with all the beauty by taking and obliterating these assets, using them to construct a city. The Canadian Pacific Railroad, which had acquired title over much of the local land from the federal government of the day in return for building a rail line to Vancouver, also discovered basalt under the vegetation. They quarried this for road construction until there were two huge holes left atop the mountain. One was eventually filled with water to make a reservoir and paved over, with the second being made into a public garden filled with flowers, ponds, and pathways. The garden became so successful locally that it drew weddings, graduations, any celebration calling for memories to be captured in picturesque family photos. The reservoir remained hidden; most people ignorant of what they were parking their cars on top of.

So GreenSide was in as central a location in the city, as well as the minds of Vancouverites, as you could possibly want, or not want, depending on how things turned out. Any architect worth their salt would tell you not to make your mistakes public. Even the best architects had those projects, not something Stanley Dunbar was aware of when he decided that Little Mountain would be the site for Vancouver's state-of-the-art GreenSide project.

The residential project was to consist of three tall condominium towers with residences for sale on the west or park side of the site. Four shorter and stubbier below-market rental buildings were to occupy the remainder of the site, accessed from the east side near Main Street. Small shops and office space occupied some of the street level space, with a daycare filling up the remainder. Heat and power for the buildings were to come from a neighbourhood energy system powered by Stanley the Mayor's newest love interest, hydrogen. This system would be located in the centre of the GreenSide project. It was over-sized so that any adjacent new development could also tap into it. The city planning department would make certain that developers wished to partake, by neglecting to give permits to anyone not signing on, or alternatively, slowing the process down so much that the applicant might conclude they'd be better off developing property in 100 Mile House, British Columbia or Moose Jaw, Saskatchewan.

Chas, or Charles Burrows, to use his correct name, liked to joke around. He was also a pipe fitter, a member of a union in Vancouver that had gas fitters, plumbers, steam fitters, and sundry other technicians and tradespeople included in its ranks. Chas had a ruddy complexion surrounding twinkling eyes, with an outsized gut, the beneficiary of a beer or three. Chas also had a Red Seal affixed to his trade certificate, which gave him a leg up on others in his field. In theory, a tradesperson's training being confirmed under the Red Seal program made them outstanding technicians, as well as citizens of the world. The designation meant they could ply their trade across Canada and garner trade recognition in countries around the globe. Another facet of this theory was that Red Seal tradespeople were highly skilled and the best at their chosen trade. This was generally true, but only if they paid attention and rigorously applied themselves to their work at all times. After obtaining his Red Seal, this standard, sadly, didn't always apply to Chas. Liquid Metal, one of dozens of subcontractors working under the control of Bamboo Construction, who were building GreenSide, currently employed Chas.

Where public money is being spent, sometimes a project manager will hire a firm to do independent quality reviews, if there is a hint that the company providing the service is not up to snuff. This, in effect, is a second check, paid for out of project funds, that may or may not detect problems that the provider didn't detect, but regardless, becomes another process inflating construction costs while providing extra safety—in theory. GreenSide indeed had a second firm looking at Liquid Metal's work, however, their focus was on the primary containment vessel. The primary vessel was deemed fit for installation, and the whole assembly was duly set up for operation.

At GreenSide, the location for the mechanical room housing the hydrogen power system was under one of the residential towers designed for low-income renters. Sometimes, mechanical rooms are placed at the bottom of a project, beneath several layers of parking. In this case, new parking regulations brought into play by the city let the designers choose how many stalls to provide. In reality, designers don't usually rise to that level of decision making, the client's project manager usually dictating such things. The architects then get to plan and figure out how to make the parking conform to the myriad of regulations set up by the city. At the cost of a shiny new high end German sedan per stall, it didn't take a genius to figure out that the project wouldn't be building many underground stalls for people not paying market rates for their new home. Public transit was going to be their ticket to ride, the closest subway stop at least a kilometre away. In the end, the room housing the hydrogen system was directly under the lobby of one of the rental towers. Because the power system needed to be functional for the rest of the project as each building was completed, it was an integral part of the first phase.

Part of completing a project involves education for the people who ultimately operate the systems needed to make the buildings run smoothly. The mechanical company Liquid Metal worked under provided these services. The novel workings of the power system also meant an interest was taken by the city, so they detailed a few people to attend the walkthrough and seminar as part of the owner's team.

The volatile nature of the hydrogen fuel meant close attention to procedures and safety precautions was essential for anyone running the system. The fuel was in liquid form at low temperatures, stored at extremely high pressure in the primary tank. A few sensors were located around this tank, in case of leaks, because the human nose cannot detect hydrogen. The main danger arose when tankers came on-site to refuel, so this point was hammered home by the contractor, with the procedures for this emphasized over and over. That there was a second, backup tank, to be used if the primary tank had problems, was mentioned, but that was the extent of it. The second tank was located across the room from the first tank and was connected with some overhead piping in the event that the liquid hydrogen needed to be shunted over to the second tank to make it usable, keeping the system fully functional.

What was not mentioned in the seminars was the huge explosive power contained in the fuel tank, hydrogen containing three times the energy of gasoline in a tank of similar size. This put the GreenSide project in a totally different category of hazard compared to the traditional method of fuel supply to a site, piped-in natural gas with no storage tanks involved. But this hazard wasn't talked about, certainly not by the project's boosters, the mayor being number one in this regard.

CHAPTER 5

Several days after occupancy was granted for the first two residential towers, the mayor had his people organize a press conference, not being one to miss out on the opportunity for some self promotion and celebration. A few days earlier, he had found out that Oslo's mayor was taking a North American tour at Oslo taxpayer's expense. Stanley had his public relations people contact the mayor's people to see whether he would like to visit Vancouver as a guest of the city. Naturally, they accepted, as their last American stop was very close to Vancouver. They were due to arrive in a few days, after a tour of Seattle, but not in time for the press event at GreenSide.

Invited to the opening were some community homeless advocates, a couple of provincial politicians whose ridings were close to the GreenSide site, and all the city councillors from the Eco Party. Several attendees were from City of Vancouver's planning and housing departments. Most of the companies having a stake in the project's success offered at least one person, so the event was packed with people congratulating each other.

One of the mayor's public event minders started the proceedings. The day was partly sunny. A low stage was set up just outside one of the completed tower's entry lobby.

"Welcome everyone, to what we envision as the start to a new sustainable era in this beautiful city." The public affairs consultant led off. Nile Gecko kept a watch on things from the edges of the crowd.

"We are pleased to finally have completed two magnificent buildings on this piece of unceded land belonging to the Musqueam, Squamish, and Tsleil-Waututh nations." She continued in this vein for another couple of minutes before reluctantly giving the microphone over to Mayor Dunbar. Stanley was resplendent in a shiny new grey suit complete with a lime green tie, just in case anyone was unaware of what the agenda was at the event.

He launched into his greenest city in the world spiel. "Thanks to all of you in attendance, we are well on the path to being the world leader in sustainable projects. I was in Oslo last month for a conference and believe me, we are the envy of the world. You should be proud of yourselves." A few of the planning staff clapped at this news. It was a terrific feeling knowing you are the best in the world, even if it wasn't remotely close to the truth. Stanley wasn't the kind of man to let a few stray facts get in the way of his gushing speech.

Stanley wasn't done. "And I'm not sure whether you all are aware of this, but the project is powered by hydrogen, not fossil fuels!" This last came out triumphantly.

Nile stood silent, shaking his head ever so slightly. He checked out the attendees. In addition to the guests, there seemed to be people from at least three news organizations watching. Included in the equipment present were a couple of television cameras. Nile was tall and dark-skinned, courtesy of some Arabian blood somewhere in his family history. A beak-like nose supported wire-framed glasses. He affected a professorial air and wasn't afraid of pointing out intelligence deficiencies of those around him. He grinned slightly at the memory of Stanley sitting in the club with his pants around his ankles, being attended to by a concerned 'schoolgirl'. Nile had heard that Kristian was due for a visit in two days and was looking forward to seeing him.

Nile took out his cell phone and called the admin assistant for the Eco Party, who had been working on an unusual task for him. He was interested in who the owner of a certain Club Otta in Oslo was. Given his condition that evening, he was justifiably proud to have remembered the name. He didn't want his fingerprints on the search, just in case.

"Hey, it's Nile. Any luck on that search?"

"Yup, just a second, it's here somewhere." Nile waited while he could hear papers being moved around. "Yes, there are two owners listed, a Dag Larsen, and a Kristian Axness. Is this what you wanted?"

"Ahh, thanks, that's good. Keep this to yourself, please." Nile hit the stop button and pocketed his phone. Interesting. Now he really wanted to talk with Kristian whenever he showed up. He eventually realized that nothing important to Nile's world was happening at the event and called it a day.

Something was happening, only it was one level below the large group, and out of sight. The newly installed head technician in charge of the hydrogen power plant was having an issue with the system. It was not functioning as advertised; not unusual for a new project, but he was having trouble making sense of what was wrong. Hydrogen systems hadn't come up in his training, or anyone else's that he knew. He was aware that people were continuing to move into their new homes—a couple of families per day in each building, so a solution was needed, or he would be hearing complaints, and he hated whiners. He tried a few possibilities to get some energy going but came up empty. Temporarily defeated, he'd try tomorrow. If he couldn't make progress, he'd be calling both the contractor responsible, and the suppliers of the system for advice. For now, the buildings were functioning minimally by using the backup generator system. Luckily, the time of year did not call for much heating to be supplied.

The next day, the tech and his assistant tried some more things after consulting their operations manuals. By noon, they admitted defeat. They called the contractor and vented their grievances. Naturally, the contractor would have to run it up and down the chain of command. The earliest they could get some people to the site would be the next morning. Some cussing ensued before the tech decided to leave for the day, not really wanting to be on the receiving end of more phone complaints from new residents.

It was two days after the press event when the hydrogen system experts showed up. The four of them met the lead technician on the plaza in front of the tower, and they went down into the large mechanical room where the hulking apparatus of the hydrogen system rested. After about thirty minutes of trying to get the hydrogen moving from the primary tank, it appeared that something was blocking the transfer. A group huddle was convened, and they decided to activate the backup tank, to do what it was supposed to do, according to the design. A couple of technicians started the transfer process, moving the highly compressed liquid over to the second tank. After about a half hour, the second tank was three-quarters full. A sharp buzzing started, as if warning of something, just as someone turned on a light at the far end of the room where the second tank was resting, in anticipation of the next step.

The resulting explosion was enormous. The initial shock wave crushed the people in the room into two-dimensional forms against the far wall. The roof blew off. Above, the erupting plaza destroyed several concrete columns supporting the front of the tower, causing half of the twelve-storey tower to cascade down onto the deck below. Debris landed all over the area, some of it in the mechanical room. It was a testament to the sturdiness of the structural design that the whole tower didn't come down—one of the benefits of applying the latest seismic codes during design.

About two kilometres away, Robert Lui was eating toast in his kitchen when he felt first a thump, then heard something suspiciously like a tremendous explosion. Robert had been fingering a small audio cassette that an undercover policeman from Delta had given him the previous spring with a warning attached—be careful. He lacked two things to find out what was on the tape: motivation, and something more prosaic, a tape machine. He looked out his window, but couldn't see anything, so he went to the front door, then out onto the street and looked south. A couple of other neighbours were also on their front walks. They all looked south, then at each other. A cloud of dark smoke southwest of where he was standing was ballooning up into the still air, sirens already wailing their alarm in the distance.

Farther west, Mayor Stanley Dunbar was talking with Kristian Axness in his city hall office at the corner of 12th and Cambie when they felt the shock, then heard the roar of the explosion. Kristian looked at Stanley expectantly, as though he could instantly explain things.

"That didn't sound good," Kristian offered helpfully.

Stanley rose and opened his office door, eyes raised at his assistant, who was sitting a few feet away. She shrugged. "I'll see what I can find out." Sirens could be heard in the distant, so she dialled 911 for some intelligence. A few seconds later, she walked over to Stanley's open door, face pale. "Sounds like something exploded at GreenSide, probably multiple fatalities." She didn't know what else to say, knowing this was the mayor's pet project.

Stanley frowned. "Let me know what you learn." He was torn, wanting to drive up to the site, but loathe to show visiting VIPs anything but honey and roses where Vancouver was concerned.

Kristian wasn't finished however, "Isn't that the project you were using hydrogen to power up?"

Stanley looked back at Kristian, but all he could do was nod slowly. He re-joined the meeting and slowly closed the door to his office, all the day's wind taken out of his sails.

Over at the VPD offices, a few blocks north of city hall, a call came in from a 911 emergency tech asking for additional cars to be sent to GreenSide. Thomas Harrow had heard the explosion. At least now he had a destination to send officers to. He thought for a moment, then decided that also sending a detective wouldn't be out of order, so he called Tony Bortolo into his office.

"Trouble at GreenSide Tony, can you get out there pronto?"

"Was that the explosion?"

"Yes. Go take a look and assess what happened, then call me, okay?"

"Sure, no problem." With that, Tony was off to start the first case of his new career as a detective.

An ambulance was the first vehicle on-site, the two paramedics aboard in disbelief at the scene awaiting them. They couldn't drive closer than sixty metres to what appeared to be the epicentre of hell on display. The driver got out and promptly stepped on a hand that was laying beside the vehicle. Part of a forearm was attached, no sign of a body. He felt his stomach roll as he jumped to one side, leaning over to expel the lunch that he had recently consumed. His partner also dismounted, walked around the vehicle, and noted her driver's non-professional behaviour. This is what happened when you linked up with a new guy, she supposed. Not that she was feeling much better as she surveyed the carnage on offer. Looking over at the hand laying next to her partner's foot, a wedding ring still on the third finger jolted her, stark reminder that more than just lives were lost in this disaster. Whole families would be torn apart by this.

She looked over at the remains of the residential tower, curious how it could remain upright with the entire front of it missing. Some small fires were burning on the deck. After a moment of inactivity, the pair quickly started to search for anyone remotely saveable at ground level. Another two ambulances were making their way close to the site by this time. More sirens could be heard as fire engines and police cars drew near.

After a quick visual assessment, the veteran paramedic called back to the Emergency Operations Centre to let them know the extent of the situation, then asked for a command post to be made available. Her voice conveyed the urgency of the situation to the woman on the other end of the phone. GreenSide instantly became priority number one for all first responders in Vancouver. The two techs then stared at the remains of the newly completed twelve-storey tower, contemplating how they were going to rescue any survivors who might be waiting in the remaining half of the building. Looked like a job for the fire department, the veteran surmised.

Unsurprisingly, the next vehicle to pull in was a news van sporting roof-top aerials. The technician wondered if they drove around aimlessly, looking for tragedy. There must be some reason they were amongst the first to arrive at any potential crime scene, not that there was anything to indicate criminality at GreenSide.

CHAPTER 6

C hanges had been made down at the Vancouver Police offices on Cambie Street since Robert Lui had been sent on his way. Steve Christie, who had been nominally in charge of the investigation detectives under Deputy Chief McKnight, was a problem. After David McKnight had done some assessing, he shuffled some officers around. Steve had been fundamentally useless at running investigations, so naturally, he was promoted to a higher position on the force. This left a void that needed some intelligent being to fill, someone who could hopefully get results. These types were getting rare in the investigation department. Robert Lui, the best detective on the force by a mile, was gone. This left a certain Rodney Fister as the senior detective in the division. No one was a fan of Rodney, save for maybe Rodney himself. So, David McKnight plucked the head of the gang task force, Thomas Harrow, back into the VPD investigative unit. This decision didn't please Rodney one bit. He had been sure that he'd be tapped to run investigations.

Thomas was happy enough to be getting a promotion and a raise in pay after dealing with gangs for a couple of years, but he worried about the lack of talent amongst the detective group.

Initially, he had had a few regrets about bringing Robert onto his gang task force, especially after the events of a year earlier, but had softened his attitude as Robert's performance review had stretched out into a kind of low-grade torture. He now would have loved to have Robert back on the force but supposed that door was firmly closed.

One person he took with him was Norma van Kleet, a very capable admin assistant that he had stolen from the very department he was now returning to. Norma had also been a Robert Lui fan, just not in the way Thomas was. After Camille Laurent had resigned, Thomas was left in worse shape. Norma began calculating how she could influence Robert's return to the force, if at all possible, after finding that not only did Camille leave the force, but that she had returned to Montreal.

Norma smiled as she considered this news. She had naturally long eyelashes framing her green eyes, the kind many women would kill for, above slightly freckled cheeks framed with chestnut hair sometimes gathered in a ponytail. Her build was athletic, with legs that spoke of a skating background, and wasn't shy about promoting the benefits of her Dutch ancestry to anyone listening. She had been less than thrilled when Camille had moved in with Robert, so the latest developments were heart-warming, to her at least.

Thomas noted the promotion of Tony Bortolo to detective; good, but green as a golf course fairway, or so he assumed. There were a few other junior detectives who he really didn't know yet. It seemed he would, of necessity, be taking a more hands-on approach until he could fill the apparent personnel gaps in his roster.

Tony drove south on Cambie Street in one of the police fleet cars, idly wondering how long it would be before the mayor started demanding that all officers ride bicycles to their crime scenes to reduce greenhouse gas emissions. He slowed, then turned east onto the extension of East 33rd Avenue. Smoke still rose from the GreenSide site, which was just behind the crown of Queen Elizabeth Park. He turned south at Ontario Street and pulled over, stunned at the amount of debris littered everywhere. Some patrol officers were already unspooling yellow tape, shooing the reporters back, who were trying their best to muck up the scene. A large part of the site was still a construction zone, so after checking in with the officers, Tony carefully walked over to what he assumed to be the general contractor's trailer and entered. The site superintendent was the only occupant at the moment, all the others dispatched to check on-site workers.

"Hi, I'm Tony Bortolo, detective with the VPD." Tony was thrilled at the way this sounded.

"Arby Knutson, site super with Bamboo." He responded, not thrilled. Arby was large, with rough looking hands resting on his drawing table.

Tony had seen the tower, or what remained of it. "Think you could get the structural guys out here to take a look? I reckon there may be some rescuing going on, and I'm betting those fire guys will want to know the risks before they go in." It was a surprisingly cogent question for a detective to make. Arby looked at Tony cock-eyed and nodded after a moment's thought.

"I've already called him, be here in about twenty minutes."

"Any idea what happened?"

"I think the hydrogen system exploded."

"The what?"

"This project is, or was, to be powered using hydrogen. It is kept in tanks under extremely high pressure, in a room below that tower, or what remains of the tower."

"Wow. Seems like kind of a shitty idea, don't you think?"

Arby rolled his eyes. "Easy to say now that it hasn't worked out so good."

"That's putting it mildly. Any of your workers missing?"

"Two or three got injured by flying debris, one pretty badly, I think. The rest, including the other subcontractors, are being checked on as we speak."

"Anyone in the room at the time?"

"Unfortunately. Reps from the hydrogen company were here looking at some issues in the room. It seems likely that they found the problems. I think they are all toast. Extremely burned toast."

"Okay, thanks. I'm going to walk your site." With that, Tony exited the trailer, heading over to the tower where a fire truck was setting up to attempt rescues of the residents stuck in their new suites. Tony could hear screams from some of them. It was hard to tell if it was the situation, or pain, at the root of the noise. A fire chief came his way. Tony waved him over, explaining who he was, and that an engineer was on his way to the scene.

He crept over to a large hole in the plaza, smoke still curling up from the blackened edges. An enormous pile of pancaked concrete from the tower lay to one side along with twisted pieces of the exterior cladding. Broken glass glittered everywhere. He gingerly sidled to the hole's edge and looked down. Sure enough, he could make out shards of a large steel tank at one end of the room. At the far end, another tank had also exploded. Remains of what could be people were imprinted against the side wall, a dark liquid stained the floor. What a mess, Tony thought. He had no idea construction could be so dangerous. He stepped back, retrieving the phone from his vest.

"Thomas?"

"Yes, what's happened there?"

"Un-holy hell, that's what. Looks like a couple of hydrogen tanks exploded and took out half a tower. The other half is standing, but it's a little unsure for how long. The fire guys are about to start a rescue operation for some people still stuck in the remaining piece."

"Any indication of foul play?"

"Hard to tell, Thomas, at this point anyway. I don't know if there is much I can do here. There are body parts all over. It's not a very pleasant scene. The press are here already."

"Thanks. Stay there a while longer just to keep an eye on things, then get back here."

Thomas sat back in his chair, looking out the window, west, at his new panorama. It didn't appear any criminality had taken place at GreenSide, at least overtly, so he relaxed slightly. Sounded like a mess of an accident, however. He knew about the mayor's boosting of the project, so he expected a reckoning would be coming his way. The view towards Granville Island from his office wasn't bad but was marred by a forest of new residential towers. He'd had to change some furniture out, but Steve Christie's old office was pretty nice as well as being spacious. Thomas was already feeling at home, his previous job of chasing gangs around the Lower Mainland fading from his mind as newer problems crowded the memories out.

Since Tony was expected to hang around, he went to watch the drama at the tower. As he threaded his way through jagged pieces of concrete and broken reinforcing bar, he tried not to look at the body parts laying amongst the desolation. The structural engineer had arrived and, after a quick assessment, seemed to have given some reassurance about the stability of the remains. Nothing guaranteed mind, but enough for the firemen to attempt the rescue. Not that they had much choice in the matter. Leaving some families in a teetering building because the rescuers were worried about their own safety was not on. Arby told the fire chief that maybe no more than five families were living on the floors of the remaining part of the building, the moving in process having been slow. With the screaming subsided, the firemen climbed their ladder, aiming at a third-floor balcony. A second ladder with a bucket on the end was being directed to the same spot.

As Tony watched, a most peculiar sight appeared. Pairs of what looked to be teenagers were being helped off the balcony to the rescue bucket, oddly linked to each other. He moved over to be closer to where the bucket would land. Once two pairs were in, the bucket was lowered to the ground, quickly surrounded by paramedics. Tony walked up to the group, trying to listen to the conversation. It wasn't going well. The teenagers weren't speaking English, although it seemed they could understand some of what was being directed at them. A bolt cutter was wielded by a firefighter to separate the couples, who were connected with handcuffs. They were then whisked away to waiting ambulances. Tony confirmed from one of the technicians that Vancouver General Hospital was their destination.

Having fulfilled his duty to keep an eye on things at Green-Side, Tony decided that a trip down to the hospital would be in order. He was curious as to the story behind handcuffed teens, who appeared to be immigrants, being found in a new apartment.

He called Thomas again, "Something stinks here, and it's not the bodies. I'm heading to VGH to see what I can learn." He then told him what the firemen had found.

"Interesting. Let me know what happens, and if any adults are involved." Sounded to Thomas like Tony was already hip deep in his first case. He would need to keep a close watch on this file.

Tony drove as quickly as he could, thinking about using his siren, but in the end, forgoing this aid. VGH wasn't very far away, and he liked to follow Robert Lui's advice—'keep a low profile' being one of his mantras. Tony wanted to question the kids as soon as possible. He expected to deal with roadblocks put up by the nurses but was determined to find out what he could. He drove west along 10th Avenue and into the large emergency receiving area at the hospital where he abandoned his car, making sure to stay clear of ambulances coming and going.

Tony made his way into the chaos of the admitting department. After showing his badge to a nurse, he was told the patients were being examined and getting treatment as necessary. He would have to keep calm and wait.

"As you may or may not have noticed, they had handcuffs on. I really need to understand what was going on in the apartment they were rescued from." Tony gave the nurse his most imploring look.

"Okay, I'll call you over when they are ready. I don't think any of them speak English, so we're calling in what interpreters we can muster."

After forty-five minutes in the waiting area filled with all manner of people with various ailments, some seemingly serious, Tony was beckoned to follow an orderly down a corridor. He walked past curtains and beds into a small room where a young girl sat with another older woman. The girl shrank away from him, edging towards the woman. Tony sat in an offered chair, knowing he needed to be as gentle as he knew how.

"What language does she speak?" This directed at the interpreter.

"Spanish."

"Does she have any identification on her at all?"

The interpreter shook her head. "Nothing."

"Could you ask her what her name is?"

"I have tried. She refuses to talk."

Tony noticed that the manacle had been removed. "Was she hurt?"

"She seems to be good, no injuries that the nurses could discern."

"Could you ask her how old she is?"

"I'll try." The question was asked in Spanish. The girl pondered it before finally answering.

"She says, fifteen."

"Can you ask where her parents are?"

"She says Ocotal."

"Where is that?"

After more questions, it was evident that this was all the girl was going to give up. Tony went to the door and tried to get the attention of a nurse. When he had one at his side, he asked, "Has this girl been checked for recent sexual activity?"

"No, is that an issue?"

"She was found in the company of five other teenagers, handcuffed, in an apartment with no adults present, so." Here he paused. "So yes, it could be. Could I talk with one of the boys?"

"They seem to speak an eastern European language, for which we have no interpreter as yet."

"Still like to talk with one of them. I think they might understand some English."

"Okay, I'll see if I can get one to meet with you."

"What is going to happen to them?"

"Social services has been called. They'll probably end up in a group home somewhere while their stories are being established."

Tony thought about this while he waited. Ten minutes later, a boy followed by a nurse came into the room.

"Hello." He started as gently as he could, "Could you tell me what you all were doing in that apartment?"

"Sex." That was it. He didn't say anything else.

Tony tried something else. "I'm with the police department."

The boy's eyes went wide, and he cowered behind the nurse, starting to cry. The nurse looked at Tony angrily, "I think that's enough for today." She ushered the boy out of the room, leaving Tony to ponder what the boy had just said, and what he hadn't.

After some thought, he went into the corridor to find the nurse he had been talking to. "Do you think you could let me know where these teens end up? We may need to keep an eye on them for their safety." He handed her his card, which she palmed after looking at it suspiciously. With that, Tony thought he better get back to Thomas. This was feeling complicated.

Up on the third floor at city hall, Stanley Dunbar wanted to head for dinner with Kristian. He had called Nile Gecko into his office after Kristian had asked about him, which annoyed Stanley. Why was that guy always horning in on his social life? It was relatively early, especially by European standards of what constituted an appropriate hour to dine, but Stanley was tone deaf to such niceties.

"Come on, there is a great restaurant a rather illustrious local Indian chef opened just up the street from here. The food is outstanding." What Stanley neglected to mention was that you couldn't make reservations. Rather, you had to stand around if there was a wait line to get in. And there was no way around it. A previous prime minister of Canada had famously endured the wait at the restaurant's previous location. Just another potentially awkward moment in Stanley's life. Nile shook his head.

As it turned out, they were so early to dinner, they were able to get in without a problem. A further stroke of luck happened to Stanley; the owner/chef was in the house and made a big fuss over the three guests, as he usually did with all his customers, famous or not. Kristian was eventually impressed, the early hour aside.

As they were chewing on their lamb popsicle starters, Kristian couldn't help himself. "So, hydrogen maybe is not the answer after all? Wasn't that what they had inside the Hindenburg a while back?" He wasn't smiling, but he didn't look sad either.

Stanley shook his head. "The Hindenburg? There will be an investigation. Someone will answer for this. I don't think you can cross off hydrogen just because someone screwed up." He looked questionably at the Norwegian, then at Nile.

Kristian threw up his hands. "Nothing intended, just observations, that's all. Is there another project we could look at tomorrow? We have one day left before returning to Oslo." He was starting to seriously wonder how Stanley had become mayor.

"We can do a tour if you wish."

Nile asked, "Where are you staying, Kristian?"

"Downtown on the waterfront. The Hotel Pacifica I believe."

"I can give you a lift down there when we're done if you wish." Nile wanted to get Kristian alone somehow, having a few things to ask.

Kristian looked at the other two. "No clubs?" He was smiling expectantly.

Nile did an internal eye roll while Stanley stumbled over a lame answer. If only Kristian knew how boring Stanley could be, Oslo apart. Nile was sure such clubs existed in Vancouver, but he didn't know where. "How about some whisky?"

Kristian's smile broadened as Nile signalled the waiter. The mayors, meanwhile, started talking to each other about mayor things.

A few blocks north, Tony had parked his vehicle, and he made his way up the stairs to his floor. He cocked his head at Norma as he pointed to Thomas's office. She nodded, so he went up and knocked on the door frame. After a grunt from within, he entered and closed the door.

Thomas shot Tony a questioning look. "What's with the closed door?"

"Because something weird is going on. I talked to a couple of the kids rescued from the GreenSide tower at the hospital. Number one, they are all from other countries, and don't speak English. Number two, they seem to be frightened out of their minds and are hardly saying a word. Number three, they are being used for sex, I think."

"The tower that got hit. How long has it been up and running?"

"Only a few weeks at most."

Thomas stared at the wall, thinking.

Tony continued, "There is more, and I don't like what it may imply. When I talked to one of the boys, things were calm until I said I was with the police. The boy reacted immediately in fear and started crying, hiding behind the nurse. The nurse took him away before I could get anymore out of him. He didn't look much older than twelve or so I think. I also talked to one of the girls. She said she was fifteen and from Ocotal, but that was all she would say. Spanish was her language. I'll find out where Ocotal is."

Thomas was silent, then, "Why was the boy so afraid of the police?"

"Hard to tell, Thomas." Tony waited while his boss evaluated the ways this could go.

"None of this leaves this room, understand? And find out where these kids are being taken. We may have to put a watch on them. Better get some good sleep tonight. There could be long days coming." Thomas waited while Tony exited his office, then stood and walked over to the window to ponder where this might all end up.

A couple of blocks south, Nile finally paid the restaurant bill after everyone had gotten themselves sufficiently soused with their after-dinner drinks. Stanley seemed to have forgotten the events of the day, at least temporarily. Nile was careful, slowing his drinking to a crawl, as he wanted to drive Kristian downtown to their hotel. Nile asked the hostess to call a taxi for Stanley, then walked with Kristian back down to city hall to retrieve his car. Once in the car, Nile remained quiet, as the drive to the hotel wouldn't take more than ten minutes, and he was assessing what he would say. After manoeuvring through downtown, they pulled up to the hotel on the waterfront and Nile stopped in front of the busy *porte-cochère*. As his guest was about to get out, Nile asked Kristian for a word. He remained in the front seat, looking across at Nile expectantly.

"So, Kristian, remember our night at the club in Oslo?" Nile twisted his body so he could look directly at Kristian.

"Of course, Nile. You missed out."

"Club Otta, correct? What I was wondering Kristian, is if there are any memories of that evening, you know, for my scrapbook."

"Let me understand. You want to know if there are pictures of that night?"

"You can see right through me, Kristian."

Kristian remained silent, then, "Why would you want such things? And why do you think I would have these items?"

It was Nile's turn to be silent. So, they existed! "Items like that are always valuable, as I know you understand. I believe that you have an interest in Club Otta, which is why I am asking."

"Sounds like you have been doing some research. Supposing such things even existed, what would they be worth to you?" Kristian now understood who was really running the City of Vancouver.

"Let me think on your last question and get back to you. Enjoy the rest of your evening, Kristian, and your tour tomorrow. Safe journeys back to Norway!"

He sat for a moment, watching Kristian's back as he headed for the lobby doors. His hospitality over with, Nile decided that a short jaunt over to the local casino near False Creek wouldn't be out of order. It had a been a while, and he was feeling the itch.

CHAPTER 7

The morning after the explosion at GreenSide, several people were getting concerned about the impending ramifications, for different reasons. First, and not least, were the people and companies who had financially backed the project. Government funding was only a minor part of the large money pie used for the construction of the non-market rental residences. The market condominium towers were funded by a consortium of lenders, all of them worried at how things had gone off the rails so quickly after the much-publicized opening day. Construction had barely started on the condo towers. Calls were coming in non-stop to the insurer of record for the project.

Bamboo Construction's president was trying to forecast how much the building schedule was going to be affected by this. It sounded like the site might be off limits for a while as an investigation was launched. Without even knowing who may have been at fault, he instructed his minions to start preparing a delay claim.

A second insurance company was involved, not as an insurer, but as a lender. BC Coastal Insurance Company directed its senior claims manager to do some investigating. Dan Prudence was a veteran of the claims business, and he knew something subtle would be needed due to the cast of characters involved in the project, especially the people at the City of Vancouver. His problem was that his most senior investigator had up and quit; heading to a competitor, poached like an unrestricted free agent. He started asking questions of his people. Outside private investigators were sometimes used by his company, but they generally could only get so far when dealing with the city. It was an admin assistant, recently hired, who came up with a name, Robert Lui. The assistant had formerly worked at the Vancouver Police Department and knew Robert to be the best of detectives. Her name was Gladys Chu, and to date, she had been an excellent addition to the office team.

Another person with some mild concerns was Manny Dhillon, head of the Two Tigers gang. His new Department of Extortion had supplied some personnel to the GreenSide project. He wasn't sure which tower they were being kept in, but after hearing about the disaster, he directed Bobbi to find out. Bobbi Atwall was relatively in the dark about this new department at Two Tigers, despite his new position as assistant to Manny, so he asked a few questions of Paneet, who was leading the charge on the sex side.

"Manny asked me to find out where some people were staying at the new GreenSide project in Vancouver. Do you know?"

"The kids?"

"I guess."

"Tower number One at GreenSide."

"What were kids doing there?"

"Don't be a complete idiot." Paneet's brow furrowed as he studied Bobbi.

This didn't clarify anything for Bobbi, but he dutifully called the information in to Manny.

On finding this out, Manny exploded and after a few curses, broke the phone connection. He then dialled another number. "Those teens taken out of GreenSide—where are they now?"

"I'll find out and get back to you."

"Don't waste any time or things will not turn out well."

The mechanical consultants who had designed the energy system were mortified to learn about what happened on-site. They informed their liability insurance company immediately, fretting about what this might mean to their company, then the project. Somehow, the poor souls who had perished or were injured in the disaster came in farther down the concern ladder.

Down at city hall, several departments were in semi-panic mode; planning, permits, housing, and the legal teams that worked on the never-ending issues the city faced every day. Some of the more junior city staff were scratching their heads, wondering if they had somehow screwed up. Senior members were reviewing records, more an exercise in making sure their rear ends were covered than anything else. Media companies had already unleashed their attack reporters, looking for any soft targets at city hall to give up some juicy angle on the disaster. Naturally, the hydrogen aspect was first and foremost on their list of queries. A couple of reporters even took some time to familiarize themselves with the issue, but most couldn't be bothered.

It was midday and Robert Lui, after a challenging night of not drinking, was considering his life. He knew he needed to be a better role model for his children. He felt it was time to right the ship. Getting some regular exercise was a good first step. He had tried calling Camille, but there was no reply. He realized he needed to clear his mind of her. Enough with re-analyzing all his mistakes. This was not a healthy way to spend one's time.

He made a short list of employment options. Other local police forces would probably have some questions about his VPD experiences. Perhaps private security firms might be on the lookout for someone with a resume like Robert's, perhaps not. He had seen plenty of bad luck situations play out in his police career, and the outcomes weren't pretty. He would review the list of jobs while running and was about to go out when his phone rang. "Is this Robert Lui? Former detective Robert Lui?"

"Who wants to know?"

"My name is Dan Prudence, with BC Coastal Insurance. I have a proposition that you may be interested in."

"Don't need any insurance, thanks." Robert was about to hang up when Dan caught him.

"I'm not selling insurance, Robert, I'm looking for an investigator. Someone of your reputed calibre."

Robert was silent, thinking about his nearly empty bank account, wondering if this was a coincidence. "To do what?"

"GreenSide. You may have heard about the mess up there. Our company has an interest in the project, and we need some delicate examination of the state of affairs, so to speak."

"I would need to be paid in money, so to speak."

Dan chuckled briefly. "How mercenary."

"Maybe, but necessary, don't you think? What do you get paid with, apples?"

"Ha, very good. Could we meet?"

"Sure. I'm about to go for a run. How about later this afternoon?"

"Three then? Our offices are on West Hastings."

"Consider it a date." Robert hung up and pulled his runners on. The run would be a perfect time to consider what his new opportunity might mean; although he was not looking forward to it, the second run being always the awful one when fitness had been neglected and atonement was on order.

After returning and showering, Robert made an internal promise never to let himself go soft again. His legs ached and his stomach didn't feel much better. He dressed, then looked up the address for the insurance company. He left a note on the counter for his kids — 'Investigating employment opportunities'. He got into The Silver Streak, his pet name for the old car he drove, and headed to the downtown peninsula, carefully parking where it hopefully would not be poached by a tow truck while he was in his meeting. After three, rush hour prohibitions meant easy pickings for alert truck drivers spotting any car on the wrong street.

He entered the lobby of BC Coastal Insurance offices on the tower's twelfth floor, taking in the expansive view of the North Shore mountains behind the receptionist. There seemed to be some money in this insurance business. He hadn't been sitting for more than a minute on a modern tan leather chair when a bookish-looking man swept into the foyer and came over to shake his hand, then led him to a conference room. Dan had dark, short hair, greased into place, horn-rimmed glasses, and a thin build upholstered in a very dark suit. Indigo? Black? It was difficult to distinguish, but it looked expensive and classy.

"Welcome. I'm sure this must seem a bit sudden. Would you like some coffee?" He knew Robert would refuse, having done some research on this potential new team member.

"No thanks." The pro-forma offer seemed suspect, but Robert put that thought aside. "How did you get my name?"

"A mutual acquaintance, name of Gladys Chu. She works here for us."

Robert considered this information without saying anything. It didn't sound like they did background checks on everyone they hired. "GreenSide."

"Ah, to business. How very direct."

Robert stared back at Dan, waiting.

"We would like some subtle digging done into this project, how it was set up, why certain decisions were taken. Our company has significant funding tied up in GreenSide. We'd like to know it is safe, or as safe as these things can be."

"I would be working alone?"

"Yes. We have a few assets should you have need for them, but we don't want a big ruckus made."

"Hmm, the development world. My first foray into that was somewhat sticky, shall we say."

"I remember reading things a year or two ago." Dan looked at Robert, assessing him.

"As you are aware, that world can get complicated."

"For which you would be well compensated." Dan pushed a piece of paper over to Robert with some numbers on it. The amount was well over half of what he used to make in a year on the police force. Dan waited a few moments, then started drumming the table with two of his fingers, nerves evident.

"I'll do it." Robert stood up. "Email me a formal offer, with your ground rules, which I will attempt to respect if I can. I'll do some thinking and get back to you tomorrow. Sound good?"

Dan smiled. "Thank you. We'll be in touch, then. You may leave your contact info with my receptionist." He appreciated Robert's efficiency.

Robert left the premises, happier than he had been in months. He started thinking about making something for dinner that would be a celebration with his children. For him, today that meant homemade pizza. In his car, he called home and talked to Robin, explaining his dinner choice, then proceeded to a grocery store to pick up ingredients. Robin was flabbergasted and happy. This was a new dad. He yelled up to Sophie to tell her what was going to happen.

After shopping, Robert headed home, driving up his lane and parked at the rear of his rented townhouse on the east side of Vancouver. He walked into the kitchen past the blooming tulips that mysteriously came up every year in the small patch of garden that made his home complete. He called upstairs to announce his arrival, then immediately started in on the dough preparation. Sophie and Robin came slowly down the stairs, astonished to see their father doing something that had been almost forgotten, making a good dinner from scratch.

"Hi Pops." Robin opened. "What kind?"

"Prosciutto and lemon, number one. Potato and onion, number two."

Both children smiled, but Sophie asked, "What is the lemon about? What happened to hotdog pizza?"

"We are moving up in the world. It's a new type. You don't want to get scurvy, do you?"

"What's scurvy, Pops?" Robin asked.

"Don't they teach you anything in school these days? Look it up on the inter-web. Wait, there's more." He announced, like a television huckster. "I landed a job this afternoon!" He plunked the dough into the mixing bowl, covered it, putting it on the stove top to rise. "Looks like your dad is going to be a private investigator."

Robin was the first. "Wow, neat."

Sophie didn't care what her dad was doing, just glad that he was finally doing something. "That's great, Dad." The worry that had clouded her mind for weeks lifted slightly. "Do you want some help?"

Robert looked over and rolled a lemon across the counter. "Slice extra thin, no seeds. Thanks." He prepared the cheeses, olives, rosemary, then sliced the potato and onion thinly before coating them in olive oil.

"So, what are you investigating, Pops?"

"You heard that explosion the other day? That was GreenSide. I'm going to look at the mess it has become."

"GreenSide?" Robin wasn't up to speed on things like development, but Sophie knew about it because of the sustainable aspect, which she and some friends were concerned about.

"I'm sure your sister can fill you in."

Sophie rolled her eyes, not going to waste time trying to educate a philistine like her brother about such important matters.

"You can go cool your heels if you want, I'll let you know when I put the first pie in the oven." Both children retreated up the stairs to their phones and homework, in that order. After he had finished slicing the toppings, Robert looked at his whisky cabinet longingly, but kept moving, opting for a celebratory glass of chardonnay instead. New habits, that's what he needed, not slipping back to where he had been. But he realized that he still had that longing for the relaxation that wine or whisky could bring.

As he pondered what he had been asked to do that afternoon, he realized he would need to develop some research skills, tasks which he previously had pawned off on people under him at his old job. Instead of a whole department to help him, he would be relying on one person, Robert Lui. The thought was sobering, but wasn't that what made life interesting, learning new things?

He took another swig of wine, then went to check on the dough. When the first pizza came out of the oven, mozzarella bubbling and the prosciutto slightly blackened, Sophie and Robin came downstairs. Sophie came over and hugged her father, Robert grunting in pain from the remnants of a wound from almost a year earlier. He smiled at his children, while inwardly remembering the cause of his broken ribs—a rifle shot to his mid-section from an unknown assailant while at the last fateful meeting in Steveston to rescue his son. Body armour saved his life but couldn't prevent everything. His chest ached most days, and the person who had taken the shot was still out there, unaccounted for.

The lemon pizza was a hit with the kids, the tang of the fruit a counterpoint to the cheese, rosemary, and olives. The second pie was just as pleasing, the thin potato and onion slices sitting in a bed of gruyere cheese, with a sprinkle of parsley laid on top. Although they earnestly attempted to eat both pizzas, in the end, some slices survived the carnage.

Over at the police department offices on Cambie Street, earlier that same afternoon, Thomas tried to build a team to help Tony should he need it. He decided against adding Rodney Fister for the moment, as Rod's primary case was a recent east side murder that didn't look to have gang implications. Instead, he added two seemingly capable younger officers, Finn Black and Vito Cotoni. Thomas led a meeting to review the devastation at GreenSide, to the extent that it could be summed up one day after the event.

Thomas sat behind his desk, reading the scene notes, the three other officers ranged in front of him. "Looks like five dead males in the hydrogen room, seven children and adults dead from the tower collapse, with several more injured, including four construction workers. Quite the mess. Then there are the teenagers rescued from the tower. Where did they get to Tony?"

"Social services have located them into a couple of special residences for the time being. I'd sure like to question them."

"Do you know their exact location?"

"No, it is being withheld for the moment."

"Do your best to find them. If you can't do it by first thing tomorrow, let me know and I'll try to throw my weight around. Any other avenues being explored?"

Tony responded, "Our forensic people are in the hydrogen room, trying to figure out what set off the explosion. No hint as yet. We will get a team into the apartment where the teenagers were being kept as well. First, we need to confirm it is safe to do so."

"Well, we will assume the explosion was an accident, but don't rule anything out yet. I don't know what your assistants here can do for you but keep them close. No talking to anyone else about this, understood?"

"Yes. I can fill Finn and Vito in on the teenagers?"

"Okay, but only them. Get going." Thomas watched the three leave before turning his attention to some manpower paperwork for his department, all part of his new duties. The days were going to stretch out very quickly for him if he couldn't find more experience to bolster his group.

Shortly after seven the next morning, a 911 call came into the Deer Lake RCMP detachment in Burnaby from Emergency Operations. No sooner had a couple of cars been dispatched to the location in question when a second call came in—same thing, different place. As the cars raced to their destinations, the information came up on their car screens about the address, group homes, so probably domestic disputes playing out. The officers hated these calls, outcomes so unpredictable and sometimes extremely dangerous. Each car called for more backup, just in case.

Later that same morning, at the more civilized hour of half past nine, Tony Bortolo rolled into the office after spending time at Cafe Paulo up the street. Tony had taken up where Robert had left off, spending more and more of his money purchasing the coffee and pastries on offer. Today, the proprietor, Gilberto, had asked after Robert, not having seen him for several months. Tony had to explain a few things, finishing with a promise to get Robert back in soon for a visit. Tony's first business was to locate those kids from the tower, so he called social services again, identifying himself.

This time, the response was different, and immediate, "You haven't heard? We have lost two valued people early this morning, both killed. Those teenagers are all missing as well. This place is in an uproar."

"What?"

"Two group homes were attacked last night, people murdered, and those teenagers taken."

"Geez. I'll get back to you." He hung up and went to Thomas's office. Norma signalled that he was in. Suddenly, Tony felt way in over his head. He tapped on the door frame and entered. His face was a light shade of grey. "Thomas?"

"What's wrong?"

"Those kids are gone, and two people where they were being kept have been found dead."

"Shit. Excuse my language. Where did this happen?"

"Burnaby."

"I'm going to call someone I know at the RCMP. You can go get the other two." Tony went out into the bullpen area to retrieve his teammates as Thomas was talking to the RCMP. The trio returned to the office, Thomas signalling them to close the door, then hung up. He sat, thinking.

"Two different group homes. The two boys were sent to one, and the four girls sent to another one, both in Burnaby. The other kids in the homes woke up this morning to find the adult dead, and our kids gone. The RCMP say two bullets to the head in each case." He paused. "Nobody heard anything. Silencers. Professional, I'd say, and I don't like where that puts us." The other three remained silent, each thinking through the ramifications of what Thomas had learned.

"I understand that social services wouldn't tell you where the kids were being kept, correct, Tony?"

"Yes. And I told them I was VPD."

"Well...." Thomas paused. "Someone found them, and pretty damned fast."

Vito spoke. "Think they were in the system yet? The computer system? That might be one way of locating them."

Thomas responded, "That would almost be preferable to what I'm thinking, that someone pushed buttons, brought persuasion to bear. No one at social services is going to give that information to an outside party unless they are compromised somehow."

"But after what happened, wouldn't it go right back to the one pushing for the information?" This from Tony. "You would need to hide yourself, wouldn't you? Use a cut-out or intermediary to obscure your identity."

Thomas was quiet, assessing avenues of action, staring into the middle distance at nothing, his hands flat on the clear desk in front of him. "Finn, I want you to find out what surveillance was in operation at the homes. I'll give you the contact at the Horsemen to get you started. Vito can ask social services about the computer angle. Tony, you dig a bit to see who knew where the kids were put, but extremely carefully. Let's meet again after lunch. I'll try to sort out the jurisdictional issues with the RCMP." The City of Burnaby used the RCMP for its policing services, and the Horsemen would be in charge of the murder investigations.

Other avenues of enquiry would be back at the site of the explosion. Who saw those people move in? Was there any interaction with people in that suite from other families in the tower? The survivors would need to be interviewed again. Was there evidence in the suite that would give clues as to who was running it, or who were acting as clients? Thomas had a head full of questions, enough to keep his team busy for the coming days.

CHAPTER 8

It was mid-morning, rain falling gently onto the rear garden. Robert Lui sat at his dining table, laptop open, looking out at the mauve/black tulips sprouting haphazardly throughout the planting beds. Unfortunately, the flowers weren't the only things growing. More than a few weeds were competing for space as well and looked to be winning. He didn't recall planting any bulbs, so how the tulips got there was a mystery. Now that he had renewed purpose in his life, the likelihood that the garden would receive some attention any time soon just shrank close to zero. Robert was only an occasional gardener, not a rabid practitioner like some Vancouverites he knew. A mess or not, he still appreciated being able to look out at green space instead of the side of the neighbour's house.

He needed a plan of action to tackle his newfound job, but first, more coffee, or there'd be no plan, at least nothing likely to work. He poured himself the last of the pot, then returned to his chair. An email had arrived from a Bernard Lily. Why was that name familiar? As he scanned the contents of the message, he remembered. Bernard was a young reporter who had stuck his nose into a case of Roberts' a couple of years back. He seemed to be trying to do the same thing here, referencing GreenSide in the email. He surely must know that I got turfed from the VPD, and how did he get my personal email address? Whatever else might be said about Bernard, he obviously had some sleuthing talents that might be of use to Robert now that he was flying solo.

Putting those thoughts aside, he concentrated on a plan of attack. He guessed that a project this large, with a few governmental entities involved, would have quite the organization chart. This would be his first task, and while mapping this out, he would do his best to find out who was financially involved.

It wouldn't hurt to find out what the VPD was up to as well. Yesterday, the news had revealed the apparent killings of two group home leaders in Burnaby. He shook his head. Violence between family members was sometimes the worst, but to have social services bear the brunt of it was terrible.

He decided to take Tony Bortolo up on his offer of coffee to see how things were going at his former workplace. He called Tony's cell. "Hey Tony, it's Robert. Got time for some coffee today?"

Tony had been feeling the pressure of his new case and was instantly on guard. "Kind of busy right now." But it only took a second to feel guilty, so he relented, "Okay. Just have a complicated case all of a sudden. Could we make it end of the day, say five-thirty or so?"

Robert sensed a tension that Tony had never exhibited before. He wondered what was up but agreed. There was enough left-over pizza in the fridge to keep his kids occupied while he was out. "Sounds good, Cafe Paulo?" An additional benefit of the later time would be less likelihood of running into other officers he knew. The cafe was only a few blocks up Cambie from the VPD offices.

"*Si.*" Tony hung up.

With that organized, Robert turned his attention to the Green-Side site. Start at the beginning, he told himself. Find out who the owners of the site were, originally, and today. See if the lands had been torn apart, making smaller lots, or consolidated into larger parcels. Once that was established, he would find out who put money into the project. The money trail always led to interesting things. He pulled his laptop closer and looked for legal descriptions and then searched titles. He asked his new employer by email to confirm the title numbers as a double check. For the moment, he ignored the email from Bernard. After a couple of hours of this mind-numbing task, he called it a day, and went for a run while organizing his thoughts. Returning, feeling slightly better this time, he left a note for his kids, then headed west in his car to meet with Tony.

He parked a few blocks east of Cambie, then ambled along Seventh Avenue, noting that nothing much had changed in his absence. He turned at Cambie and walked through the door of Cafe Paulo. Gilberto, partially behind his La Cimbali machine, caught sight and a huge grin came over his face. "Roberto!" His voice boomed.

"Gilberto," came the loud reply. He looked around. Tony had not arrived yet, so he went over to the counter to make up for a lot of lost time. Only a couple of young people, maybe in their twenties, were sitting at a table, eating the last of the sandwiches that were usually on offer in the glass display case. Otherwise, it was empty, the cafe normally shutting down around six-thirty.

"How are you a-doing?"

"Good, good. You heard why I don't spend so much time here?"

"Yes, yes, unfortunate Roberto. But you are well? And how about that girl?"

Robert knew this was going to be brought up at some point but had tried to pretend it wouldn't. "She's gone, Gilberto. Back to Montreal. It's all over." He looked down at the marble counter, shaking his head slowly.

"Too bad." Gilberto nodded his head in solidarity, then jumped to something more positive. "Coffee?"

"Of course, small Americano, please." Just then Tony came through the door, a big smile breaking out. "Make it two. Hey Tony! Still employed?"

"Pretty funny, Robert. Good to see you."

"Ditto, let's grab a seat." Although his hair was still jet black, Tony seemed to have aged more than the several months said he should have. A few more wrinkles surrounded eyes above the can opener he used for a nose.

"So how is the detecting going, Tony? Everything you imagined?"

Tony exhaled, then, after a moment, "A tad heavier than I thought it might be."

"Some cases get that way pretty quickly. I won't ask you what you're working on." Which was Robert's way of saying he wanted the exact opposite. "I have news. I got a job the other day."

"Excellent, another police force?"

"Better, a private eye. Kind of like Humphrey Bogart in one of those Dashiell Hammett stories." Getting his media mixed.

"Any dames involved yet?" Tony knew all about Camille leaving.

"Still waiting for that part of it." Robert laughed lightly. "Actually, I'm working on that GreenSide thing."

Tony froze, not knowing what to say. He blinked a couple of times, something Robert had never seen him do.

"S'matter?" Then Robert realized, "Your case as well?"

Gilberto brought the coffees over at that moment, breaking the tension ever so slightly. Robert took a long sip while he waited.

Eventually, Tony realized he could offer little resistance to the man who had helped his career so much. "Yes." Then, "Who are you working for?"

"An outfit called BC Coastal Insurance. They lent some money for the project. Guess they want to know it's still okay."

"You been up there yet? It's quite the mess."

"No, I haven't. Why are you involved? Thought it was an accident."

"Related malfeasance, we think."

"Hmm, mysterious. I'm going to see how the whole thing was set up, see who is involved, and follow the money, as usual. Who are you working with? Not with Rodney, I hope."

"Finn and Vito, for now."

"Good guys. Thomas treating you well?"

"Yes. We're lucky he came back, I think."

"Well, I won't poke anymore. We may be able to help each other, though. I'll keep in touch if that's okay with you."

Tony paused, then issued the warning. "Be careful, Robert. You know those murders the other morning in Burnaby?"

"Heard something."

"It's related, so really, be careful. This is going to be a lot more complicated than it appears."

Robert stared at Tony, then, "So that wasn't family violence playing out?"

"No. Something larger. All I can say right now."

Robert stared at Tony. "Got to get going. My kids may need help finding the leftovers." He finished his coffee and, with a nod at Gilberto, walked out into the evening.

Tony sat a while longer, nursing the last of his Americano, thinking about the chances that they would both be working on the same case, but from different perspectives. Somehow, he felt better knowing this.

CHAPTER 9

A t Vancouver City Hall the next morning, George Ascot, lead lawyer for the city legal team, was reviewing some of the paperwork that had been assembled and signed as the development agreement was put together for GreenSide. His office was on one of the upper floors in the building with the stripped-down Art Deco style built in the 1930s. Although city departments had grown so much that they had been spread out to several nearby buildings, the legal offices were kept in the same building as the mayor's suite. People thought nothing of the building's location today, but at the time of construction, the site was controversial, seeming to be far from the commercial centre of the city. Now, it was classified as a heritage building in a city that had precious little in the way of older built history, meaning any needed renovations would be tricky and expensive.

What George was studying at the moment could be equally controversial if it ever got out into the public realm. On his desk was a signed agreement to provide liquefied hydrogen to the GreenSide project over twenty years for an ungodly amount of money, to be paid by the City of Vancouver monthly. There were two signatures, a Ken Jalla of Sun Energy and Mayor Stanley

Dunbar, with some witness scrawls added for good measure. A mayor signing a contract was very unusual. Now that the hydrogen system at GreenSide had exploded, George was looking for a way out of the contract. It didn't take much of a genius to figure that whatever system replaced the existing one, it wouldn't be based on hydrogen.

He reread the document twice more and couldn't find an exit. His anger built as he wondered who amongst his staff had reviewed this before it was signed. He rose and walked outside his office to find a paralegal who could tell him what had happened. He wasn't so sloppy as to give the document to the paralegal. Rather, he asked him to find out who had reviewed the energy purchase contract.

Half an hour later, the paralegal returned to George's office, entered, and offered the results. "Nobody here reviewed that document. No one thinks it was part of the package that came through here."

"They are sure about that?"

"Yes. We have a copy of the whole document that we reviewed. It is not part of it. Must have been added later?"

"Okay, thanks." The paralegal correctly took this to mean he should leave. George thought a bit about this, wondering how such a thing could have happened, and more importantly, who was behind it. After a few thoughts along those lines, he changed course. The issue really didn't matter to him anymore, now that it had been determined that his department was in the clear. If people were going to bypass his department, then they could live with the results. He turned to other matters, such as the never-ending lawsuits levelled against the city by all and sundry for imagined slights or real accidents on city property.

While George was busy ensuring his department's reputation, a Delta Police squad car was creeping along the extension of 64th Avenue, just west of the main north-south commuter route, Highway 91. The officers were searching for someone on the other side of the road. They were responding to a call from a golf course about a body being discovered at the north edge of their property. The driver spotted a man waving at them from across a ditch, where it was heavily treed. The car stopped at the side of the narrow road and the officers got out, walking over to opposite the man on the other side. He looked down, pointing. The officers followed his direction, and there it was, in the bottom of the ditch, laying like a rag doll that had been carelessly left behind. One of the officers immediately called for more cars and a forensic vehicle. The other officer stood at the edge, trying to understand the cruelty at work for this to happen. It was a young girl from what he could see, but it was impossible to determine what had propelled her into the ditch. It was about two metres deep, with some standing water sitting amongst the weeds and grass.

"One of our golfers was looking for his ball, and found her, about thirty minutes ago."

"Is he still around?"

"Yes, in the clubhouse."

"Please ask him to stay. We'll need to talk with him." It wasn't raining, but the sky was leaden, matching the mood of the scene.

After dozens more officers showed up to complete the scene documentation, the girl was finally removed from her ignominious resting place. Her injuries suggested she had been killed somewhere else and dumped here to be discovered, but the coroner would have to confirm or deny this explanation. The media had shown up, trying unsuccessfully to get a comment from an unguarded officer. The story, or what the media could make of it, was already spreading.

Back at the VPD offices on Cambie Street, Tony, Vito, and Finn were sitting in a small meeting room, musing over what they didn't know about their latest case. Vito was a friend of Tony's, bound by their semi-common background. They seemed to have acquired their noses at the same dispensary, both sporting pronounced aquiline profiles. Tony was originally from Modena in Italy's industrialized and wealthy north. Vito hailed from farther south, Naples, so naturally was considered half criminal from the outset by Tony. The Jesuit priests who had given Vito some of his education in Montreal would have been mildly taken aback by this assumption, but they weren't ignorant of the types of prejudices people carried around. Finn Black was native, hailing from up BC's coast on Haida Gwaii.

The three were talking softly, no confidence in the walls of the room they were in. After a summary of next to nothing was made by each of them, Tony expressed what all three had been thinking. "I wish Robert was back here."

Vito responded, "Well, he isn't, so get over it. We're grownups. We'll have to make do without him. But that said, I agree with Tony."

Finn nodded as well. "Let's get out of here."

Several minutes later, Thomas looked outside his office and beckoned the three detectives from their bullpen desks into a late morning meeting. After the group assembled, Vito looked at Tony and Finn first, before leading off. "It appears that the information about the teenagers was entered into the computer system near the end of the day on which they were apprehended. So, if someone was very good, and very quick, this might be a way to locate them."

Thomas remained silent for a moment. "Bit of a long shot."

"I'd say so. There wouldn't be much preparation time to organize a killing and a kidnapping, two of them at that. But still, not impossible." Vito responded. Tony and Finn remained silent.

"Cameras?" Thomas asked.

Finn sprang to life. "Yes. Shows someone entering, well disguised, then leaving with the kids. Both places were similar. But they must be different people because of the time; nearly the same, just after two in the morning. It will be hard to get any useful information out of the footage. Both people were average height and build, faces hidden."

"Fingerprints?"

"My guess is that they won't find any from the killers, but the scene people are running through what they lifted."

"Ballistics?"

"The RCMP are still working on that aspect."

"How far apart are the group homes?"

"About five kilometres."

At that moment, a knock sounded on Thomas's door. Norma entered with a message for Thomas, then just as quickly, vanished. She had written the note, disturbed by its contents.

Thomas read the message, his face darkening. "A body of a teenage girl has been found in Delta, beaten to death, it appears. Marks on her wrist as well." He paused, as if digesting this unfortunate news, his face growing redder. "Tony, you talked to a couple of these kids. Maybe you should check with the coroner's office and find out where the body was taken. My guess would be Delta Hospital. See if it is one of those kids. And on your way back, I think you should go over to GreenSide and check on the residence where they were found."

Tony stood up, prepared to leave. He paused, looking straight at Thomas, almost telling him about Robert, but decided to keep it to himself for now. It took some self-control to do this.

"I haven't got any further with seeing if someone applied pressure to release the whereabouts of the kids. I'll get back to it when I return." With that, he went off to do something he had no wish to do, view the body of a beaten teenager. The other two remained with Thomas, as he went through his list of what they could chase after while Tony was doing his gruesome duty.

Robert rolled out of bed around eight, his children already gone. He was really appreciating the no commute thing, even though his former drive over to Cambie was no big deal. He knew he would eventually need to land a real job after this adventure was over, so enjoyment at being his own boss would need milking for all it was worth. After a long shower, he went downstairs to start the coffee operation. While the water was getting ready, he looked at his emails, noting the message from Bernard still sitting in his inbox. He'd answer him today, see what Bernard was up to. There was another email, this from Dan Prudence noting Robert's communication with his people as the title search was started. Looked as though Dan would be a nosy boss.

Coffee in hand, he returned to his research. The site had been one parcel at some point, owned by the city, but had since been sub-divided. There were now two parties as owners, with the Province of BC as an interested party to the city's parcel. The city owned the piece of land under the rental towers. A company called Fern Developments owned the remainder of the site, for the building of condominium towers. Fairly straight forward. The new titles told the money story. The rental site had a couple of large Canadian banks bankrolling progress. They wouldn't hesitate putting money into a government backed project, as long as the province was paying the bills. It also looked as if a lien had already been filed against the rental project by a company called Liquid Metal. Robert made a mental note to check on the people behind all these entities.

The condo site told a different tale. There were no traditional large banks involved at all. Five lenders were listed; The Bank of Vancouver, BC Coastal Insurance, Fern Developments, Bamboo Construction, and something called *Deux Tigres*, whatever that was. The first two names were normal: a small local bank and an insurance company that also dealt in mortgage lending. Robert was no development expert, but even he knew it was unusual for a developer to have his own money in a project, not unheard of, however. The last two were more unlikely. He hadn't heard of a construction company ponying up some money for something they were building. And *Deux Tigres* would need some investigating. He immediately did a quick web search, coming up with nothing that made any sense. Maybe this would be something the intrepid cub reporter, Bernard, could help him with. Robert then turned his attention back to the other players, trying to flesh out a picture of each entity, with names and positions. That there were five lenders painted the entire enterprise a questionable colour, but perhaps it was common in the development world.

After another hour of computer research, he took a break to make some toast and think. While chewing, he responded to the Bernard email, '**Interested in meeting?**' He was making a second pot of coffee when a reply came back. '**Absolutely. Name a time and place.**' Hmm, pretty keen, this one. It matched what he remembered from a year or two earlier. He set the meeting for the next day over at Olympic Village, giving him a chance to find out what he could about the recent adventures of Bernard before the meet. He did some online research into Bernard. It only took a minute to find him at the people's network, CBC, working for the local television broadcast group. Well, he would get trained correctly, at the very least. Bernard obviously had more going for him than Robert thought.

It was time for some fresh air, so he laced up his runners and went for a longer and slower run. The more times he went out, the better he felt. Strength was slowly returning to his legs, but every time he went running, a different part of his body complained. Today it was his abdomen, the first thing to go as people aged. Was he really getting that old?

While loping along, he remembered that he shouldn't take anything for granted. First order of business would be to check out both the Bank of Vancouver, and his employer, BC Coastal. Sometimes, seemingly conservative institutions had the most to hide. He was starting to quite like his new employment. He just didn't know how to turn it into a lucrative career that excluded trailing people cheating on their marriage or their insurance claims, which he suspected was the bulk of the work available.

Tony found that the Delta Hospital had indeed received the remains of the teenager found in the golf ditch, so he got into his Ford and headed south on Highway 99, turning off west as he left the tunnel under the Fraser River behind. After entering the hospital admin area and presenting his credentials, he was led down a long corridor to a small room where it was obvious to Tony that few autopsies were done. It didn't appear to be set up for anything other than as a holding area. A doctor shook his hand and took him to a stainless steel table covered with a white cloth.

"Whoever did this was a monster. From how the blood pooled, we can tell that they broke all her leg and arm bones before caving in her skull. Some of her fingers were broken as well." He didn't move. "And there are some bite marks, which we are assuming came from a dog, quite savage markings. These are preliminary observations only. The autopsy will probably happen tomorrow."

The comment about the fingers grabbed Tony's attention. He waited.

"The girl is around sixteen years of age. Judging by her dental work, she may have come from Central or South America, certainly not from the U.S. or Canada. I assume you wish to see her?"

"I don't wish to, but I am afraid I must," Tony responded reluctantly.

The doctor folded back the cover. Tony shifted backward with a sudden intake of breath. "It's her. Jesus, I was talking to her only a couple of days ago. She wouldn't say much. Frightened to death, I thought."

"It seems you were correct to think that." He paused. "Anything else?"

"Sexual activity?"

"Yes, recent."

"Okay, thanks. Could I have your name in case we have any further questions?"

After writing this down, Tony thanked the doctor and slowly made his way back to his car. He sat behind the steering wheel, thinking, and what he was thinking again was that he wished Robert was back to lead this case.

He shook his head and started the car, then returned to Vancouver and the GreenSide site. To serve and protect. Wasn't that the motto of some police agencies? To know that he had that girl within his grasp and was unable to prevent what happened was hard to reconcile. Some anger was building, towards who was hard to determine, but the injuries told him that maybe Manny and his gang were involved. Manny had a thing about fingers.

Tony kept turning events over in his mind as he drove, until he eventually pulled into the construction parking lot at GreenSide. He looked around at the seemingly lifeless site. Some of the mess had been cleaned up, but the tower that had been cleaved by the explosion still sat with a pile of stacked concrete slabs in front of it. He went over to the Bamboo trailer and knocked, then walked in. Again, only Arby was present.

"Hi. I'd like to get into the tower. The third floor, to be exact."

Arby looked at Tony like he was some insect, then turned back to some drawings that he seemed to be inspecting on his layout table. "Go ahead. At your own risk, though. It's a little shaky." He waved his hand at Tony like he was shooing a fly.

"Is there a stair at least?"

"Yes, one of the exit stairs survived. The door is unlocked at the rear. The elevators aren't working so good." Arby smiled at this thought.

"Thanks for all your help." The insincere comment was left hanging as Tony exited the trailer. He approached the tower and looked up at part of a short, exposed corridor with two elevator doors on each floor. He headed to the left, where the stair door might be. He walked around the side and there it was, with a sign saying 'Danger—No Entry' on it. Well written, Tony thought, as he opened the door. He knew what he was doing wasn't safe, but he reasoned that if the rest of the structure was going to fall, it would have done so by now.

He walked slowly up the stairs, past gaping cracks in one of the walls, reinforcing bars exposed like ribs in a chest. A handrail had fallen off and lay by the wall on the risers, as if left carelessly by a labourer. At the third floor, he pushed the door open to the now open-air corridor. Suddenly, he felt less sure of himself. No safety railings or netting had been installed at the open edge, so he shuffled along the wall to what he thought was the approximate location of the suite where he had seen the teenagers rescued from.

He entered through a partially open door into what looked like a new apartment. Some shards of concrete that had spalled off the ceiling lay scattered on the floor. The drywall displayed a multitude of cracks. Otherwise, it didn't look too bad. What did look weird was the number of beds in the place. There were two large beds in the living area, and another one in the bedroom. He entered the bedroom and saw a hole neatly cut into the wall, leading to what he realized was the adjacent suite. He stepped through and saw it was set up the same way. A couple of pieces of clothing lay on the carpet. He guessed that there would be a treasure trove of DNA information for a forensic team, so he snapped a few pictures with his phone and decided to get out while getting was good. After he had descended the stairs, and forgoing the courtesy farewell with Arby, he headed straight to his car and back to Cambie Street.

It was two by the time he ditched the car in the underground parkade, so he strode up Cambie Street to Cafe Paulo for some sustenance and thinking time before he met with Thomas and the group.

He walked in, but there was no sign of Gilberto. It seemed that Carmelita was in charge today. "*Espresso, dopio, per favore Carmelita. Grazie.*" He then looked into the glass case and selected a panino with a tuna salad filling. He went to the table by the window that formerly was the preserve of Robert Lui. As he waited, he realized that Carmelita had probably come from a similar area as the poor girl who had been beaten to death. His quick search had found that Ocotal, where the girl had said she was from, was a small town in Nicaragua. His family had come from northern Italy, so he was un-used to the travails of people from poorer regions of the world, but he knew life was hard for them. Didn't matter, there was no excuse for what had happened to those kids, particularly the girl found this morning. As he was pondering the chances of Robert working on the same case and what this might lead to, Carmelita brought over the sandwich and coffee. He wasted no time devouring the offerings, and nodding to Carmelita, left the cafe to go update his superior.

Tony walked onto his floor and towards his desk, where he had spent scant time lately. He nodded to Norma, who beckoned him over to her desk. "The chief would like to see you, if it is convenient?"

The chief? Did Thomas get a new title? Tony looked at Norma with a crook eye. "I am sure it is convenient, Norma." He proceeded to Thomas's door and knocked on the frame, peering in as he did so. Rodney Fister was standing in front of Thomas's desk, looking like he was getting ready to leave. Tony nodded at Rodney as he brushed by him, not really feeling like talking. The look Rodney sent Tony's way as they passed wasn't exactly full of hatred, but it wasn't far off. If Tony had to guess at the source of this antipathy, his new case would be a good starting point. Rodney being stuck with a fairly standard murder case on the east side on top of all his other cases was likely not sitting very well. In addition, Rodney was a rank above him, a sergeant, so the exclusion from the GreenSide affair probably drove him crazy.

Thomas waved at his guest chair. Tony closed the door, then slumped into the chair.

"I remember Robert once telling me what enthusiasm you could display on the job."

"I believe I am starting to appreciate why Robert was the way he was." Tony answered.

But Thomas had made his point. What he expected Tony to do about this was left unsaid. "So, what did you learn?"

"The girl was the same one I talked briefly with three days ago. She was beaten to death, Thomas, and apparently savaged by a dog as well. It was pretty horrible. In addition to all the other broken bones, they broke some of her fingers. Remind you of anything? The complete coroner's report should be available in a day or two. I also went by GreenSide. It was a tad dicey, getting up to the third floor. The apartment had been linked to the adjacent suite by a hole in the wall, a crude doorway. The whole place seemed to be fitted out like a brothel." Tony felt compelled to add. "Not that I would know what one looked like."

Thomas smiled briefly, "Of course not, Tony." He glanced out his window at the lowering sun, clouds having left the scene. Flocks of crows in waves were making their return journey east to their homes somewhere in Burnaby, a process that happened every day. What was the correct term for them? A murder of crows? Who figured that one out?

"So, we have a brothel set up in a city-run rental building where the paint hasn't even dried. And found only by the unluckiest of events. I'm guessing the girl was made an example in front of the others."

"I feel ill," Tony confessed. "She also had had recent sexual activity."

"Go home Tony. I'll get a forensic team out to GreenSide."

Chapter 10

The next morning, Robert headed over to his meeting with Bernard at Olympic Village, an area of high-priced condominiums formerly used as athlete's accommodation for the 2010 Winter Olympics. He weighed his options and decided to drive rather than use the transit system, wanting to arrive the same day. He parked The Silver Streak close to the plaza with giant bird sculptures, house sparrows the size of elephants, and walked over to the cafe at the west edge of the open space. Bernard was sitting outside at a table, looking his way. Robert remembered that this used to be Bernard's neighbourhood, and maybe still was for all he knew.

He walked up to Bernard, touching his finger to his forehead in a casual salute. "Coffee?"

Bernard smiled. "Yes, that would be nice." Bernard was smartly decked out in freshly washed black jeans; a green checked shirt partially hidden by a dark blue anorak that looked like it had recently been purchased at one of the local mountaineering shops. A striped yellow and black scarf loosely wrapped around his neck completed his ensemble. Perhaps Bernard had aspirations of being an on-screen reporter, who all sported scarves, the bigger and more intricately tied, the better. Robert imagined there was probably a school of scarf knots somewhere in the bowels of the CBC, a mandatory course for the on-air talent. Bernard had a decently fresh face atop his neck, so there were possibilities.

"I'll be back." Robert went inside to order. It was mid-morning, and the place was packed. He wondered, not for the first time, who in the city actually worked.

He returned with two drip coffees, placing Bernard's in front of him. "Don't know how you take it." Then he sat down, the action implying he didn't much care how Bernard took his coffee. After Bernard returned from filling his coffee with sugar and cream, Robert stared at him for a few moments, enough to generate an uneasy feeling in the reporter.

Robert sipped his coffee, waiting, "So, you found my email address. You must know then that I am not with the VPD anymore."

Bernard didn't know what to make of this directness. His previous experience with Robert had consisted of being treated like something a small step up from a dog. He sampled his coffee. "Yes, I heard some things."

"Ha. How's it going at the people's network?"

Again, direct and to the point. Bernard now knew he wasn't the only one who could do research. He had to remind himself that he was dealing with a detective, and a very good one from what he had learned. "It's going fine. Learning a few things."

"I'll bet. They train you right from what I hear." Robert paused to increase the tension, looking directly into Bernard's eyes. "So why are we meeting, Bernard?"

"GreenSide. You saw the news clips. Those kids rescued with handcuffs on them. Something's not right. I think they have disappeared again from what I have been able to learn."

"Why do you think I care? I'm not with the force anymore."

"You responded to my email, so I am inclined to think there is a reason. Or am I wrong?"

Smarter than I thought, Robert mused. "Yes, there is a reason. I am working for one of the companies involved and doing some research. That you found me indicates that maybe we may be of some use to each other."

Bernard was silent while he thought this through. Inwardly, he was rejoicing. Here was a way into what could be a really juicy story. And it could be his to command. "How could I help? Who are you working for?"

Robert estimated it was all Bernard could do not to drool over the table. "*Deux Tigres.* French company, maybe. I'd like to know more about them if possible. They are apparently an investor in GreenSide." Tony's warning to Robert about danger two days earlier, already forgotten.

"And in return, once I have this information?"

"Let's see what you learn first, then we'll discuss *quid pro quo.*"

"Could I have your cell number?"

"No. I'll contact you. There's always email, anyway."

Bernard sat back, smiling slightly at this stroke of luck, finishing his cup. Robert wasn't smiling, but considered where this all might lead.

"I'll be in touch. Let me know if you find out anything. It has been a pleasure." He then got up, wheeled around, and walked back towards his car. Bernard was already on his cellphone, communicating with the mothership. Robert thoughts shifted to dinner, thinking it felt like a Chinese night, so he turned and went over to the local grocery store, and after wandering the aisles, purchased a couple of bags of frozen dumplings and some fresh-looking *dau miu* before heading to his car.

On his journey home, he remembered something and stopped in front of an electronics store on Fraser that he had used previously. He entered, nodding to the proprietor. The place was otherwise empty. Maybe the whole day was like this for the gentleman. It was hard to gauge.

"Slow time of day?"

The older man spread his arms apart. "Larger stores take my business away," he said helplessly. The accent didn't give Robert a clue where he hailed from.

"I'm looking for a tape machine. I have a small audio cassette that I need to play."

"Do you have the cassette with you? There are many different types."

"Sadly, not."

"Okay, let's see what I have. Let me know what matches if you can." He wasn't about to let Robert escape easily. He pulled open a drawer, taking a handful of examples out, laying them on the counter in front of Robert.

"That's the one," pointing to the smallest cassette. The owner smiled. After paying for the mini-machine, making the shop-keeper's afternoon, Robert completed his trip home. The purchase wasn't directly related to his current employment deal, as far as he knew, but he would be adding it to his expenses for recovery later. After stowing the groceries in the fridge, Robert pulled out some soup and heated it up for a late lunch. As he stacked the dishes after finishing, he had his eye on the cassette sitting on the table, wondering what surprises were waiting. The only thing he knew was that it had been liberated from the Gupil gang a year earlier, along with a few other items which Robert did not care about. He sat down, inserted the cassette, and stared at it. Maybe a cup of coffee might be in order. What he had been drinking at his morning meeting was marginal at best. Yes, I better get some more caffeine. Another delaying tactic.

After finally running out of reasons to procrastinate; he re-turned to the table, sat down, inserted the cassette, pressing the play button.

'*Is this Edward?*' Robert thought he recognized the voice.

'*No names, you fool.*'

'*Calm down. We need some cleaning done. I heard you have someone who could help us.*'

'*Help me, not us. I have a diamond in the rough, so to speak.*'

'*What the fuck does that mean?*'

'*He is on the inside at Gaming and Enforcement. He gives us advice on where we can clean money. I can give you an option, but this service is not free.*'

'*I thought not. I would be grateful for some leads.*'

'*I'll let you know.*' A click signalled the end of the conversation.

Robert let the machine play, but there was nothing else on the tape. He opened his notebook. Edward had to be the man he knew as the head of the Wide Bay Boys triad. He was still in remand, awaiting trial for the events of a year earlier. Robert guessed that the other speaker was the gang leader known as The Guru. The triad had used The Guru's gang, the Gupils, to do some of its less savoury tasks on occasion. The Guru was no longer around, so Robert assumed that the Gupils had disintegrated since, having heard nothing about them in the interim. Robert previously guessed that the triad had someone on the inside within government. It was the way they operated, planting moles so that surprises were kept to a minimum.

Gaming and Enforcement—very good, Robert thought. What better place to have someone who could help with money laundering? A rather broad clue was referenced by the diamond in the rough phrase. There was no other hint in the conversation that meant anything, so he would start with that, carefully, of course. Edward had been sloppy with his boast. From what little Robert knew of the man, it was uncharacteristic.

He decided to leave the sleuthing for now and concentrate on dinner. His children would be home soon, and they were always hungry. Fortunately, the dinner he was planning didn't ask for a lot of prep for a change. He pulled out the rice maker, and a jar of chicken stock from the fridge. He prepped the *dau miu* so it would be ready for blanching, then finished with garlic and a *hoisin* sauce when the dumplings were close to being ready. Next was a glass of wine while he turned on the local news to see what other shenanigans the criminal element was up to in greater Vancouver.

He didn't learn anything, other than that the GreenSide explosion was still in the news, the reporters trying their best to assign blame somewhere. The sad roll call of those who had perished was read out, along with those injured and still in hospital. The missing teenagers were not mentioned, but Robert guessed that Bernard would change that pretty quickly if he could.

Once his children were home, he prepared the dipping sauce for the dumplings by shaving some ginger, then adding it to a mixture of vinegar and soya sauce. He put the dumplings in a large pan, browning their bottoms before adding some stock and covering them for fifteen minutes before the final sauté. Dinner was ready a few minutes later, and there was no conversation.

Next day, Robert suffered a slight interest downturn with his research work. After seeing his children off to school, he made a phone call, something he had been putting off.

"Hey Mom, it's Robert."

"Good to hear from you, Robert. How are you?"

"Fifty-fifty, Mom. Camille has left, gone back to Montreal. It wasn't working out."

"Oh Robert, that is a shame. I liked her."

"Yeah, well, it's what you get when you mix work with your love life." He wasn't going to say any more than that. "But on a brighter note, I landed a job. Private investigator for an insurance company. I'm looking at that GreenSide mess."

"That is good news, Robert."

"Kids are great, as usual." He heard a contented sigh from the other end. The children were what his parents really wanted to know about. "I'll call again soon, Mom." He hung up then mulled over calling Camille again, finally deciding to at least try. He dialled her number. Of course, there was no answer. She could probably see who was calling. He considered leaving a message, but in the end, didn't, regret working its way through his emotions. What was the point, anyway? It wasn't like he was going to pop over to see her and try to reset the relationship, Montreal being some four thousand kilometres away. Maybe it was time to think of the future and be more positive for a change.

After breakfast, Robert did a computer search of personnel in the Ministry of Attorney General, Gaming and Enforcement Branch. He took his time but didn't find anything to attract his interest. He sat, perplexed. The tape he had listened to was over a year old. Perhaps the person had moved on. After all, with Edward in jail, maybe there was no one pulling any strings or paying the mole for information. Robert pondered the idea of a visit to see Edward. One would think he'd be keen to have some visitors after a year sitting in remand, even if it wasn't exactly a friendly visit. He would mull that over. One thing he could be certain of was that Edward probably didn't know that Robert was no longer with the police force. Something he could possibly use.

He then mapped out a visit to the city planning department to see what he could find out about the process for GreenSide. He knew one thing for sure, that it would be tortured and span several years. His deceased wife had been a planner, both for Vancouver, and at the end, Surrey, so he knew second hand about the intricate machinations of attempting to get a project through all the approvals, never mind getting it built. He was familiar with one planner left from his wife's tenure at Vancouver, if she was still at the city. People tended to jump around from place to place looking for that bump in pay and the chimerically perfect job that always lay on the horizon of one's career. Before he met her, though, he would go through the public record of decisions and votes on the matter, as the information all existed on the city's website. Deciding to leave that task for another day, he got changed, donned his runners, and went out for some exercise and a think.

He headed south, running up Fraser Street, then cutting west through the huge main city cemetery, always a relaxing place to run. GreenSide wasn't far away, so it wouldn't hurt to swing by the site. His second thought was his bank account. Nothing had appeared from BC Coastal to bolster its diminishing numbers. He supposed a call to Dan Prudence was in order. On reflection, the holdup in funds transfer was probably intended to provoke this very call so Dan could keep tabs on progress or lack there-of.

As he ran up Main Street just to the east of the site, he could see some VPD vehicles near the damaged tower, probably doing some more investigation. He turned west again, intending on running into Queen Elizabeth Park to get above the site to see what else might be going on. He slowed to a stop as he looked over at the site, then glanced down at a sewer cover, a manhole lid, that was more like a work of art. The inscription read, *No dumping, salmon stream below*. He supposed it was evidence of what used to be.

After a couple of moments, he started jogging between the par three golf course in the park and the site below. He looked over, but the only new thing he learned was that a forensic unit was sitting by the tower. A call to Tony might help illuminate things. Then he slowed and stopped a second time. He looked west, across a fairway, at two wispy figures walking slowly. One was a woman, half naked, wearing what looked like a bark skirt. She had a basket on her back with the strap wrapped around her forehead, long black hair waving slightly in the wind. The man was similarly dressed, naked torso with only a breechcloth covering his lower half. He had some kind of knife attached to his side. Robert blinked, looked back at GreenSide, then returned to the vision. The natives were no longer there. Instead, two golfers were tugging spindly carts towards a green.

After returning home and showering, he called his employer, pointing out that the twenty percent up-front payment had mysteriously not appeared. After some back and forth, and Robert's revelation about the four other investors in the project, Dan was sufficiently mollified to agree to make the deposit that afternoon. Turned out Dan knew about the number of investors but was unaware that both the contractor and *Deux Tigres* were also noted on the title, agreeing that Robert was making some progress.

Robert was coming to the unpleasant realization that working for yourself also meant making sure you were paid. It was a bit of a wake-up to find that money wasn't coming into his bank account once a month, no matter what happened. Still, the freedom that came with being your own boss was exhilarating, for now at least.

After checking his account later that afternoon and finding the money had indeed been deposited, Robert celebrated by ordering in some pizzas for dinner. His children would never say no to this extravagance.

It wasn't until dinner was over, and the few plates had been tucked into the dishwasher, that Robert checked his email. In amongst the usual garbage was a message from his new pal, Bernard.

'Just out of sugery. We ned to talk soon as can. VGH. Bernard.' The message had come via a phone. Robert was not impressed with the spelling from someone who called himself a journalist. Robert didn't waste any time.

"Going out for a bit, should be back in an hour," he yelled as he walked upstairs. He went into his bedroom, to the bottom drawer of his dresser, where he kept a strongbox with his only gun. He strapped on his shoulder holster, made sure his gun was loaded and the safety on, and yelled "See you soon" on his way out.

After he parked at the hospital lot and walked over the sky-walk to the main lobby, he went up to the smiling girl behind the information kiosk. "Looking for a Bernard Lily. I believe he was admitted today."

The girl checked her screen, and a few seconds later, "Room 981, main tower. He just came out of surgery a while ago."

"Any information on how he is?"

"None so far. Visiting hours are over at nine sharp."

"Thanks." He proceeded in the direction she had pointed, wondering what the hell had happened to Bernard. The elevator opened its doors on the ninth floor and Robert got off, hesitating slightly. He hated hospitals. The admin desk wasn't far away, so he went over and asked for 981. After a short trip past carts, beds and all manner of medical devices clogging the corridor, he came to the room. He entered and saw that Bernard had a roommate. His conversation would have to be controlled. He walked past the dividing curtain and immediately saw the reason for Bernard's less than one hundred percent email spelling. His right arm was in a full-length cast extending from his shoulder downwards. Only the tips of his fingers could be seen.

"Geez Bernard, what did you do?"

Bernard started talking softly. Robert leaned in closer to make out what he was saying. Bernard looked woozy.

"Got attacked in my garage. This guy beat the crap out of my arm; broke a few bones. Came with a warning; if I didn't stop asking questions about *Deux Tigres*, next time I'd be dead. I believe he meant it."

"Didn't know you owned a car, Bernard."

"Moved up in the world." He tried to smile, but the pain turned it into a grimace. "It was actually pretty scary. There was no telling if he was just going to beat me, or maybe kill me. The guy was the same size as me, not an ape."

"I am sorry Bernard. I had no idea this could be dangerous. How long are they going to keep you here?"

"I expect to get the boot tomorrow if my pain is manageable."

"Do you have family in town, or a girl?"

"Other side of the country, and no girl."

Robert pondered this lack of support. "If you want, I can come get you tomorrow, drive you home. Least I can do for you."

"That would be nice. Think I'll put this research for you on hold, if you don't mind."

"No worries. Somehow, I thought you'd be better at it than this." He pointed to the cast, smiling slightly. "I think you should be safe for the night, but I'll have a word with the nurse. Can you email me when you are set free? I'm not far away. Maybe you should go visit the police and make a report."

"Not sure about that, Robert. Let me think about it. I'll let you know when I'm released."

Robert touched his brow with his right index finger and left the room.

He went to the nurse at the desk he had just talked to. "Do you think you could make sure Bernard doesn't get anymore guests this evening? His arm wasn't an accident. I understand he is being discharged tomorrow?"

"Probably. And you are?"

"A friend. Ex-police officer."

Her eyes widened slightly at this. "Is there danger?"

"I believe not, but I would keep people alert here while he is incarcerated." With that, he left the floor, then the hospital, heading for home and a whisky while he thought about his case. He'd have to find out what exactly Bernard had been doing to provoke this type of response. He didn't feel his children were in any danger so far, but he was very attuned to such things after what they had been through a year earlier.

After Robert got home, he yelled up to his children. They both answered, so he expelled his breath and headed for his whisky collection. After pouring himself a scotch, he sat down and texted Tony. **'Think we could meet tomorrow? Unexpected developments.'**

That done, he settled back and contemplated what he seemed to have got himself into. Undoubtably, this *Deux Tigres* thing was attached to some kind of criminal element. He wondered how many of the other investors in GreenSide knew about this. It would be wrong to assume they were all ignorant. He knew from his conversations with Camille that back east, criminals had been long entrenched in the construction industry. Maybe British Columbia was just catching up. It was hard to tell. It shouldn't surprise anyone, he thought. Laundering money was a wide-ranging enterprise, construction being one of many vehicles enabling this.

CHAPTER 11

Morning dawned with clouds and spotty rain, a spring day to help things grow. Robert woke to hear his children preparing for another school day. He checked his cell; sure enough, Tony had answered, **'Where and when?'**

Robert thought Cafe Paulo was too close to the station, so he suggested another place on Main Street, the Apollo Cafe. Tony agreed. The meeting was on for half past ten. He hadn't heard from Bernard, so assumed he wasn't being let loose from the hospital just yet. After seeing his children off to school, he made some toast. Finished, he walked over to the meeting, despite the rain. It was a bit of a hike from his home east of Fraser Street, but good exercise and a change from running.

This time Tony was waiting for him, sitting by the rear wall of the cafe. Robert waved and signed the question. Tony nodded, so Robert went up to the barista and ordered two Americanos, then went over to Tony's table. There were five or six other people in the place, mostly studying their phones or laptops, which seemed to be what passed for socialization in most cafes these days. It was hard to see how the proprietors were able to keep a business afloat with deadbeats filling the chairs.

"How are you keeping Tony?"

Tony tilted his head from side to side. "Okay, I guess."

"Sounds about right. Got something to report." Robert then fell silent, as the barista had succeeded with Robert's order and called out his name. Robert went over and retrieved the two mugs of coffee, returning to the table. "Here you go."

"You drink more coffee than anyone I know."

Robert smiled. "I know. Anyway, I seem to have poked someone. Remember that reporter from eighteen months ago? The Eden Gardens case? He found me, so I thought he would enjoy doing some research for me. Thing is, he ended up in the hospital yesterday. Someone beat his arm into pieces and left a warning. Ever heard of *Deux Tigres*?"

Tony's eyes widened. "Did you say *Deux Tigres*?"

"I believe I did."

"French for Two Tigers, right?"

"You're a living French-English dictionary, Tony. I'm impressed."

Tony took this in the spirit it was given, smiling. "The Gupils new name is Two Tigers."

"Uh oh. Bernard was asking about *Deux Tigres*. They are one of five investors in the GreenSide project. Who or how he asked, I don't know yet."

"That should make the other participants happy, to know they are partners with criminals." Tony said.

"Yes. I wonder which of them know this already? Don't think two of the lenders would knowingly get into bed with a gang. I feel bad about using Bernard like that. Whoever did it threatened to kill him next time if he didn't leave off." Then, "I thought the gang disbanded after last spring."

"From what Thomas told me, Manny stepped up and is now running things."

"Great. That thug wouldn't think twice about killing anyone, and brutally. It's hard to believe that he hasn't been nailed for something yet."

Tony didn't consider what he said next; maybe he felt like Robert was part of the team again, or maybe he just screwed up by spilling information he shouldn't. "We think there was a brothel set up at GreenSide, populated with teenagers, essentially. It was in the tower that got the alterations done to it."

"But that is a new project."

"Yes, so this was planned, not an opportunistic thing. Another thing, the teenagers that were pulled out of there disappeared and two den mothers killed the night after they were apprehended. Two separate locations, and very quickly done."

"Don't think you're supposed to be telling me this, Tony."

He smiled, "I know, but it feels good doing it. There's more. I talked with one of the girls at the hospital before she was taken away. She was found yesterday morning in a ditch, beaten to death, multiple fractures, and broken fingers. It's bloody sickening Robert." The smile was gone, replaced by a haggard look that Robert hadn't seen before on his former partner.

"The speed of the responses is a little unnerving, don't you think?"

"We're looking into it but haven't unearthed anything yet. They may have inside information."

"Great. That's all you need, another mole. The fingers sound like Manny's work. I'm going to continue my research into the project, how it was set up. It's generating a certain odour already."

"Yeah, I'm thinking Manny is behind the violence. Thanks Robert. Let's keep in contact."

"Agreed. One other thing, is Roy still available? Need to replace that Beretta I lost last spring. It's in the drink in Steveston."

"Yes, he is still working."

"Thanks Tony. Keep your head up." With that, Robert stood and, leaving the cups on the table, left the cafe to head back home. Tony remained seated, puzzling how much of this he should tell Thomas. Decision reached; he also left, and like Robert, walked back the way he came.

As Robert headed east, he considered what he needed in the way of armaments. Roy was a procurer of weapons, the kind that a police force didn't give to its officers. Robert was certain that Roy had customers other than police personnel but didn't ask questions. A SIG Sauer, which was used as a service pistol, was all well and good, but sometimes, other things were useful. Robert had, of course, given up his weapon and badge when he was forced to resign. He had a second SIG Sauer of his own with a shoulder holster, and used to have a Beretta Tomcat before it had unfortunately been dropped by a fellow officer into the Fraser River. So, he wanted a replacement, and he thought that a tranquilizer pistol wouldn't be out of order either. Sometimes, a little discretion was required. As he made his way closer to his townhouse, he called Roy and put in the order. Roy was always happy to get requests like Robert's. The way things were heading,

Robert would expense these two items as well. Dan Prudence hadn't warned this was going to be hazardous work.

Robert arrived home and rummaged through his fridge, looking for something similar to lunch, when he heard his email ping. Sure enough, it was Bernard, being ejected from VGH. Robert answered that he'd be there in fifteen. While travelling to the hospital, Robert came up with a lunch idea. He'd take Bernard, if he was up for it, to his favourite noodle house on Broadway. Bernard would no doubt need fortifying after eating hospital food for a day. After the pickup, Bernard agreed to the detour, and as he and Robert were settling in for a noodle fest, Tony was preparing for a meeting with his team at Cambie Street.

Just after one, Thomas asked the GreenSide team into his office. Tony walked into the office, nodding at the other two detectives, who were already sitting, waiting.

"Anything to report, anyone?" Thomas led off.

Finn started. "Ballistics are still checking the bullets pulled from the two women killed in Burnaby. No report back yet. And no progress with the surveillance videos. Dealing with the RCMP isn't like talking to people around here. I don't know whether I am being told everything or not."

"Don't take it personally, Finn. So, a big bunch of nothing. Vito, anything?"

"I've been talking to our tech guys down in the basement. No progress on the computer angle so far. It apparently is going to be difficult to find any digital fingerprints."

Digital fingerprints—the others looked at Vito as though he was talking about an alien landing. Thomas shook his head.

Tony at least had something to talk about, but he wasn't going to reveal Robert's presence just yet. "I found out that a company by the name of *Deux Tigres* is a lender to the project."

"Shit." Thomas knew immediately what this meant. "Now we have a reason for the violence. The Two Tigers are a much more brutal gang ever since the demise of The Guru."

"The violence is spreading."

"Meaning what?"

"Remember a reporter, name of Bernard Lily? From the case Robert worked on a couple of years back?"

"Vaguely."

"He was doing some research into *Deux Tigres* and got beaten up for his troubles."

"How would he know about them?"

"Someone pointed him in their direction. I'm not sure who yet."

Thomas took this at face value, the white lie undetected, but he was suspicious. "Find out who."

The direction didn't leave Tony much wriggle room. It was just a matter of a day or two until he would need to reveal Robert's participation. "Okay, but he is a reporter—sources, etcetera. I believe he is working for the CBC now."

"Great." The media weren't fast friends with any of the officers at Cambie Street. "Anything from the site yet?"

"Still processing all the evidence found there. It's going to take a while to sort it all out." Tony responded.

Thomas said nothing, nor was he looking at the other officers. His gaze was fixed on some unknown entity hovering above their heads. Finally, "We have someone inside the gang. But I don't want to use him just yet. It has to be important or a threat because we probably only have one shot at this. And of course, this stays in the room."

Tony looked at Finn and Vito. All three had slightly wider eyes at this news.

After Robert and Bernard had finished their noodle extravaganza, Bernard using his off arm; Robert ordered a couple of more dishes to take with him, drove Bernard to his rented condo, then headed home to restart his research task. Bernard thanked Robert for the excellent meal, then went into his tower home to ingest more painkillers. Robert shook his head as he watched Bernard disappear into his lobby. Tony's warning came back to him, 'Be careful'. He needed to pay more attention to things.

Back at home, instead of chasing the money for now, Robert looked at the early days of the project, who was involved with the land deals, how companies were set up. He looked at the private side, then the public side. The ultimate goal would be to see who might be profiting that shouldn't be. Developers did their thing to make money, everyone knew this. It was the 'sucker fish' swimming along and trying to latch on to this enterprise that Robert was after.

He went back five years into the public record to see where the initial idea came from. Making the project both for profit and building social housing wasn't a new idea, nor was it usually problematic. It wasn't uncommon for a developer to derive some extra condo units and more height for a project by offering to build some social or rental units into the bargain. GreenSide was different, however. The city had owned the entire land parcel, and then gave or sold some of it away to Fern Development. Robert wanted to find out if it was a straight money transaction, presumably done to fund some social housing, or something else at play. The location of the site was prime, and there was no indication that there was anything wrong with the soil, which is generally where much of the project risk lays, so any developer would have done whatever it took to secure the property for their use.

Robert obviously would not be finding out about what backroom deals were done, but he could check on the voting records of city councillors as a start. He looked at the rezoning process, which would have been when the basic outline of what GreenSide was to become was laid out. All rezoning applications must appear eventually in front of city council, once for a public hearing, then again for the final vote after inevitable revisions have been made to the application. The public gets to have a say, with those against the project usually the most vociferous in their arguments. Complete records are kept, so this is what Robert waded through online. It didn't take long for the effects of both the search and the noodle lunch to degrade Robert's brain functions. He eventually stood up and walked around the main floor to get some blood moving.

He sat back down and reviewed what he was learning. The amount of vitriol from some of the public in these council meetings was astounding, and he assumed the content had been watered down by the note taker. Each councillor's vote was accompanied by a rationale explaining their decision. By far, the biggest booster of the project seemed to be Councillor Nile Gecko. Robert was unfamiliar with who he was, but he'd keep an eye out for the name in future searches.

He then moved on from the rezoning process, which was when the site had been split up into two parcels. The development process that followed rezoning was more fragmented, as each tower needed its own development permit, going through much of the same process again. He started to appreciate why developers complained about the city process so much. A development agreement also became one of the city requirements at this stage. Far as Robert could tell, it was a nitty gritty legal document laying down who was exactly responsible for what between the developer and the city. He'd like to get his hands on this but couldn't find it online. Maybe he could find it through his contact in planning, Jean Kwok. From what he could tell, it also seemed that Fern Developments was to take both the condo tower's site and the social housing site through to completion. He anticipated that Fern would get quite the financial sweetener to do the rental portion but puzzled how to find this out. Again, maybe in the development agreement?

He changed tactics and went back to the title search documents. He looked closer at the lending amounts, which was when he found something immensely interesting. He knew that anytime money was loaned for anything, the largest and most traditional lender would make sure they got first rights. If something screwed up or someone went bankrupt, the first in line would get their money out. The small investors usually would be left holding the proverbial bag, with nothing in it. Somehow, in this case, *Deux Tigres* seemed to have first rights, leaving BC Coastal Insurance in third place. The amount of money that the gang had fronted was the smallest of all five lenders. Robert wondered who among the other lenders knew about this, and how it happened. Probably threats and some violence secured the front of the line. Plenty of things to tell his new employer, so he sent Dan Prudence an email saying he'd be calling in tomorrow with an update. He didn't want Dan getting fidgety enough to hold up his payments again.

As Robert was setting the table for dinner, which he had had the foresight to purchase at the restaurant after lunch was done, his cell pinged. It was Roy, texting that he would have his order the day after tomorrow. That was quick, Robert thought, wondering, not for the first time, what it was exactly that Roy did for a living when he was not running weapons.

After a successful dinner, during which Sophie actually talked about an environmental course she was taking, he called his parents to broach something on his mind.

He waited until Sophie and Robin retreated upstairs to their lairs, then dialled, "Hello Mom."

"Robert. This is unexpected. Two calls in a week."

"Yes, I know. How are you and Dad?"

"Good Robert." Then silence, while Mary waited for whatever was to come.

Robert felt bad asking this, but he didn't have much of an option. "If they needed to, could the kids come stay with you for a couple of days?"

"I'm sure they could, Robert. What is happening?"

"Just being cautious, Mom. This new job has turned out to be slightly more complicated than I anticipated."

"Complicated, as in dangerous?"

"That kind of complicated, yes." His mom, a former university professor, was nobody's fool. "It may not come to anything, but I'll try to give you some warning if it needs to happen."

Mary responded slowly, "Okay. Would you and the children like to come for dinner this Sunday?"

"That would be nice, Mom. We'll be there." With that, he hung up, wondering where GreenSide was taking him, and his family. There was no way in hell he was going to be caught out again.

The next morning, Robert got up after his children had left for school. He felt lethargic, so pulled on his runners and immediately went for a long run. While he was on his circuit, he went over what he would and wouldn't say to Dan. Finally satisfied with his logic, he returned, showered, and readied himself.

He called his employer. "Dan? Robert here. Are we feeling grand today?"

"Yes, yes. Odd choice of words, but I was wondering when you would call."

"Wonder no more. How much do you know about the other lenders on the GreenSide project?"

"We know there are four other lenders, but only the top two put in the lion's share of the money."

"Is this something your company has done before?"

"On a much smaller scale, we have done it a few times. This is a relatively new part of our business, and this is the first time we have gone in with this much money."

"Yes, forty-five million seems like a large sum to me, but I'm no expert on lending practices. Again, what do you know about the other companies?"

"There is the bank, then the developer, contractor, and a small French company named *Deux Tigres*. Why?"

"I'd say you are keeping some pretty questionable company." There was silence on Dan's end, so Robert continued, "I've found out that BC Coastal is not second in line, but third. *Deux Tigres* is first."

"How could that be? Their lending amount was small, five million, I believe."

"Probably because it is not a French company, but a notorious criminal gang based in Surrey called Two Tigers. I would guess that they used a combination of threats and violence to get to the top of your little pyramid. That in itself may not be all that big of an issue but, combined with the other things that have happened at GreenSide, I would say there is potential for much more trouble. One other thing. Someone I was having do some research for me ended up in the hospital. You didn't warn me this could be dangerous."

Dan was speechless for a moment, then went on the offensive, "I thought I was hiring only you."

"Correct. This other person doesn't know about your company." Switching topics slightly, "I am going to look at Fern and Bamboo next. I'll check with you in a couple of days. And I would expect that my next payment will be made per the agreement. I hate having to remind people."

"Geez. Okay." Dan ended the call and with that, Robert's day felt done, even though it was still mid-morning. His mind immediately flipped to food. If he got his act together, he could do a lasagne for his family. It took him every bit of four plus hours to put together from scratch, so not something often made. First up was the tomato sauce with pork, Italian sausages, and finely chopped vegetables. Once he had that prepped and bubbling gently on the stove; cream, wine and nutmeg added, he turned his attention to making and rolling out the pasta noodles. The last component was the *bechamel* sauce, which he would fold in as one of the layers. This was old time cooking at its best, and there was nothing quick about it. Because of the effort involved, he always doubled the recipe so that he could fill a couple of smaller dishes to freeze for future dinner emergencies. His afternoon passed slowly in a very pleasant way, the aromas relaxing him as they had always done for as long as he had cooked.

Robin arrived home first, surveying the kitchen. He beamed when he correctly guessed the reason for the mess. Robin had played hockey in past years, but was taking a year away from it., and regretting it. He was missing the action, so had discussed with Robert about suiting up again next fall. Robert was happy to hear this, always nervous when kids didn't have enough things to occupy their time and energy. Bad things started this way sometimes, even in the best of families.

An hour later, Sophie came through the door with her closest friend, Rose, on her arm. They were inseparable most of the time, Rose being responsible for helping save Sophie from the kidnappers a year earlier when Robin was taken. They were also happy to see what was on offer.

Robert had a closely held fear that one day Sophie would declare she would not be eating some particular part of the food chain, so was always relieved when this hadn't happened. He supposed, rightly or wrongly, that if his cooking was good enough, his children would continue to eat all of it.

CHAPTER 12

At Vancouver City Hall the next morning, in the accounts department on the main floor, a staff bookkeeper stared, astonished at the amount of the invoice pried out of an envelope from Sun Energy. It was for hydrogen delivery to GreenSide for the month of April. She had seen large invoices before, but always for city wide services and maybe covering a few months, but not this amount for one particular site, so she beckoned her supervisor over.

Mamie took one look at the piece of paper and an expletive escaped her mouth before she could think. "This is bull crap. I'm taking this up to the third floor."

The bookkeeper smiled to herself. You didn't want to get on the wrong side of Mamie, which apparently was what the mayor's office had done.

Mamie followed the news enough to know that GreenSide was not functioning at full throttle, more like *non compos mentis,* or *non compos* anything, to be more precise. The third floor was where the mayoral suite was. Mamie would deliver it in person and let them handle it. She had seen a lot of financial garbage funnel through the city in her days, but this about topped it all. She happened to be a citizen of Vancouver, so large tax hikes every year were part of her burden to shoulder. That she knew where some of the money was wasted made things like this even more galling. She took the invoice and marched up the stairs, avoiding the heritage elevators that took forever to get anywhere, sometimes neglecting to let you out after arriving at your intended floor.

She walked into the mayor's assistant's office and laid the offending paper in front of her. "Perhaps the mayor could take care of this, thanks." She turned and left before the aide could even read what had been left on her desk. Mamie was under no illusion about the outcome of her action. She would eventually pay the invoice for the city. She just liked the idea of making a statement about waste when she ran across it, which was getting more frequent.

On the east side of Vancouver, Robert was entering his kitchen when his cell pinged. A message was waiting from Roy. **'Have your stuff, want it today?'** Indeed, he wanted his stuff, answering, **'Yes, can you come by here?'** A moment later, Roy replied in the affirmative, so Robert went up to his bedroom to collect the cash he had freed from his bank account the previous day. There were a lot of bills in the envelope, but he knew it was good insurance for whatever might come his way. Whether he could recover some or all of it from Dan Prudence remained to be seen, but he was going to try, not that Roy would issue a receipt for the guns. Such an item would lend an air of validity that didn't really apply to this transaction.

Robert decided to be the responsible person he used to be and emailed Bernard, asking him how the arm was doing. The response came quickly, Bernard probably not having much else to do but sit in front of his computer. **'Arm is better. Pain is going away. Are you still alive?'**

Pretty funny, Robert thought. He'd have to find some role for Bernard moving forward, one that didn't put him is too much danger. He responded, **'Good to see your spelling is back up to par - left hand?'**

'Toes.' Robert smiled, even better.

'Be in touch.' He concluded the back and forth, assuming Bernard was still being paid by his mothership and wouldn't starve. A different type of regret was wriggling into Robert's brain. It started to feel like he was responsible for a third child in his life, when frankly, two were plenty.

Robert then considered his idea of visiting Edward Su; knowing that there would be a record of the event left, and that the conversation would be listened to, probably recorded. Nothing he could do about that, so he'd move forward. The possibility of learning anything about this supposed mole in Victoria outweighed the risks. First thing would be to locate which remand centre Edward was locked up in. Maybe Tony could help with this, so he texted him for the information.

Over at Cambie Street, it was a new day for Tony, but nothing new was happening in the GreenSide investigation. Any potential lead was not fulfilling the meaning of the word, dead ends being the result. Of course, he had other cases to occupy him, but nothing that matched the interest generated by GreenSide.

Tony's cell pinged with a message. **'Do you know where Edward Su is being kept?'** Robert, as usual, exploring avenues that Tony hadn't even thought of. He checked the database on his computer and found Edward in Surrey awaiting trial. He was leery about using his phone for a reply, so went over to Norma's desk and asked her to let Robert know about the result. By doing this, he realized he had decided about Robert, so he also asked Norma if Thomas was in.

"I don't think so, Tony. He's meeting with his betters on the top floor. Should be back after lunch." With that, Tony thought a trip up Cambie to get some food and coffee would be a good idea, so he left Norma to her task.

A few moments later, Robert received a text from Norma, **'Hi Robert, we've missed you around here. Tony directed me to respond. Edward is presently cooling his heels in the Surrey Pre-Trial Centre. You should come by for a visit someday soon. I'd love to see you! Norma.'**

That was crystal clear. He definitely found Norma attractive, but after his most recent office romance soured, he wasn't interested in repeating what he felt could be classified as a mistake. Although, technically, he was no longer a VPD employee. Further consideration might be in order after all.

At Cambie Street, up on the top floor, a small meeting was being held. Three people were in attendance: Deputy Chief Constable (Investigations) David McKnight, Superintendent (Investigative Services) Steve Christie, and Special Constable Thomas Harrow.

Thomas's title was made up, as he was really the one in charge of the investigations, not Steve. But Steve held the title after David's re-shuffle, so Thomas had to be content with being 'special'. Thomas was last into the room, nodding at the other two as he followed David's pointing finger to the only empty chair in front of his immense desk. The room was furnished sparely, the massive mahogany desk taking up a fair bit of the real estate. Shimmering luminescent art adorned the wall behind David's head, perhaps fashioned by one of his offspring. A couple of photos of what Thomas assumed to be David's family members sat to one side, on the desk. A low grey file cabinet sat under a large window with a view to the west. The guest chairs were wood framed with brown leather, not especially comfortable, but then, comfort for guests was not on the menu in a top floor meeting.

"GreenSide. Where are we?" David dove right in. No small talk about hockey, the weather, or any other mindless diversion. "The mayor asked me if there was some criminality to the explosion." He stared at Thomas, eyebrows slightly raised.

Thomas looked sideways at Steve, but he seemed to be present merely for window dressing, like a stuffed parrot. He also appeared to have the smallest of smirks working his lips.

"Over here, Thomas." David was not pleased with the apparent attention deficiency.

Thomas turned his head back, considering his reply carefully, "None that we can discern, so far at any rate. We are still processing the site and its information." It was as generic as he dared.

"When will it be wrapped up, then? The contractor wishes to get back to construction. Time is money and all that crap."

"Maybe in a week or so. There is one other thing...."

He was cut off. "You mean the people rescued from the tower? I saw something on the news about them."

Only the news? Thomas thought quietly, no expression. "Yes, there were some teenagers rescued. They were sent to group homes in Burnaby. A day later, they were gone, with both home managers murdered."

"Burnaby. RCMP then and out of our hands."

"Yes." Thomas had no wish to elaborate or reveal any of his thinking on the matter.

"Good. Let me know when this is finished as soon as possible. A lot of people are waiting for a conclusion." He glared at Thomas to make sure the point was taken. "You may go."

Thomas got up, nodding at Steve. "Steve, David, thanks for the meeting." He left the room as quickly as he could without running. He was perspiring, not a huge fan of being treated like a child, but he was savvy enough to know that it came with the position. What the meeting meant to his investigation was less clear. He nodded to David's assistant as he passed by her on the way to the stairs, quickly descending to the third floor.

As he passed by Norma's desk, she raised her head. "That was a short meeting. Tony was looking for you."

Thomas raised his eyes in question.

"I think he may have gone up to that cafe where Robert used to spend his days."

"Do they have food?" He had been in there once but couldn't remember what was on offer besides coffee.

"I think so."

"I'll head up there. Anything else?"

Norma shook her head, so Thomas turned, heading back to the stairs. As he walked slowly up Cambie, he tried to sort out how he was going to proceed now that he had established the non-support of his senior officers. He hated doing underhanded things to get a case moving, but this looked to be his fate on GreenSide. Thomas walked into Cafe Paulo, spotting Tony at a table by the window. He waved and went over. "Mind if I join you?"

Tony almost choked on his panino. "Sure." He couldn't think of anything to add. He was pretty sure Thomas had never been in the cafe before.

"What's good?"

"It's all good. Carmelita will help you out. She toasts up the paninis. I think they're the best in the city." Thomas went back to the counter, standing in line behind a young woman stylishly dressed in black leather and chains as he waited to order. The woman also seemed to have as many rivets in her face as on her clothing.

Tony figured he would wait to see what Thomas had to say before he spilled his guts about Robert. Yeah, play it cool, that was the plan. All he needed was the fortitude to carry it out.

Thomas finally made his way back to Tony's table with a cup of drip coffee, the sandwich in process. He looked back at the woman in leather. "Looks like someone got a piercer for her birthday. If she would do that to herself, imagine what she'd do to you or me if she got hold of us." He turned back to Tony. "So, this is where Robert spent all his time, I believe. I've only been in here once, with Robert, a while back."

Tony looked at Thomas, waiting. It took all his determination not to talk first, but he cracked, "How was your meeting?"

"They want the GreenSide case wrapped up, by tomorrow if possible."

"But we don't even know what's happening yet?"

"I believe that is the point. We are not meant to, for reasons unknown."

Tony thought about this for a few moments. Carmelita walked over with Thomas's panino.

Thomas nodded approvingly at the plate in front of him. "Anything from the site techs?"

"Fingerprints, blood, semen, you name it, it's there. Multiple people, so we're cataloguing and organizing. Checking against records."

"Mmm," was all Thomas could respond with. He smiled. "This is darn good, Tony."

"Maybe you can appreciate why Robert spent half his life here."

"I am starting to."

"So, Thomas." Tony stopped.

Thomas sensed a confession coming.

"I have to tell you something." He stopped again, then, "Robert is working the same case."

Thomas remained silent but looked directly into Tony's eyes, waiting.

"I've met him. He is working for an insurance company that loaned money to the GreenSide project. And he has found a few things that we haven't."

"Naturally. Robert is not stupid."

"I kind of wish he was back with us." There, he had said it.

Thomas remained silent, considering options, then, "What have you told him?"

He lied, "Nothing I shouldn't have." Then, "I told him to be careful, but it turns out he has already discovered that for himself. He's the one who told me about *Deux Tigres*."

"He did, did he?" Thomas paused his chewing.

"Robert is also exploring other avenues that may be closed to us."

"How so?"

"He's going to see that Edward Su character."

"Why?"

"Not quite sure yet."

"Well, if Manny has his fingers in GreenSide, it might not be a stretch that a triad is somehow involved. And you are correct. If one of us went to see Edward, it might sour the case against him."

"I thought the Wide Bay Boys were defunct in Vancouver."

"Maybe, maybe not." Thomas looked down at his panino and started eating again.

"If we are getting shut down from above, perhaps a back channel to Robert might yield things."

"That's what I was thinking." Thomas answered.

"Like old times."

"Not exactly Tony." He finished eating, studying his coffee cup. "I believe I may come back here." He stared at Tony for a moment. "You may continue conversing with Robert. Just don't screw up any evidence that would cause a case to get turfed."

Another responsibility of his job that had previously been the problem of his superiors. Tony was starting to appreciate why he had been given a raise with his new position. He would earn every penny of it. They piled their dishes together and went up to the counter to pay, Thomas grabbing Tony's bill as well. "Let's get out of here."

About the time Thomas and Tony were vacating Cafe Paulo, Robert was receiving a guest in the front sitting area of his townhouse. It was a room seldom used. He didn't even know why it was there. His family spent all its time in the family room beside the kitchen and eating area. Perhaps he would start calling it the gun room after what was about to take place in it. He shook hands with Roy, pointing to a small sofa.

"Thanks for the delivery, Roy."

"My pleasure. What happened to the other Beretta I brought you? Not working so good?"

"I loaned it to a fellow officer who managed to drop it in the ocean after getting shot by a gangster. Not really his fault."

"Survive?"

"No, it probably drowned, but the officer made it, thankfully. He was from Hong Kong, over here as a favour, so there was some guilt on my end."

"I won't ask further." Roy opened a small knapsack, pulling out a Beretta with an ankle holster and then a dart pistol. A couple of boxes of cartridges for the gun followed, before he pulled out a tray with five darts sitting under a plastic cover. "Have you fired one of these before?"

"Never. Just thought it might come in handy."

"Maximum range of thirty yards, or metres, if you wish. But for accuracy, I'd be closer. The darts can take down a large animal, but of course the effects aren't instantaneous. Some kind of neuroleptic agent, whatever that is. I'm guessing you won't be using this on cattle, correct?"

Robert handled the Beretta, checking the action on it. "No. Thanks, this should do nicely." He turned to his coffee table. Picking up the manila envelope, he handed it to Roy, who deposited it inside his pack without looking at the contents.

"Can I ask a nosy question, Roy?"

"Maybe?"

"What else do you do for a living?"

Roy studied Robert for a second before grinning. "I run a gun club in Richmond. Perhaps you've heard of it? It's not a full-time job by any means."

"Ah yes, makes sense." Robert knew better than to pursue things further.

"So, you are on your own?"

"For now. See how I make out. Try to get paid, and not get killed."

"That's all anyone can ask, I suppose." Roy smiled again. "Good to see you. If you have any further requirements, let me know." With that, he left, and Robert sat and looked over his new items. He loved getting new things. It was like Christmas. Eventually he leaned back and considered whether he should start wearing the Beretta while on his runs, for insurance. The reactions resulting from his limited poking to date strongly suggested that he do just that. He decided not to pursue any further research for the rest of the day, instead going up to change into his running clothes. He generally wore long baggy track pants when running, so today would be as good as time as any to try strapping on his new purchase and take it for a tour.

As Robert ran, he started his deliberations on the visit to Edward, which he intended to make tomorrow if nothing else got in the way. He'd be reserved, and maybe make a few promises that might not get kept. He was certain that Edward wouldn't know that Robert was no longer with the VPD. Yes, deceit and deception were how you handled a triad member. There was no guarantee that Edward would agree to the meeting, but Robert was betting on curiosity getting the better of him. After settling this in his mind, he ran harder for the rest of his route, feeling almost nauseous by the time he circled back home, breathing heavily.

At Cambie Street, Tony had received the results from the forensic scouring at GreenSide. Not surprisingly, some of the DNA matches were for the teenagers taken out of the tower. Their clothes had been swapped out at the hospital before they had been delivered to Burnaby, so these were in Vancouver Police's possession, not the RCMPs'. There had been two other matches made to data on file, both for gang members attached to an Asian based group operating out of the Vancouver east side. The remainder were coming up blank.

Thomas called a meeting of the GreenSide team at four in his office. After the three detectives filed in and sat down, Thomas went around the group, asking for any progress. Both Vito and Finn had little to say. Tony related his forensic findings from the brothel discovered in the devastated tower. Nothing very surprising was revealed by this.

Thomas took over. "I have some news for you. Number one, the top floor needs this wrapped up quickly. The contractor wants to resume work." Vito and Finn looked at Thomas like he had lost his senses, uncomprehending.

Finn responded. "I get that the explosion was probably an accident, but that hasn't even been confirmed yet. What about the other stuff?"

"Upstairs thinks it's in the RCMP's capable hands now."

"Shit."

"Let's try to be professional here. There is another avenue apparently. Tony has been busy. News item number two, he informs me that Robert Lui is working the case, from a different perspective. He has been hired by an insurance group that is one of the lenders to GreenSide, BC Coastal Insurance, I believe?" He was looking at Tony.

"Correct."

"Tony informs me that he is already uncovering things that we haven't. Not a very good judgment on our own skills, but not surprising either. Robert is Robert, so I really wouldn't expect any less from him."

Vito and Finn were surprised, but nodded.

"So, we will bend on this for the top floor, but we will not break. We will continue our enquiries, but with discretion. Understand? Tony will liaise with Robert and within certain parameters, information will be exchanged. Tony can tell you what Robert has learned to date, and from my perspective, this is going to be a dangerous case for all involved."

On the Eastside, Robert relaxed for a few moments after returning from his run, then realized that he hadn't told his children about the possible alternate living arrangements. They weren't going to be happy living a few kilometres farther from school, and their friends. He'd tell them over dinner about just the outside possibility of it happening. Probably nothing to worry about. Right. He knew deep down that danger was present. This time he was going to be prepared, and one step ahead of whoever came after him or his family.

CHAPTER 13

In Surrey the next day, Bobbi attended a meeting that featured Manny, Paneet, and a couple of newer members to the Two Tigers. They were in Manny's club headquarters, one street east of King George Highway, in the heart of the new Surrey downtown. Internally, Bobbi wasn't doing well. He exhibited nerves most of the time; eyes darting around and hands that wouldn't stop moving. Bobbi couldn't discern any reaction from Manny to this, but he noticed Paneet eyeing him almost constantly.

Bobbi came by his feelings honestly. He was scared out of his mind some days, and it stemmed from a year earlier when he had been arrested in Steveston for his small part in a hostage exchange gone wrong. He lingered in remand until Thomas Harrow had realized that he was the weak link in the Gupil gang and could possibly be turned into an asset. After a few discussions, Bobbi revealed his desire to escape the clutches of the gang life. A deal was signed that returned Bobbi's freedom in exchange for future unknown action or possible testimony if Manny was finally charged with something serious. It was enough to cause Bobbi permanent anxiety. He had a younger sister who tried to keep Bobbi even-keeled despite the pressure he was feeling. After confiding in her, she also hoped he would get out and return to a responsible life exclusive of crime. She had had her own run-in with a former member of the Gupils, who was now deceased, thanks in no small part to her protective brother.

Up on the second floor at club headquarters, Manny looked around the long table and called his meeting to order. "Where are we with those kids, Paneet? Do you have them re-located and working again?"

"Not exactly. I'm still working on an alternate set-up. Then I'll need to get the word out."

"That means they're costing us money instead of making money. I don't like that, understand?" As he said this, his gaze wandered across Bobbi as well. As second in command, everything generally fell under Bobbi's oversight, even if he couldn't affect much change on anything that happened. No one feared Bobbi, unlike their leader. Sometimes it took a small meeting to remind people how things really worked in the Two Tigers.

Looking directly at Bobbi, "You dealt with the two guns used to get the kids back?"

"Yes, Manny." Bobbi neglected to tell Manny that instead of dropping them into the Fraser River as he was told to, he had hidden them in his condo as possible future insurance. Of course, there were no fingerprints, but the bullets extracted from the victim's heads could be matched to the guns.

"I have talked with the head of Bamboo about getting into another project. I don't think they know what they're doing over at GreenSide. I mean, who lets a building blow up just after it's completed? They are incompetent, is what I think. I'm going to get our money out and into a better run development." Manny scanned the table again. "Anyone find a computer hacker yet?" He was still after what he considered to be the holy grail of criminal enterprise.

There were negative mumbles around the table as the other members looked at each other. Bobbi remained silent while a thought crept into his head.

"Anyone heard anything from that reporter since his reminder about where not to stick his nose?"

Again, only shaking of heads.

"Keep an eye on him." This directed at Bobbi.

Paneet smirked at this. He knew Bobbi was no fan of violence and didn't have it in him to control anybody with threats. It was Paneet who had administered the beating on Bernard's arm, doing his best to make up for his lack of size by being enthusiastic.

The meeting ended with Manny considering how to get his money into a better project. He'd call Bamboo and tell them what he wanted to do. He did not realize how difficult this would be, but he wouldn't be concerned. His view was that it was other people's problems to solve.

Robert headed to south Surrey along Highway 10, where Surrey's judicial district resided. In addition to the Pre-Trial Centre Edward called home these days, sat one of the busiest provincial courthouses in the entire country, as well as a sizable police detachment. Surrey's city hall had formerly inhabited the same compound but made the move into a brand new structure in central Surrey a few years earlier. The old city hall was now full of crown attorneys who had previously been crammed into the courthouse.

Driving along the internal road of the campus, he swung into the courthouse underground parkade, knowing his chances of finding an empty stall were slim given the time of morning. Sure enough, after driving fruitlessly to the bottom, he turned around with difficulty, re-surfaced, and drove west, eventually ending up parking on the side of a road. On reflection, given some of the clientele who parked in the parkade, he'd be happy to leave his car up in the sunlight.

As he trudged back toward the remand centre, he composed his thoughts for the encounter, knowing that Edward was at least partly to blame for the abduction of his son a year earlier. It could become a complicated conversation. He entered the building's foyer, heading for the security checkpoint. After surrendering everything in his pockets and going through the body scanner, he signed a logbook and made his request to visit with Mr. Edward Su. Then he waited.

After a half hour of staring at walls and starting to think maybe this was all a waste of time, a sheriff the size and shape of a bear came into the waiting area and beckoned him.

"Ed will meet with you. Follow me."

Robert followed the sheriff through dour corridors lined with olive painted concrete block and paved with grey linoleum. They came to a door, which the sheriff opened, gesturing that Robert should enter. The space was tiny; more like a closet, but it boasted a chair, a counter, and a glass window. It was decorated like the corridor he had just left.

"Lunch starts in a half hour, so I'm guessing that's how much time you have. The guests usually don't like to miss their meals. One other thing, your conversation may be recorded." The sheriff then grinned. "For quality control purposes." Robert was unaware that sheriffs had senses of humour. He smiled just as the door closed.

Robert sat back, staring at the window sitting atop a stainless steel counter as he waited. He supposed inmates had conversations with their lawyers in this closet as they protested their innocence, trying to finagle their way out of custody. After a couple of minutes, the door on the opposite side opened and Edward, dressed in the palest of orange jumpsuits, entered the tiny room and sat. He could have been mistaken for a brain surgeon if it were a different setting. He seemed to have aged several years.

Edward stared at Robert as he sat. "To what do I owe the pleasure of your visit?" He spoke in Cantonese.

Robert appreciated the attempt to mess with the listeners. Now they would be forced to find their interpreter. He answered, also in Cantonese. "I was in the neighbourhood. Thought I'd drop by, on the off chance you were in, and in the mood to receive guests."

"Unfortunately, I am here most of the time, thanks to you." In English now, a slight smile accompanied the response.

"I realize you had your fingers in many pies."

"I am not familiar with that idiom. How is the police work going?"

"Oh, you know. Some days you are winning, some days, losing." Didn't sound as though Edward knew about Robert's present status. "I have come to ask about a certain contact of yours across the water in Victoria."

Edward stared back at Robert; his mind suddenly fully engaged. "I am not sure who you are referring to."

"Someone you used in your business dealings."

Edward sat back, waiting, then. "What would it be worth to you?"

"Some leniency when your case comes up."

"I would need more specifics."

Shit, thought Robert. So close. "Someone took a shot at me that day, not with your group. A long gun."

Edward smiled at this memory. "You seem to have survived. I will say this, it would be very dangerous to try to find out who this person is. Thanks for your visit. It has been a pleasant diversion to the day. I must go for lunch now. Sadly, they don't have a late sitting in the cafe." With that, he rose, turned, and knocked on his door, then he was gone.

Robert decided it was time to make himself scarce before any bright bulbs in the remand centre understood what had just happened. He knocked on his door and was let out. He returned the way he came, retrieved his few possessions, signed out, and left the Pre-Trial Centre. He took a deep breath once he was outside, thankful to be free of the dreary institution.

Robert didn't know how people could work in such a place, let alone be incarcerated in it. And the prisoners in the facility hadn't been found guilty of anything. They were merely waiting for their day in court. He hastened to the street and headed for his car, wasting no time. He wanted to be out of there as quickly as possible.

While he drove across Richmond towards Vancouver, he considered what little he had been told. The 'diamond' guy would be dangerous if he sensed someone nosing around. Robert got the impression from Edward that the shooting and the mole in Victoria were linked somehow, although it could have been because he had brought both things up. The smile from Edward as he responded said something, though. Maybe Edward had been the one to organize it.

He decided to return to his research work when he got home. He'd call up the planner at city hall, see what he could find out about the deal that had been cobbled together to bring GreenSide to life, then contact Tony.

Back at city hall in Vancouver, Mamie's prediction came true. The mayor's aide returned the hydrogen invoice to the accounts department, expressing the sentiment that she trusted it would be paid promptly. She by-passed Mamie and left the invoice with the bookkeeper who had originally opened it. Mamie had that effect on many of the people working at city hall. If they could avoid antagonizing her, they would. When the bookkeeper reported back to Mamie, all she did was nod. The bookkeeper took this to mean it was okay to proceed. Mamie went back to her desk and sat down, staring into the middle distance, at nothing. She had never even considered leaking anything to the media thus far in her career, but she was starting to think along those lines. Someone needed to put a stop to the fiscal madness.

CHAPTER 14

After Robert returned home from his Surrey adventure, he took a quick run, then a long hot shower to rid himself of anything he might have picked up at the remand centre. Not that he thought any germs would attach themselves to him. It was more of a mental thing. He hated prisons and intensely disliked being in one. He understood perfectly why they were necessary, but the visit reinforced a personal motto—never get convicted for anything.

He called Jean Kwok at the city planning department.

"Hello?"

"Hi Jean, it is Robert Lui calling. How are you faring?"

"Hi Robert. It is great to hear from you again. Kids well? I seem to remember a ruckus about one of them being kidnapped a year ago?"

"They are good, Jean. They survived and have mostly forgotten about it. You know youngsters. Thanks for asking. Still planning for a better Vancouver future?"

"Haha. Something like that, anyway. What can I do for you?"

"I wondered if you had some time to meet with me. I am doing some investigation for one of the lenders for the GreenSide project and thought I'd get a planner's perspective on how it was put together."

There was a moment's silence on the other end. "Is there a problem? Why would the police be interested in the planning?"

"I'm sorry Jean. I should explain. I was let go by the VPD earlier this year. There were some differences of opinion about how I rescued my son. So, I am free-lancing, for now anyway. I'm working for BC Coastal Insurance who are lenders to the project and have found a few unusual things. I'm just trying to complete the picture."

"I didn't realize Robert."

"No reason you should have known Jean. I'm fine now, but I had a bit of a bad patch earlier this year." Robert was shamelessly working the pity angle.

"Okay. Can you come in tomorrow, say, around ten?"

"That would be great, Jean. Thanks for this. I'll see you then." He was slightly ashamed of himself. He knew his late wife would not have stood for such antics.

With that set, he went back to his computer to review the planning documents that were accessible on the city's website. His next thought was Tony, so he texted him, asking how it was going, and if they could talk soon. Tony responded within a few minutes, suggesting they get together tomorrow at Cafe Paulo. Robert could set the time. This was a change of tone. Something must have happened, so Robert responded that an early lunch might be in order. He knew Jean wouldn't have much more than an hour for him. Planners were constantly besieged by developers and their consultants as they tried to move their projects along. He considered himself lucky to even get any time from her.

Cafe Paulo—pretty public, so something really must have changed. With this all organized, he thought about giving his client a call, but decided to wait until he had met with Jean. Tomorrow being Friday, it would be a good way to wrap up the week, and making sure he got the next payment from his employer into the bargain. He reluctantly turned to his laptop and resumed his slog through the documents for GreenSide, learning much more than he wanted about developing property in Vancouver.

Friday dawned, and as it was mid-May, the sun was rising earlier and earlier each day. Wrens, robins, and sparrows enjoyed being back in the city and made a racket every morning, before the sun had even started thinking about coming up. Robin moaned that he could no longer sleep in with all the chattering going on. Robert smiled at this manifestation of normalcy in his family. The smile slowly faded as he contemplated what might be waiting for them as he dug further into GreenSide. He rose, saw his kids off to school, then showered, eating some cereal for a change before heading over to the city hall area where the planners camped out.

Whereas only a year or two earlier he had been able to park his car in a city hall lot central to several city planning and engineering buildings, the lot was now littered with signs forbidding a normal car to park in it. If you didn't have an electric car, a co-op car, a bicycle, or worked for the city, you were out of luck. So, he circled the block a few times looking for a street stall, trying to avoid the bike lane only streets, the one-way streets, and of course the cyclists who, without exception, sneered at his car. After confirming that he would not likely get towed away from his place for the next hour or two, he locked his car, plugged the meter, and walked over to the planning building.

Once inside, he didn't get very far, but had to wait until Jean came down to the lobby to lead him back up to her floor. Security seemed tight. Were planners so important that they needed this type of protection? Maybe it was developers they needed protection from. While he waited, he passed the time reading some of the handy brochures on offer, telling him how to improve his neighbourhood, and where bike lanes were going to be installed soon. He was given a tag by the security guard to attach to his clothing. Now he was someone!

Finally, an elevator door opened, and Jean came out. She smiled. "Nice to see you, Robert. Follow me." Robert tailed her back into the elevator and they got off on the fifth floor, making for her small office.

As Robert sat down, he held up his hands in mock surrender. "I give up. I'll never bring my car to a meeting again. This place has become merciless."

Jean laughed, "Yup, that is pretty much the intent around city hall. The mayor hates cars. He tries to hide it, not very successfully though."

"But you are still here. Never thought about leaving when my wife opted for Surrey Planning?"

"Not really, although I've considered it a few times since."

"Must be difficult in a city like this. So many pressures."

"There are a few." Jean smiled as she nodded, her short black hair swinging side to side. "So, GreenSide. What do you want to know?"

"Where did the idea come from initially?"

"I believe the mayor was approached by someone in housing from the province, something about getting social housing built. Probably a deputy minister. Those conversations happen regularly, action, not so much. The city had the land, so it looked like a go. Then Fern got involved."

"Do you know how that happened?"

"Not really. Back room deals?"

"I understand them wanting to build the condo towers, but any idea how they got to do the whole project?"

"Again, above my pay scale."

"Do you know what the terms are for Fern?"

"That would be referenced in the development agreement, which is not a public document."

"I'd love to get a copy of that agreement." He raised his eyebrow at Jean, knowing he was skating towards thin ice.

"That is not possible, Robert. You mentioned some unusual things when you called yesterday."

"Yes, but this isn't for public consumption. In fact, you should keep this to yourself for a while until the story all comes out, which I am sure will happen eventually. I've found some weird things on the financing end. Turns out there are five lenders for the condo side of the project, one of which is a criminal gang out of Surrey. I don't think the more traditional lenders are aware of this, but Fern is one of the lenders and I am interested to see which side of the line they are on."

"What line?"

"The criminality one, Jean. And that's not all, by a long shot. The police are looking into some other malfeasance mixed up in the project. Pretty unsettling violence, actually."

Jean was silent after hearing this news, staring at her computer screen, obviously contemplating something. She punched in a few keystrokes, waited, then some more. She glanced over at Robert. It was impossible to discern what was going through her head.

"I seem to have the document in question on my desktop. My email program is open. I have to go to the washroom for a few minutes." With that invitation unfinished, she rose and left the room, closing the door softly behind her. Robert wasted no time in sitting in her chair to compose an email to himself, adding the PDF of the document as an attachment. He pressed send. After waiting a moment, as it was a large PDF, he went back and deleted the sent file, then went into the trash folder and deleted it again. He knew this would not erase the email trail entirely, but he trusted that no one would investigate the minutia of Jean's computer. He returned to his chair and waited patiently, looking out the window north at the skyline of downtown Vancouver with the mountains beyond, admiring the view. Pretty nice for a public servant.

Jean returned, looking at Robert with a raised eyebrow. He gave the barest of nods, then went back to his questions. "How did the hydrogen thing happen?"

"I don't know how much you know about developments in the city, but using natural gas as a fuel has been outlawed for new construction. This means using hydro or getting creative. Electric rates are expensive relative to natural gas, but the mayor and council don't care what people have to pay to keep warm. I doubt if they would get away with it if Vancouver were a colder city. Hydrogen has always been a bit of an outlier. You've probably heard about a local fuel cell company that was all the rage several years ago, then, not so much. Someone, and we don't know who, got close to the mayor's ear and started whispering sweet things about using hydrogen. Next thing you know, we have a district energy system based on hydrogen, or had rather." She grimaced as she concluded her dissertation.

"Do you know who was tagged to supply the hydrogen?"

"It's in the development agreement. Just a second and I'll check." She turned back to her monitor and made a few keystrokes, then, "A company called Sun Energy. I don't know anything about them."

"I'll look into them and let you know if anything is off kilter about their set-up. Change of topic. What do you know about Nile Gecko, a councillor?"

"Well, we are now wandering into the land of hearsay, but I will say this, he was the most ardent supporter of the Green-Side project from the beginning, always sticking his nose into the planning department to see how things could be speeded up. I assume he was doing the same thing with the Permits Department when it came time to process the development and building permits for each building. Then there were the rumours. Some say Nile liked to spend time gambling. One or two of our co-workers may have seen him in the local casino down by False Creek."

Robert stared at Jean, re-living some moments a year earlier where a VPD employee had been compromised directly due to such behaviour. The moment quickly passed.

"I won't bother you any further Jean, I know how busy you must be. A thousand thanks for taking the time. Your daughters are well?"

"Thanks for asking, yes. Both in university now. It's why I have to keep working. Tuition, you know?" She smiled. "Good luck with your investigation. I'll walk you out." They walked to the elevators, where she said goodbye.

"Wait a minute, aren't you coming down the elevator with me? To make sure I leave?"

"I think they have it rigged so you are pretty much obliged to leave." She smiled as she turned and left. Robert checked his watch. Time to meet Tony.

Just after eleven, he entered the cafe. After the usual yelling of greetings with the proprietor, he went over to his favourite seat and waited for Tony to make an appearance. As he scanned the clientele, he couldn't help himself. Shouldn't some of these people be gainfully employed somewhere? Of course, he was employed, and he was sitting there just like the other customers, but it didn't stop his prejudiced thinking. Ten minutes later, Tony came through the door, smiling as he spotted Robert. He came to Robert and sat down across from him. Robert promptly rose and went over to the counter to order, then returned.

"I thought I had bad breath or something," Tony complained.

"Just taking care of business. How are you?"

"Surviving." He was no longer grinning. "I've talked with Thomas. He now knows what you are up to and wants me to be a kind of liaison to you."

"Like you are running a spy? Really? I kind of got the impression that I was not flavour of the month anymore. Don't know where I got that idea."

Tony shook his head. He was smiling slightly. "We have some internal problems, so it looks like you may be part of the team — unofficially, of course."

"Internal problems at the VPD? What is the world coming to?" Robert laughed. He looked over at the bar as Gilberto signalled that their coffees were ready to fetch. He pointed past Tony, who looked confused until he realized what he was being asked to do.

Tony returned to the window table with the two Americanos and, as he sat, noticed the slight bulge in Robert's jacket. "Hardware?"

"I think it may be the prudent thing to do, unfortunately. Not going to get caught out like a year ago."

"Don't blame you at all. Changing subjects, we have been told from the top to wrap up our investigation."

"Really? And what does Thomas make of this directive?"

"Well, even to a dull-witted detective like me, it seems like someone is covering their arse."

"How cynical of you, Tony. I recall the days when you had a gleam in your eye and were panting to be a detective. Wasn't that long ago either."

"The contractor wants to get back to work." Tony paused after Robert waved his hand across the table slightly. Carmelita came up behind Tony with their paninis, laying them gently on the table with some cutlery. Robert smiled thanks to her and took a bite of his sandwich.

"Sounds like a reasonable excuse to me."

"Maybe, but we don't really know what's going on yet. The boys upstairs want to leave the murders and the kidnapped kids to the RCMP in Burnaby."

"Again, sounds reasonable."

"Whose side are you on?"

"My own side, these days. I'm sure Thomas knows how to play it. Steve and David can't follow everything you do. You just have to be cagey about it. So, I take it that you'll keep me abreast of developments, correct?"

"Yup."

"I will reciprocate. Big word, I know, but I'd like nothing better than to nail these sinners."

Tony was grinning as he was chewing, kind of the mixed-up facial expression that he was known for. "I don't have too much else to tell you right now. We have lots of forensic evidence from the rooms in the tower, much of it linked to people not in our database."

"We probably shouldn't meet here anymore. A little too close to the station."

"I thought with Thomas giving us the okay...."

Robert cut him off. "It's not Thomas, it's others. Just better if we meet over on Main Street, if you can make it there."

"Okay, good point."

"I have some information. I went to see Edward yesterday."

"You hate prisons."

"You don't have to tell me that. Anyway, I was trying to find out something about his mole over in Victoria. Remember Farhad? He gave me a tape last year which I played only a couple of days ago. Big clue as to who the Victoria guy is, but I haven't figured it out yet. Edward only told me one thing, that it would be dangerous to identify this person. I get the impression that the mole and the shooter who tried to nail me last year are connected. Edward smiled at the memory of that day. It may be nothing, but I have a feeling."

"Not much we can do for you on this, Robert."

"I get it. I met with a planner this morning. I'm going to be looking into a company called Sun Energy. They supplied the hydrogen to GreenSide. Ever heard of a city councillor, name of Nile Gecko?"

Tony had opened a small notepad and started writing the names down. "No, I haven't."

"I'd check into him, carefully, of course. He may have a gambling problem, which, as you know, can generate all kinds of interesting outcomes." With that, Robert concentrated on his food, taking his time, enjoying being back in the cafe he used to think of as a second home. After finishing up and yelling goodbyes to Gilberto and Carmelita, Tony and Robert left the cafe, shaking hands on the sidewalk before heading their separate ways.

Steve Christie had stepped out to get some lunch and was across the street, waiting for a traffic signal to change. He looked across the intersection and noticed the two men parting. His eyes narrowed slightly while his heart rate elevated. He would need to do something about young Tony.

CHAPTER 15

R obert checked his email after arriving home. Sure enough, the development agreement was waiting. He moved it to his GreenSide folder, then started trawling through it. It didn't take him long to realize that it was written in a foreign language, legalese—similar to Latin, yet harder to understand. At least Latin could be found embedded in the English language. Robert wasn't sure where legalese came from, but he knew he'd need another pot of coffee to keep his attention from drifting as he struggled through the dense paragraphs. After some moments, he changed course and scanned the whole document, which ran to a few hundred pages. He wanted to understand the structure and what topics were covered. Much of it was mind-bending, boring writing. Sewers were a big issue, who was obligated to upgrade which sewers on which streets, and when. Well, he supposed, crap had to be taken care of. Traffic lights, bicycle parking, bus stops, public art — the list seemed endless. Then, bingo, the energy system had a whole section. He scrolled through the pages, then came to an agreement on hydrogen supply. He was looking at the same agreement that had attracted George Ascot's attention several days earlier. After reading this section through and staring at the signatures to the agreement, he decided it was time to release his bloodhound.

Robert dialled Bernard's number from his landline. "Bernard?"

"Robert?"

"How's the arm?"

"Aching."

"When does the cast come off? Do you have to do PT?"

"What is PT?"

"Physical therapy."

"Probably. They haven't said much about that."

"The patient is usually the last to know. Take advantage if it is offered. I'm sure your mothership will cover any costs." Robert paused before explaining the real reason for the call. "Are you interested in helping out again?" He knew that Bernard could hardly say no to being on the inside track of potentially one of the biggest stories of the year. He felt temporarily guilty taking advantage this way.

"Not sure if I want my other arm smashed up before my broken one is healed."

"Good thinking. Maybe you should be drinking more milk. This should be relatively safe. Sun Energy. I've looked it up. It is a legitimate company. I want to know its set-up, who the owners are, etcetera. Sun Energy is supplying hydrogen to the GreenSide site or was. When you are done, let me know and we'll do lunch again, okay?"

"Okay. Sun Energy."

"And Bernard? Be careful." He hung up, grinning to himself. This wasn't school anymore. Bernard was going to have to learn how to take care of himself in a world that sometimes played for keeps. He sat back and thought about the cost of the hydrogen in the document. He was no expert, but the price seemed steep, especially on a monthly basis. Could this be one of the things causing his rent to go up, all because city taxes relentlessly rose year after year? He shook his head. It was part of the pageantry of living in Vancouver. He could always leave, he supposed, go live in one of the surrounding communities if he tired of the fiscal nonsense.

Bernard looked at his dead cellphone. 'Be careful.' Great. This was all he needed, more danger. Robert had been correct, however. He had a story to build, and so far, it was his. Robert. Honestly, he was beginning to be attracted to him, even though he seemed to treat him like a pet dog sometimes. Bernard was pretty sure Robert played solely with the other team.

He had alerted his boss at the CBC and said he could get back to work in a few days. At the same time, he also hinted that he had something going on with the GreenSide story, to stoke the fires. His boss was interested. So far, the other media outlets hadn't found out many pertinent facts about the story, so Bernard felt like he was on stable ground. He had also intimated to his boss that his arm problem stemmed from the GreenSide story. That definitely got attention.

Bernard was realizing that danger had an upside to it as well. Still, he would follow Robert's advice and conduct his next research project with the utmost discretion. He didn't fancy having both arms broken and having to walk around like Quasimodo for the rest of his life, or, even worse, being dead for the rest of his life.

Robert contemplated the next phone call, to his brand new employer. He wouldn't let any information about the police side of things out, other than to issue warnings. He picked up his phone again and dialled.

"Dan?"

"Yes, who is this?"

"Your newest employee, Robert."

"Ah yes. How is it going?"

"Great. How much research did your company do before you decided to sink forty-five million into this project?"

"I don't like the tone of that question. Maybe not enough?"

"Yeah, that's what I am thinking. The more I dig around, the more like a viper's nest it looks. Can you get your money out?"

"Don't think so. Not unless there is some criminality involved. Even then, the lawyers would get rich as it wound its way through the court system. Take years at a guess."

"Hmm. Well, I got my hands on the development agreement today. I don't think you should let that get around, by the way. I'm just starting to go through the contents, but the energy section is fascinating. Someone is making a pile of money off the hydrogen. Oh, and something else, I've had to draw arms, so to speak. I'll be sending some reimbursable items your way."

"Don't think so. Your overhead, so to speak."

"Maybe. Let's say if I don't need to use them, then it is my overhead. Otherwise, I'll send the invoices on. Believe me, I'd prefer it to be overhead. Also, it turns out that I now have an inside link to the VPD investigation. What I learn will be held close. If it affects your company, I'll keep you apprised."

"That sounds good, Robert."

"My payments will be made on time?"

"Absolutely."

"Okay, until the next time, then." He terminated the call, satisfied that he had rattled Dan's cage.

Once Steve Christie returned to his office, he called a meeting with Thomas. Norma let Thomas know he was wanted on the top floor, so after a few moments, Thomas took on his most benign appearance and made his way up to Steve's office. Inscrutable, that's what you had to be when dealing with the top floor. He knocked on Steve's door, which was always closed. Thomas understood this on one level; when you had as little to contribute to the efficient running of the VPD as Steve did, then a closed door was a wise option.

"Come in." Steve bellowed.

Thomas entered, noticing the change in views. Steve was now facing east, not nearly as enticing as his previous view of Granville Island and the mountains beyond. Thomas knew that Steve was miffed at this. Meanwhile, Thomas had Steve's old office, lower in the building, but facing west. He sat in the offered wooden chair opposite Steve.

"I won't keep you long. Do you know what your new detective has been doing?"

Thomas was instantly alert. "Which one?"

"I saw Tony today with that Robert Lui. I want him suspended."

"You already fired Robert, now you want him suspended?" Thomas couldn't help himself, even as he knew the futility of humour in the situation.

"Don't play silly buggers with me, or I'll have you fired as well. I want him disciplined for talking to Robert."

"Steve, forgive me, but last time I checked, we still live in a fairly free country. Tony can talk to whomever he wants to, especially when he is conducting an investigation. In fact, it is incumbent on him to do so."

Steve was silent while he digested this piece of news. "What case is he talking to Robert about?"

Thomas spread his arms wide, palms up, "I don't know that he was discussing any case, Steve. They are friends. They spent the last two years working together. Thomas helped Tony to become the detective he is today. Why wouldn't they talk to each other on occasion? Besides, I am a little short of detectives these days. Losing another one would not be good, not that I could think of any good reason he should be suspended, anyway." He sensed Steve was dangerously close to losing control. He was blinking rapidly, stress induced.

"I want you to keep an eye on Tony, understood? You are dismissed." Steve mustering all the curtness he could command through his raised voice.

Where am I, in the army? thought Thomas as he left Steve's office, then the top floor. Not for the first time, he was trying to parse reasons for Steve's hatred of Robert. As he walked by

Norma's desk, she looked up and noticed Thomas's red face, the usual sign of stress in Thomas's work life.

"Didn't go so well up top?"

"Loons, Norma. Crazier than loons up there."

As it was Friday, Robert felt he had already put in a full day after his busy morning of meetings. He decided to relax all afternoon. He was blissfully unaware of the pressure that was building on his former co-workers after being caught out with Tony post-lunch. He looked at his rear garden and headed outside for some long overdue weeding and general cleanup. If he was diligent and got some soil cleared, he might even get some tomato plants into the ground. The garden faced west, so it was a pleasant afternoon, as the sun warmed the ground and Robert's body. It was a short mental holiday as much as a physical one, for a change not worrying about the machinations of the people who put GreenSide together.

He clipped off the early daffodils that were far past their prime, then re-potted some herbs that had survived the winter. He left the tulips for now, even as they were starting to fade. The terracotta pots which were home to the herbs had suffered some damage from the previous winter's freeze/thaw cycles. A couple would need replacing. The rosemary, sage, thyme, and parsley plants were the most important plants to Robert, for all the food that he put together for his family. He had tried a few other herbs, with less success. He was thankful that whoever had planned the townhouse group had neglected to plant trees in his tiny back oasis. He valued the sun far more than any shade that might occasionally be needed in the hottest days of summer. He swept the pavers of his tiny patio and cleaned up the all-important grill, readying it for its next action.

After a couple hours of this, he pulled out a chair from the tool shed, went inside, and grabbed a beer. The sun was lowering, so it wasn't long before the warming rays caused a drowsiness impossible to fight. His son spotted him from inside after arriving home, knocking on the rear window to catch his attention. Robert started as he woke, his neck sore from leaning at a cock-eyed angle for the previous twenty minutes.

Turned out Robin was curious as to dinner ideas, which, for a change, Robert was bereft of. He went inside, rooted around the freezer drawer for something; eventually coming up with a dish of lasagne, which would suffice for the two of them, Sophie being out with Rose for the evening.

Two days later it was Sunday, time for a visit to the parents for a delicious meal and catch-up. The day following would be a provincial holiday, Victoria Day, not that it mattered so much to Robert now that he was self-employed. Robert's Cantonese born father had been a top-rated chef in his working life, so dinner was always a treat. After picking out the nicest Riesling he could find from his limited wine collection, he gathered his children and drove north to Renfrew Street where his parent's modest condominium could be found. Once inside and after his mother,

Mary had hugged both children half to death, they sat down in the living room, glass of wine in hand.

"So, Robert. A new job! How are you doing? Must be an adjustment after being with the VPD." Mary started the interrogations. Robert assumed she knew nothing about his issues with alcohol earlier in the year, but it was just an assumption.

"The commute is way better." He smiled, "But I'm having to learn a few things that formerly staff would do for me. I don't think it is a permanent thing, but the money is not bad for all the freedom I seem to have."

"But the danger? You mentioned something last we talked."

"We'll see, but this GreenSide project is not exactly as advertised. If some toes get stepped on, there may be some reactions. Can't tell you too much else. It is early days so far." Robert tried to change the topic. "What are you cooking tonight, Dad?"

"I've been thinking of a pork stir fry with steamed baby *bok choy* and rice. Maybe some dumplings as well." Ethan answered. "I think I'll start the prep work, if you don't mind." With that, Ethan repaired to his kitchen domain.

"And Camille? Is she really gone, Robert?"

"Afraid so. I've tried contacting her, but no success." He neglected to mention the lameness of his attempts. The children wanted no part of a conversation about their father's failed relationship, and had already tuned out, studying their phones intently.

"Don't worry about me, Mom. I'll be fine." Sophie made a face, having been witness to all the drinking that Robert had been doing until recently. Conversation then drifted into school matters after Mary had pried the kid's attention away from their phones. Dinner eventually was served, and everyone left the table fuller than they could have imagined; Ethan smiling and accepting the accolades with grace.

The next two weeks did not bring much new to the investigation, either by Robert, or Thomas and his crew of detectives. At the VPD, the top floor had assumed that Thomas had moved onto other matters and radiated a more relaxed demeanour. Steve actually smiled at Thomas as they passed each other on the stairs. Tony learned that *Deux Tigers* was the name on the lease for the two apartments that had been transformed into a brothel but found out nothing else of use. He also checked with the RCMP in Burnaby as to how they were doing. It seemed that they were making even less sense of the case than the VPD, if that were possible. Thomas had a quiet word with Tony that reinforced what Robert had said. They should meet farther afield from the Cambie precinct. Tony guessed something had happened, but Thomas didn't reveal any details about his discussion with Steve.

Meanwhile, at city hall, the accounts department received a second invoice from Sun Energy. The bookkeeper who had opened the first invoice was the lucky one to open the second version. She smiled as she got up and walked it over to Mamie's desk. She watched the news, so she knew darn well that no hydrogen was being used at a site that had been blown to smithereens by the same product. Mamie wasn't around, so she left it squarely on Mamie's keyboard where it wouldn't be missed, and returned to her seat, anticipating the fireworks to come. She didn't have long to wait.

Mamie returned from the coffee station, holding a cup of tea. She didn't even sit down, just stared down at the offending invoice. She looked up, then over at the bookkeeper who had received the first version. She nodded to Mamie, smiling slightly. Mamie didn't swear this time, but calmly took the paper by its corner, as though it had an offending odour, and proceeded up to the third floor where, once again, she deposited it on the desk of the mayor's aide. This time, she was absent, so Mamie couldn't leave an accompanying editorial comment. Satisfied nonetheless, Mamie returned to her desk on the main floor and turned her attention to more pressing matters.

Bernard had been making progress. His cast had been cut off at the hospital, to be replaced by a lighter and shorter protective brace. The doctor told him that the arm was healing well, and that maybe he should reconsider any future skateboarding. This had been the story that Bernard had given the attending nurses and doctor when he had gone to emergency to attend to his arm. The doctor knew damn well that what Bernard had suffered had nothing to do with a skateboard fall. However, this doctor was used to bogus excuses for physical trauma. In a large city, things happened, and sometimes, the victim didn't feel like talking about the cause, for a variety of reasons. Rehab was offered to Bernard on an out-patient basis at the GF Strong facility just east of Oak Street. He accepted, without knowing what it would entail. However, he was also told that the cost for this was on the house, another health care expense covered by the BC medical system.

A further sign of progress was his imminent return to work. The CBC, being a quasi- government run institution, put him on light duties while his wing healed. Bernard knew he was being spoiled, and if he didn't watch it, he would never be able to return to the dog-eat-dog world of for profit media. But he accepted the proffered sympathy of his co-workers. These people were told a slightly different version of the cause for his wonky arm; more along the lines of what he had told his boss, that he had been threatened due to his work on a story. Naturally, they wanted to know what story he was chasing that came with such danger. He demurred, smartly letting the theories build as to what he was up against.

The last signal of his return to action was his research on Sun Energy for Robert. He had naturally done preliminary work online. He found that the company was privately held, so no financial details were available to the general public. There was a list of corporate officers, but the roll call of directors was missing. He puzzled about how to get a list of the owners. At a guess, all the officers would have shares, but the directors? He determined that the company was provincially incorporated, so he would go through the provincial apparatus to find out the owner's identities. He had met a good-looking government functionary a year earlier at a social event, so this would be who he would tap. He stayed away from directly contacting the company, trying his best to keep things at arm's length, which he realized was a good strategy as he looked down at his battered arm.

When he thought he had enough to report, he called Robert. "Hi, it's me."

"Bernard?"

"The same. I have some information about Sun Energy."

"Care to discuss it over lunch—same place as last time?"

"Thought you'd never ask."

"Pick you up in an hour, at the curb." Robert ended the call. This sounded promising. He hadn't made much progress the last two weeks, spending it principally digging through the development agreement that he had taken from the city. He had read the signed energy agreement a few times and had come to the same conclusion as the city lawyer: that the city was on the hook for a lot of money, with no visible way out. Dan Prudence had called him the day before yesterday, and for the first time, Robert didn't have much to tell him. He could tell that the lack of substantive progress did not sit well with Dan. But then, to date, all Robert had unearthed was bad news, so perhaps the lack of news was a good thing. Robert tried to sell it as a positive, however, a hint of skepticism was detected on the other end.

Forty-five minutes later, Robert hopped into The Silver Streak and made his way west to the land of recently built residential towers that Bernard called home. Robert threaded his way through the brand new neighbourhood that had sprung up like a field of buckwheat from what had been an empty industrial wasteland only a couple of years earlier. He couldn't see much in the way of green space. It seemed that the newly arrived citizens would be making do with the seawall pathway for their recreation and dog-walking. He arrived at Bernard's tower, and there he was, lolling against a *port-cochère* column, looking more dapper without the ponderous piece of plaster hanging off his right arm.

"Hey Bernard, get in." Robert called through the open window. "I'm curious. How is this area?" He started once Bernard had settled into the seat.

"I don't consider it really as a proper neighbourhood. Don't you think it might need a couple of more decades before it gets some character?" Bernard responded after some thought.

"But it's new."

"I guess. Not totally sure how much longer I'll stay. It has all the charm of a big box store."

"Because all the buildings are made from the same kit of parts. I'm guessing the city planners have something to do with that. They like to keep their thumbs on things. At least that's what I've learned from my wife. Once you get a formula, you follow it."

"What does your wife do?"

"Did. She passed a couple of years ago, cancer. She was a city planner."

"Geez Robert, I'm sorry. I didn't know."

"S'okay. Let's head for lunch. Enough about architecture. Don't want to ruin our appetites." Robert put the car in gear and drove the short distance to the noodle house on Broadway, parking right in front of its entry door. Once they were seated and had ordered their lunches, Bernard started in on his findings.

"So, Sun Energy is not a publicly traded company. It has a smallish list of owners, half of which are on the board of directors. One owner is city Councillor Nile Gecko." Bernard smiled as he said this.

"Really?"

"He is not on the board of directors, nor is he listed anywhere that the public could access."

"So, how did you find this out?"

"Inside source." Bernard's smile broadened. The waiter appeared with a plate of noodles for Robert, and a rice dish for Bernard. He returned a minute later, holding a plate of steamed pea tips with garlic and a bowl of minced pork over tofu. Talk ceased while the two concentrated on their food. Chopsticks were not an option for Bernard, with his right hand still less than one hundred percent, so he worked with a fork.

After the food had all but disappeared, Robert returned to the topic at hand. "That is pretty good research, Bernard. I found out that their contract with the city seems unbreakable. In other words, they keep paying, whether GreenSide uses the hydrogen or not."

"Wow. Who signed that contract?"

"The mayor."

"Doesn't he get advice before he does things like that?"

"Apparently not. Or he ignores the advice given. Either way, this nonsense is kind of what I've come to expect from our civic government."

Bernard thought about this, but Robert could see something else lurking. Bernard's eyes were darting around.

"Spit it out." Robert said.

"This is what we call a news scoop."

"I get it. However, there is something else going on that I can't talk about yet. I want to see if the two things are connected in any way before we go spreading it all over Vancouver. So, I'd like it if you could restrain yourself for a bit longer." Robert tried to put on his most imploring look as he asked this last favour.

"I suppose. But I don't want someone else to stumble upon this story."

"I get it. Just be patient. I'm going to order some more food to take away. Want a lift back to your place?"

"Thanks, but I think I'll walk. I'm back to work full-time tomorrow, by the way."

"Congratulations. I'll be in touch." He watched Bernard walk to the door.

As Bernard left the restaurant, he considered the ramifications of ignoring Robert, and blowing the story wide open. The only thing holding him back was the last thing that Robert had said about something else linked to the hydrogen story. He had only been at this journalism caper for a couple of years, but was already feeling older, beyond his years, and not in a good way.

CHAPTER 16

M amie was pouring through a list of payables at her desk at Vancouver City Hall when her internal line rang.

"Mamie?"

"Yes."

"It's the mayor's office, upstairs. Think you could come up here for a moment?"

"Yes. Be there shortly." Mamie was pretty sure what this was going to be about. She'd be asked to pay the next invoice from Sun Energy that she had shovelled upstairs to the mayor's office a few days earlier. She got up, smoothed her skirt, and started the trek up the stairs to the third floor, nodding to a few co-workers along the way. Arriving on the floor, she made her way over to the aide's desk and sat gently on the adjacent side chair. She tried to maintain a neutral appearance despite knowing what was coming.

"Mamie, I realize you somehow disapprove of this invoice, as you effectively displayed last month when the first one arrived. I've talked with the mayor, and he is directing us not to pay this one. No hydrogen has been delivered to the site this month, for obvious reasons. He would like you to return the invoice to Sun Energy with a short note to this effect."

Mamie was slightly taken aback. Not what she was expecting, but she smiled, then rose, grabbing the offending paper's corner. "Consider it done." She held her head a notch higher as she triumphantly left the floor. She returned to the main floor accounting department and went over to her bookkeeper to instruct her in the matter of the invoice's return. Then she decided to step outside her bounds. She would email the sender near the end of the working day and tell them what the mayor had decided. In doing so, she wasn't really offside, but the effect of the email would be to move up the date at which the legal shitstorm would be started.

In the centre of Surrey later that same day, Bobbi Atwal was caught in a dilemma of his own making. Bobbi was sitting in the club the Two Tigers called home. He was considering making a call to Thomas to fill him in on a few matters pertaining to the gang. He had visions of being found out, however, and he couldn't shake the feeling that Paneet was trailing him, waiting for Bobbi to make some kind of mistake. That his call to Thomas could not be detected by Paneet didn't matter. He was convinced he would be uncovered. On the other side, he really wanted this all to end. If he didn't start a fire, then how would things explode? The police didn't appear to have a clue how to take down the Two Tigers, and as far as Bobbi could discern, didn't seem to care.

He came to a decision. He'd call Thomas when he returned to his condo that evening. He hadn't talked to Thomas since their agreement had been ironed out while Bobbi was in remand several months earlier, so he was nervous about opening a channel of communications. Who knew what he might be asked to do for Thomas once contact was re-established.

Robert realized that he should try to track down the mole over in Victoria. He had been putting it off, afraid of what box he might open. He'd start with the Ministry of Municipal Affairs–responsible for BC Housing, one of the players at GreenSide. Robert was no better at computer searches than most people, so he took the direct route and called the deputy minister's office, asking for a chart of the department's structure and a list of the people under his wing. He might have said something about the Vancouver Police Department; but if someone asked later, he would have trouble remembering exactly what he said, one of the advantages of phoning and not leaving unwanted traces.

Apparently, it was a slow day at the minister's office, because he had an answer back within twenty minutes to his email account, which they asked for. Near the top of the long list of civil servants, there were three assistant deputy ministers, but one name stood out: Chip Diamond. This was obviously the guy that had been referred to on the tape. But why had he changed ministries? Robert was unsure as to what advantage there might be to working in this particular ministry. Despite not knowing what this all meant, for the moment, Robert was pleased with himself. What it might mean for his employer was less clear, however.

Inside an hour, he realized the mistake he had made. He should have used a cut-out or taken a less direct route in his quest for the information. Now, his quarry might very well know that his identity was compromised. It wasn't a stretch to think that a halfway competent admin support person might let on that this information had been asked for, and by a supposed police officer who went by the name of Robert Lui. He could kick himself twice, actually. Giving out his email address was less than a bright move as well. His pulse quickened a bit as he imagined the danger that he had just placed himself and his children in.

Siegfried Damler lived and worked in an industrial building atop a dike on the south shore of the Fraser River, just west of Ladner. Siggy, as he was known to his friends and foes alike, did several things to earn a livelihood, one of which was combat training for police force personnel. This was done via a referral system. People would not be able to find this service offered in the yellow pages, on the internet, or any of the social networks. Siggy formerly had served with the Canadian Armed Forces—Special Services, from which he was retired. Siggy also happened to be for hire, by anyone with enough money. In addition to his Ladner accommodations, he had a second place he could go to if needed, one hundred kilometres farther east up the Fraser Valley near Chilliwack, where he did his long gun practising. It was barely more than a cabin, up the side of a local mountain, but it was hidden and well protected. He was not in the habit of letting people sneak up on him unawares.

As the weather was warm, he was sitting on a small deck behind his home, cleaning and oiling one of his pistols. The deck overlooked an arm of the river, where various types of boats plied the waters in an intermittent stream. An occasional fishing boat would chug by, and pleasure craft sometimes ventured up what was really an industrial highway of sorts. The main channel for the Fraser lay farther north beyond some small islands, so he couldn't watch the parade of larger craft as they either struggled against the shifting tide or took advantage of it. He owned a small boat, but avoided using it unless an unusual need arose. Better to stay away from the tugs and their barges with invisible tow cables, train ferries, and the larger ocean-going freighters. His mind wandered back to almost a year earlier when he had last used his boat to motor over to the Steveston side of the river. It was not a good memory, as it was one of the few moments in his career where he had failed to complete a mission. He had tried to put the event behind him, but irritation grew every time something tilted his thoughts in that direction. Bah, old history. No one was perfect in this world, he supposed. His thoughts strayed to his cabin in Chilliwack. He should take a trip up there to check on things. He hadn't been out that way in four months.

His cell rang with the standard old phone ring that he had grown up with. He placed the gun barrel carefully on the cloth-covered table, picked up the cell, and answered.

"Hello?"

"Siegfried?" The caller was making sure who he was talking with.

"Yes." Siegfried was unsure. "Who is this?"

"A friend in Victoria."

"That's interesting. I'm sitting on my deck by the river here and was just recalling my adventure from a year ago. What's up?"

"A certain Robert Lui has been sticking his nose into places where it is not wanted again. I've decided to give you a second chance. If you are up to it, that is."

Sounded like an insult to Siegfried, but a deserved one, he supposed, given his lack of performance a year ago. "I wouldn't mind evening the ledger."

"That's what I hoped. I'd like it done as soon as possible."

"Why is everyone in such a hurry? This is how things screw up." He was sure that his failure a year earlier stemmed from a similar need to perform quickly, before proper preparations could be made.

"If you aren't up to it...."

"I'll do it. Sixty?"

"Agreed. Let me know when you are complete." The line went dead. Siggy looked at the phone for a while, then started to plan. First, a reconnaissance mission. He knew where Robert lived, but that was a year ago. Sometimes things changed.

An hour later, Siggy was sitting in his beat-up Corolla on Inverness Street in Vancouver, watching the front of Robert's home from half a block away. It was mid-afternoon. After an hour of nothing, he noticed Robert in his rear-view mirror, walking up the opposite side of the street from the south, workout clothes on. He slouched lower in his seat, watching Robert turn into the walk to his front door. He wondered why Robert wasn't working. A short time later, first his son, then his daughter, arrived home from school. Looked like domestic bliss. Siggy smiled, having seen enough. He would make his preparations and do the deed a day later. If he had bothered to complete his surveillance, he would have noticed Robert making his own preparations, but once again, haste made errors.

That evening, after dinner was concluded, Robert told the kids what he had planned for them. He had phoned his mother that afternoon after returning from his run, warning her that he was bringing his children over that very evening, apologizing for the abruptness.

Sophie was not happy, defiantly laying out her position. "I'm not going. I'm staying here."

"It's not open for debate this time, Sophie. I think I made a mistake today. I need you both out of here for your safety. I'm not going to argue about it. Get your things, enough clothes for a few days."

Sophie's eyes were blazing as she stomped out of the room and went upstairs. Robin was mild by comparison. He shrugged and went upstairs to collect whatever teens needed to live with these days. The three piled into the car and Robert deposited his children at his parents. Sophie remained sullen the entire journey.

He considered how he was going to function for the next few days. He dismissed the idea of wearing body armour. His adversary wasn't going to make the same mistake twice. Wandering around in his home with the lights on at night was out of the question. A long-distance shot would be easy to pull off. He also decided to sleep in the main floor front 'gun room' for the next few nights. When he arrived home, he took a slow walk around the neighbourhood before entering his back door. He was undecided if his adversaries were so quick as to try something the same day he was discovered, but then the memory of what Tony had told him about the teenagers came back, so he assumed they could.

He went upstairs, got a spare blanket and his gun. He also took the dart gun and did something few men bothered to do, read the brief instructions that came with it. He got a glass and poured himself a small shot of whisky, then grabbed his SIG Sauer and dart gun, making sure both were loaded and headed to the front room. He had been making his way through a book about the Burgess Shale, a sobering summary as to how much luck was involved in mankind even being around at all on this place called Earth. He picked up the book and plunged back in, his gun under a cushion, the dart gun waiting on the table in front of him.

The sun rose early the next morning, with Robert cursing the shortness of his couch, no match for his lanky frame. The night had passed without incident, more or less as he had hoped. He got up and stretched, his body filled with kinks and aches. After a shower and his first cup of coffee, he felt more human. He checked in with his mother to see that his kids had left for school, then called Tony to let him know about Chip Diamond, and the resulting paranoia this generated.

Tony considered this information. "I'll get a watch put on your place. On a different topic, Thomas got a call last night from Bobbi Atwal. He is still with the Two Tigers. He hinted he could find out where those teenagers ended up. Then he offered something equally interesting. Apparently, Manny has been trying to get the services of a computer hacker into the gang but has come up empty so far."

"Quite the opportunity, I'd say, wouldn't you?" Robert responded.

"Yes, probably a way to dismantle the entire gang. But that leaves a problem."

"The kids, right?"

"Yes."

"I understand the moral dilemma Thomas has. Do you leave those kids for months of degradation and exploitation, possibly torture and death? All in aid of taking down the entire gang and finding out where all their money is kept?"

Tony remained silent after the choice had been laid bare.

"I know what I'd choose, but this is why Thomas has a larger salary, to handle weighty problems."

"Maybe he'll do both."

"Yes, the commotion caused by getting those kids out might provide cover for whoever gets inserted. Certainly take their minds off a new hire."

"You're right Robert, Thomas has some decisions to make. I'll try to keep you up to speed. Be careful."

"I intend to, don't worry. Talk soon."

Down in Ladner, Siegfried was preparing for the killing of Robert Lui. He had briefly considered doing it while Robert was on one of his runs but dismissed it—too unpredictable and public. He would do it tonight at Robert's home using skills learned in the army. In and out quickly, then collect a nice fat cheque. He had been considering making some improvements to his Chilliwack hideaway, so this would help nicely. He pulled out his hunting knife, his night vision goggles, and a pistol with a silencer. Robert's children would probably be scarred for life by what would unfold this evening, but that's what you get for having a nosy cop for a father. He wasn't too concerned about either kid hearing anything. From his observations, most teenagers seemed to like shutting the world out, concentrating on their cellphones with earphones on. He packed everything into his rucksack, had a snack, then tried to get some rest. He planned on leaving Ladner just after midnight.

By midday, Robert was itching to go for a run, the weather being agreeable, but didn't dare chance it, settling instead for some more GreenSide research, concentrating on Bamboo Construction. He knew it was a long shot, but he was trying to see if there was any overt link between Bamboo and Two Tigers. After a half hour of this, he was finding it difficult to concentrate on his work while the perceived threat to his life was out there. Maybe it was just over the top paranoia. The uncertainty was getting to him. He knew he hadn't imagined the smile on Edward Su's face, however, as he recalled the events of a year earlier.

Up the street, a car pulled to the curb, parking practically in the same spot as Siegfried had occupied a day earlier. Two officers were in the car, out of uniform. Tony had used his newfound pull as a detective to organize this. He'd tell Thomas later about this audacity.

Eventually, Robert called it quits and watched some local news on the television while he thought about dinner. He knew how forces personnel operated. They'd choose the darkest, sleepiest time of the night to strike. He determined that he should get some early rest so he could hopefully be alert in the middle of the night. After he had eaten and cleaned up, he retreated to his front room, shutting off all the lights, settling in for another night of discomfort on his too-short couch. He set his watch alarm for midnight, finally dozing off with the help of some scotch.

Robert was startled awake by the soft buzz from his wrist. He looked back to the middle of the house, straining to hear anything out of place. His night vision was fully in gear, but there was nothing to see or hear. Eventually, he started to doze off again.

A click! He was instantly awake, wondering what he had heard. Then he realized that it had come from the rear door. He kept still as he could see someone moving towards him. Whoever it was stopped at the stair and proceeded up the risers slowly and silently. As the person turned sideways, Robert could see some kind of apparatus on his head and a hump at his back. Night vision goggles, he guessed, and maybe a knapsack. He pulled his gun out from under the cushion, taking the safety off. Then he grabbed the dart gun instead, waiting, his heart rate elevated. He strained to hear what the intruder was doing. Whatever it was, he wasn't in a hurry. He heard the stair creak again after at least ten minutes. He crouched to one side, by the jamb of the front room entry, waiting. Finally, as the apparition wandered across his view, he hit the lights. At the same moment, he fired a dart into one of the intruder's legs, aiming low at the thigh, where there would be no body armour. The man swung around and fired a couple of bullets from his silenced pistol. However, being temporarily blinded by the light, the only thing he hit was the sofa. Then he sagged, staggered slightly, dropping his gun before hitting the floor with a thud. Robert went over carefully, kicking the gun farther away from the man's hand, then reached down to take the goggles off his assailant. Siegfried Damler! The man who had been training Robert only a year earlier. Even though it confirmed his suspicions, Robert was staggered.

Robert didn't have a clue how long Siggy would be unconscious, so he went into the closet next to the kitchen to get some rope to lash him up. He had a set of cuffs, but these were in his bedroom. He thought it prudent to avoid entering that room for now. After hog-tying Siggy rather harshly, he removed the dart sticking out of his thigh and hid his regular gun in the front closet before dialling Tony's number. He left the dart gun on the table in the front room.

"Hello?" Tony sounded groggy.

"Hey Tony, it's Robert. Think you could organize the bomb squad over here? I have Siegfried Damler tied up in my dining area. Tried to take me out. I got lucky."

"Geez, Robert, I'll get some people over right away. Stay tight, okay?" Tony sounded suddenly more alert.

"Yes, I will, thanks Tony." He stopped the call and stood, looking down at the man who had tried to kill him. As he was contemplating the reasons for this, he heard a knock on his front door. That was fast, Robert thought. He opened the door to two men. They identified as officers.

"We were just up the street, tasked to keep a watch on you." They both entered and looked past Robert at the inert body of Siggy. "Apparently, we missed something."

Robert didn't say a thing, then. "He used to be special forces, so it'd be surprising if you did nab him. Don't feel badly. Let's sit down. We're waiting for the bomb squad. I believe he may have left a present upstairs for me."

"How did you get the upper hand?" one of the officers asked.

"I was waiting for something like this. It's a bit complicated. On second thought, maybe one of you could check the lane out back. He came in through the rear door. His car must be somewhere close by. Wouldn't touch it, however, just in case."

Robert got some coffee going for what looked to be a rather lengthy night. Thirty minutes later, the technicians with the bomb squad arrived. After Robert had warned them what they were up against, a couple of them suited up and went upstairs. Robert was serving coffee and tea to whoever wanted it, all the while apprehensively looking at the stairs, half expecting an explosion. A couple more squad cars arrived, and yellow tape started partitioning the area, all to keep the press and neighbours distanced. Photos were taken and explanations doled out. One of the officers recognized Siegfried, having received some training from him in the past. He looked at Robert with a raised eyebrow.

"I know, you think you know someone." He shrugged.

"Why is he still unconscious? Did you hit him on the head?" one of the other officers asked.

"I got him with a dart. He might be out awhile. The gun is on the table over there."

"Better get an ambulance. Do you know what was in the dart?"

"Not really. A neuroleptic? Didn't really want gunfire in my home, but he let off a couple of shots at me anyway before the dart took. Check the couch in the front room."

One of the officers was being pesky. "So, you were waiting for this guy?"

"More or less. I did something that I thought might have repercussions. Turned out I was correct."

"What did you do?"

"Sorry. That is on a need-to-know basis."

"Don't get smart with me."

One of the other officers stepped forward and whispered a few words into the officer's ear. Apparently, the questioning officer had no idea who he was talking to.

"You'll need to ask Thomas Harrow tomorrow," was the best Robert could come up with. He didn't fancy being arrested at the moment.

Twenty minutes later, the technicians working upstairs came down. "The top floor is clear now. You were correct, this guy was quite naughty. We found a device attached to the underside of your mattress. And a second smaller one in your dresser's top drawer. The first one would have killed. The second would have removed your hand, maybe your face as well. We checked all the other rooms. They are clean."

Robert stood still, no expression. "His car is out back, but I'd be careful before you cart it away."

A siren could be heard, drawing near. One of the officers untied Siegfried and cuffed him. He was still unconscious.

"I'd put a couple of officers in the ambulance with him if I were you. This is one slippery and dangerous guy." A couple of techs wheeled a gurney through the front door.

The officers nodded as they loaded Siegfried on the gurney, cuffed him to it, then took him out the front door. It was determined that the rounds Siegfried had fired at Robert had lodged in the wall behind the couch, so the bullets were dug out after photos were taken. Robert had hoped that the bullets had remained in the couch, so that he could be rid of it, but his luck didn't extend that far. Still, he had to consider himself extremely fortunate that he had come out on top of this encounter. He could only pray that Siegfried would remain locked up while the case was being examined.

After the last of the officers had cleared out and left Robert to clean up, he went to his cabinet and poured himself a large helping of whisky, a solo celebration of life, he told himself. He sat down in the family room and looked down at his hands. They were trembling slightly. He realized how close he had come to being killed. He took a gulp of the drink, then texted Bernard, telling him to phone tomorrow if he wanted a few inside details on what had transpired this evening. His doorbell rang once, but he ignored it, probably the press. An hour later, his nerves softened by the whisky, his hands thankfully stopped vibrating. He went upstairs, gingerly eyeing his bed while hoping for a quieter day tomorrow. However, he did text his mother before dropping to sleep, telling her he was fine, and the children could return tomorrow. After his parents saw the news tomorrow, he wasn't sure if she would believe him. He could only hope.

CHAPTER 17

In Victoria, the next morning, Chip Diamond arrived in his office just past eight. He sported a new navy suit with a contrasting tie, as he was to attend a ministerial function at lunch that day. Per his usual routine, he sat down at his desk and trolled through the latest news while sipping his coffee. He noticed a story about the reactivation of the GreenSide project in Vancouver. He smiled at this news, then noticed another story about a late-night disturbance at an east side Vancouver residence. That got his full attention.

Details were scant, but apparently the bomb squad had attended, and a man had been arrested. This was the extent of the story. He called Siegfried to see what progress was being made in eliminating Mr. Lui. He only had Siegfried's cell number, so when Siggy didn't answer, he left a brief message to get in contact. Concern seeped into Chip's mind.

On the Lower Mainland, across the strait from Victoria, Ken Jalla received some disturbing information. The Sun Energy comptroller informed him that the latest hydrogen invoice was being returned from the City of Vancouver, unpaid. He also said that an email from a Mamie in the accounts division at the city confirmed that since no hydrogen was being delivered to the GreenSide site, there would be no further payments. Ken smiled and made two calls.

The first was to Sun Energy's lawyer, who went by the name of Chopper. Ken couldn't even remember his real name. All he knew was that Chopper's name was an accurate depiction of what he did to people getting in the way of his company's progress. He had been half expecting the city to pull this kind of thing, so forcing the issue was going to be a pleasure. On the negative side was the size of the city—they could put up a good fight and maybe financially drain his company. Not the optimal outcome.

After he had unleashed his hound, he called Councillor Nile Gecko and gave him an earful of abuse. "Nile, you better explain the facts of life to your mayor. I didn't bring you in to this company for your good looks."

Nile was silent. He had just put an order in for one of the nicer and pricier German sedans.

"You there Nile? Am I talking to the wind?"

"I'm here. I have a lever I can try."

"Well, you damn well better pull it. Let me know when the mayor is back on side, so I can spend my money on something better than lawyers." He ended the call, leaving Nile looking at his cellphone. Nile wasn't at city hall, but rather had been enjoying a mid-morning latte and croissant at one of the better west side cafes on Broadway.

He called his assistant at the Eco Party offices. "It's Nile. Remember a couple of weeks ago you did some research for me regarding Oslo?"

"Yes Nile, I remember. Not senile yet." She could be a trifle short with people she considered idiots.

"Okay. I wonder if you could do some more snooping for me. I'd like to know a bit more about Oslo's mayor if possible. Like if he has a family, things like that. Also, I'd like his contact information. Is all this doable for you?"

"What, are you sending him Christmas cards? It's either very late or very early for that." She had a firm grasp on how calendars function.

"I'd just like to keep in contact with Kristian Axness, if possible."

This seemed plausible, so she finally relented, "Okay, I'll see what I can do."

That accomplished, Nile then considered whether to call the mayor about the non-payment of the invoice. After some reflection, he decided that it would be better if the mayor didn't start thinking about why one of his councillors would be interested in whether an energy invoice had been paid. He went back to sipping his coffee, idly watching the other patrons in the cafe while he fretted.

On the other side of the city, Robert called his mother and confirmed that the children could return to his place that afternoon. Mary expressed concern at what the news had said about an intruder at his place. Robert tried to allay those fears by saying that the intruder had been arrested and was in jail. He didn't tell her he thought the intruder would stay in custody due to the charges he faced. No need for his parents to know that someone had tried to kill him the previous evening. They would just get unnecessarily excited. He texted both Sophie and Robin to let them know it was good to return home after school, then his thoughts turned to Bernard. By doing this, he assumed that no one else was going to be coming to send him to his reward. It was a gamble, but he felt he was on solid ground.

Bernard had emailed him early in the morning. Robert took his time, making some breakfast as he considered how much he would tell Bernard. Then there was his employer. By mid-morning, the city would know about the ruckus at Robert's home, if anyone cared, that is. Half the people in the world seemed to pay no attention to the news, which was what Robert hoped for, publicity being the last thing he wanted.

He looked out the rear window. It was spotting rain. Wonderful, as far as he was concerned. Funny how a brush with death re-focused your outlook. He then called Bernard. "How is the ace reporter doing?"

"So, you are alive! Good work Robert. Don't suppose you could tell me what really happened, could you?"

"Well, this will come out eventually, but you can be the first to know. The guy they arrested is named Siegfried Damler, ex-special forces commando. Lives in Ladner on the dike and occasionally trains security personnel on a private basis. I will leave it to your imagination what he was doing in my home when he was arrested, but let's just say I didn't invite him over for a drink."

"So, he was trying to kill you?"

"I believe that may have crossed his mind."

"Do you know why?"

"I have a strong feeling that I made the same mistake as you. Not being subtle enough in my research. Turns out we are quite the pair. How is your arm, by the way?"

"I thought you would be better at this somehow. I believe someone told me the same thing recently—can't remember who—and the arm is doing well. Thanks. Doing the rehab thing, but I feel guilty taking up their time. It seems that everyone in there is way worse off than me."

"Yeah, there are some buggered people in there."

"How do you know? Been there?"

"Yes. I may have had something to do with one of their patients. A waste of taxpayer monies on that one."

"Anything else you can tell me?"

"Not right now. You'll have to make do."

"Okay, thanks Robert. Got some writing to do." He ended the call. Bernard was grinning to himself; finally, a story that was his and something he could get into the news without waiting around.

Before calling more people, Robert's mind shifted to dinner and what he would make to help the reconciliation with his kids. Pasta was always popular with them, so after he checked his pantry and fridge for ingredients, he decided on the tried-and-true *penne aux gratin* along with a cucumber salad. That confirmed, he considered what he would say to Dan Prudence. Between the press, his employer, and the VPD, he was having trouble keeping all his stories straight. Each entity needed to know only so much. He might want to start taking notes about what he had told to each of them. He shook his head and called Dan.

"Hi Robert."

"Hello Dan." Robert assumed Dan's call display was working. "Do you follow the news?"

"Financial news usually, why?"

"There was some local news this morning that you may be interested in."

"Going to give me a clue?"

"An ex-special forces guy tried to kill me last night."

There was silence while Dan digested this. "Geez Robert, what happened?"

"Do you know someone named Chip Diamond? Government guy?"

"I recall the name. I might have met him at one of the GreenSide meetings, not sure, why?"

"He is more complicated than advertised, I'll put it that way. Anyway, luckily for me, the killing wasn't successful, but I have to say, I believe I am earning every penny of what you are paying me."

"Maybe you should stop. We didn't intend for people to get hurt working for us."

"No. I finish what I start. There are too many snakes loose. They need rounding up. I'll be in touch." He broke the call.

Dan immediately looked at a local news feed on his computer, and there it was. A man arrested at an east side residence last night.

The bomb squad had attended as well. Robert was correct, there wasn't much else to the story yet. Dan went to talk to his boss.

Robert's cell rang. "Hey Robert, Tony here. You okay?"

"Yup. Never better. I assume that Siggy will be kept locked up for a while?"

"I would think so, but you never know with those judges and lawyers making their deals."

"I'd feel a lot safer knowing he isn't getting out. I have an idea for you to check. His place down in Ladner? I'd search it thoroughly. Look for a long gun. I assume you still have the slug they took out of my body armour a year ago? Check for a match. If I was a betting man…." He didn't finish the phrase. "Of course, I'd do it very carefully, bomb squad and all that."

"Yeah, good idea. I heard about what he left in your bedroom. I also hear he is awake and not happy."

"Well, if he really was the one who took a shot at me last year, then he'd be zero for two. I really don't want a special forces guy on my ass trying to make up for past failures. I'd like to see my kids graduate from high school, at least."

"It's lucky your kids didn't wake up last night. He must be a very focused guy to only go after you."

"Focused, yes, but my kids weren't there. I put them over at my parent's place."

"Sounds like you were laying a trap."

"No. Just being prepared, like a good boy scout. Could you quietly check out a Chip Diamond? He's an assistant deputy minister in Victoria in the housing branch. I believe this is what precipitated last night's events. His name was alluded to on the tape Farhad gave me a year ago. I started looking for him and he found out after I got sloppy."

"Robert, I wish you were back with us."

"Well, I don't know if I see that happening."

"I'm going to go talk with Thomas. We'll be in touch."

"Okay Tony. Be careful."

After the calls, Robert suddenly felt exhausted. This was all getting to be a little much. Working for yourself really meant you were on your own. The VPD was looking pretty good from this perspective. He flipped his radio on and made a real breakfast, as in eggs, some bacon, and toast. A grapefruit too, so he wouldn't get scurvy, he told himself. He smiled as he thought of his children. The rain was coming down in earnest now. The sound of it bouncing off new leaves and back terrace pavers was soothing. He'd concentrate on domestic items after he ate, and maybe go for a run in the raindrops.

After a morning of not getting much accomplished, Chip Diamond went to the ministerial event in downtown Victoria that included lunch, getting concerned by the lack of reply from Siegfried. Could it be that the person arrested was Siggy? The thought made him angry. If you couldn't trust an ex-special forces guy to do a simple task, then what was the world coming to?

After lunch, Chip headed back to his office, where he checked the news feeds again. On the CBC, he found a story about the event the previous night. Siegfried Damler had been arrested in the process of trying to kill an ex-VPD officer by the name of Robert Lui. There were few other details, but he didn't need any. Shit, was all he could think. This was in no way good. His fingers drummed on the desk while he went through his remaining options. There were two people he could call, each different from the other. He was certain that Siegfried would not blab his name to the authorities, but what guarantee did he have of this? He had also been certain that Robert would be dead by now. Twice, Siegfried had failed. Chip now didn't care if Siegfried ever got out of jail. He was off Chip's list.

After some further ruminating, he called his new banker first.

"Who is this?" Manny answered.

"Chip, in Victoria. How are you?"

"None of your fucking business, that's how I am."

"Something wrong?"

"Yeah, something's wrong. That brilliant project you got me into blew up. I'm getting my money out. They don't know what they're doing is what I think. How did you link up with those jackasses, anyway?" asked Manny.

"The mayor's vision may be clouded by a green haze, but the project is fundamentally sound."

"Well, the stupid people can stick with it. I'm getting out."

"I don't think you can just take your money out like that," Chip responded.

"Watch me. Why did you call me anyway, to waste my time?"

"Do you remember a cop by the name of Robert Lui?"

"Yes, what about him?"

"He is poking his nose where it is not wanted."

"So? Last time I checked, it's not good business to kill cops. Kind of makes you a target for all kinds of bad things." Manny seemed to have forgotten his killing of an undercover officer from a year earlier.

"He's not a cop anymore. He was let go by the VPD several months ago."

"Still not seeing why you are wasting my time."

"He is investigating GreenSide."

"As a hobby? Not my problem anymore, so why don't you go screw yourself?" With that, Manny ended the call.

Chip looked at his cell. That didn't exactly go as planned. The Two Tigers had been Chip's new source of income after the demise of the triad. Manny seemed to have already forgotten his involvement in the brothel that was set up on the site. Well, he might live to regret this dismissal of facts. Did all gangsters operate on this type of 'out of sight, out of mind' way of seeing the world? Maybe that was the reason for their relatively short life spans? Who knew?

He was now officially running short on answers to his Robert problem. Already forgetting what he had just decided, he wondered if he could get Siegfried released from remand somehow, although after two failures by Siggy, he wasn't sure a third try would be anymore successful, no matter how motivated he might be. He decided to text his contact at the VPD to see if pressure could be brought to bear.

As Robert was prepping his dinner ingredients, he heard the front door open. "Pops. You here?"

"In the kitchen, Robin." He looked up, then grabbed his son in a big bearhug as he entered the room.

"Are you okay? Nan said that someone came after you last night. It was on the news."

"I'm fine. They arrested the guy. He should stay locked up, I think. Want to see something?"

"What?"

"Don't tell your sister, or anyone else actually, okay?"

"Okay." Being let in on a secret by his dad was a new one to Robin. He followed him into the front room with eagerness and some trepidation. Robert pulled up the blanket that was covering the back of the couch, displaying two small holes in the fabric.

"Geez Dad. Are those bullet holes?"

"They are. Apparently, it comes with the job I took on. Not what I was expecting. On the bright side, I've decided that I don't like that couch anyway, so I'll replace it soon. Not a word to Sophie, okay?"

Robin smiled, "Mum's the word, Pops." He liked the idea of having knowledge of something that his sister didn't. Because she was two years older than Robin, she wouldn't hesitate to put him in his place, sometimes without mercy. For his part, Robert wondered how long Robin would last before he cracked and spilled the beans. He returned to his culinary tasks after mentioning the menu to his son.

"Pops, our stuff is still back at Nan and Gune's."

"Yeah, I'll go retrieve it after dinner, okay?" Robert responded. Robin smiled and went up to his room, everything right with the world again. A half hour later, Sophie arrived home. Robert wondered whether she would act put out by the imposition of being away from home, but she seemed happy enough to be back after only two nights away.

"Hey Sophie. Before you say anything, I'll go get your things after we finish dinner." She smiled at this, then turned and went up to her lair.

At the police offices on Cambie Street, Thomas had had a difficult day, not in any way related to ongoing cases, but due to manpower struggles. He had been trying to procure some more detectives for his group, but because it involved money, it was turning into a struggle against the forces of bureaucracy, namely Superintendent Steve Christie. Deputy Chief McKnight told Steve that he liked having a couple of fewer detectives around, money-wise. He had been eying some hardware for the force that had a hefty price tag. Prying more money out of the mayor and council any fiscal year was a struggle, so maybe they didn't need so many highly paid officers. This was the thinking that he passed along to Steve, and Thomas was struggling to come up with a cogent argument against it. It was almost as if management was happy to see him and his teams struggling. Not what he had envisioned when he had taken the offered position.

Thomas had conferred with Tony after the events of the previous night had been explained. He agreed that a trip out to Ladner was in order, but it was to be very carefully done and they were to call the Delta Police to ask for permission. A once over of Siegfried's car in Robert's rear lane had not found it booby-trapped, but there were explosives, detonators, and other dubious materials in the trunk. This was not the vehicle of someone going on a sightseeing jaunt, shopping, or visiting the cinema—more like a fully stocked terrorist-mobile.

Tony and Vito led the excursion to Ladner after lunch. A couple of Delta officers attended as well. Robert's idea of including the bomb squad was excellent foresight, the front door having been rigged to explode should anyone other than Siggy try to enter. After the door was made safe, the squad suited up and carefully searched the entire building. While they waited, Tony and Vito visited the adjacent structures on the dike, asking salient questions of the locals that provided nothing in the way of insight. Apparently, Siegfried had not been the most gregarious of neighbours. No one knew anything about him. He had minimal interactions with the locals, which the officers found odd. After receiving the all-clear, Vito and Tony entered a large space, seemingly dedicated to exercise. A lifting apparatus, free weights, and some other indeterminate equipment sat in orderly rows. The room was silent, dark. Off to the side, a picture of a human torso was attached to some plywood with several hunting knives.

"Looks like dart night at the pub," Vito commented.

In the end, several long guns were collected, some of which were the type one might find arming a commando platoon. There was so much ammunition and explosives that the team decided to come back again the next day with a truck to clear out the place. A couple of phones were found and bagged, along with a laptop computer.

Before they left, Tony and Vito went into the rear of building and found the living quarters of Siegfried's operation on the north side. A couple of large windows gave a view of the river. There were no curtains or blinds for the windows. A small wooden deck with a single chair and a table adorning it was the sole evidence of outdoor activity. There were no flowers or pots, bushes, or decoration of any kind. Inside, at the west end of the single large room, was a rudimentary kitchen, spare, but very neat. No grime could be seen on any surface.

Tony was about to open the fridge when Vito spoke. "Wouldn't do that if I were you." He wriggled his index back and forth. Tony looked at Vito sheepishly. "Yeah, good thought."

A small table with two chairs gave scant evidence that perhaps Siegfried occasionally had a visitor to dine with. In the middle of the room was a modern-looking couch of indeterminate quality with a wooden coffee table in front of it. A couple of hunting magazines lay on the table along with a paperback by Immanuel Kant—*Critique of Pure Reason.*

Tony looked over at Vito, who shook his head slowly. "German, naturally."

The disturbing part of the room was the east end, where a desk sat against the wall. A single bed lay up against the south wall of the room; nothing remarkable, however the wall above the desk was.

It was covered in photographs. Tony and Vito leaned in to study them. Several seemed to be from the remains of a fight that could have been in a troubled country in Africa. Corpses littered the ground, some with heads missing. Siegfried was standing alongside a couple of special forces men, all in uniform, grinning. It must have been from the time just before the Airborne group was disbanded because of atrocities on the battlefield attributed to some of them. There were other photos of men—civilians, alive and more recent, maybe taken in the Lower Mainland. Two were of Robert Lui. The others were unfamiliar, but that didn't mean anything. Tony stepped back and took a photo with his cellphone, then he took down the wartime photo and slipped it into an envelope. "With any luck, we might solve a few cold cases."

"I guess. I wonder where his buddies are and what they are doing."

"What kind of life was this?" Tony mused.

"The life of someone damaged, I would say." Vito responded. They decided that they had had enough. The forensic people would be sent back the next day to scoop up more evidence now that the place was relatively free of danger.

Chapter 18

E arly the next day, the rain had subsided, but pewter clouds covered the skies, threatening to unleash more moisture if someone so much as looked sideways at them. At city hall, Mamie had just settled into her chair with a cup of steaming tea sitting next to her right hand when the phone rang. She let it ring a few times before deigning to pick up the receiver. "Mamie here."

"Is this the Mamie who sent an email to Sun Energy a couple of days ago?"

"I may be. Who is this?"

"Your worst nightmare, Mamie." Chopper said loudly.

"I don't dream, whoever this is." She hung up.

Chopper sat at his largish desk, staring down at his phone. No one hung up on Chopper. He redialed the number. But all it did was ring and ring. Fuck. He should have identified himself, maybe. This Mamie was apparently no babe in the woods. Now what was he going to do? The only thing he could think of was to reply to the email. He then composed an email with a few forthwiths, heretos, and some other vaguely Latin sounding legal terms, the intent being to scare the recipient into paying the outstanding invoice immediately and stop jerking Sun Energy around. He unwisely added a paragraph about phone etiquette to finish the message, then he sent it before he had calmed down, compounding his mistake.

Chopper swore a few more times for good measure before rising. He stuck his head around the doorjamb and asked for more coffee from his assistant. She had heard this act before, so wasn't unduly rattled, taking her time getting another mug of coffee for Chopper. She, of course, knew Chopper's real name, needing to use it regularly on legal documents, but she had a theory that Chopper had forgotten his given name. He was living his own myth so thoroughly that he had become slightly detached from reality. At least, this is what she felt, and she wasn't alone in the firm with this opinion.

Mamie had been smirking as the phone rang and rang. Her assistant looked over to check that Mamie hadn't suffered a heart attack or something similar, but on seeing the slight grin, she relaxed. Mamie was obviously putting someone in their place, which she gold-medaled at.

A couple of blocks north on Cambie, Thomas convened a meeting of the GreenSide team mid-morning. As the team had not grown, due to the superintendent's belief that it didn't exist anymore, Thomas had the meeting in his own office. Rodney Fister watched suspiciously from his desk as Vito and Tony made their way into Thomas's office.

Finn Black was already in the office, so the three detectives settled into their seats across from Thomas, silent, waiting for

Thomas to say something. They didn't have long to wait. "For a case that we're not supposed to be pursuing, there seems to be a lot of action. Would you lead off with what happened the other night, Tony?"

"Robert told me that he rattled someone's cage in Victoria, who then sent Siegfried Damler to kill him. That is the short version. He gave me a name to carefully check: Chip Diamond. The name sounds made up, but it turns out he is an assistant deputy minister in the Housing Department. That is the basic story, but of course, there is a lot more to it. As far as Siggy is concerned, Robert thinks he may have been the one to take a shot at him a year ago in Steveston. We are checking the rifles we picked up at Siggy's place in Ladner; we should know by end of today. If there is a match to the bullet that was pulled out of Robert's body armour, then I think Siggy should stay in remand for quite a while. Vito and I went to Ladner and explored his place yesterday. It was like an armoury — not surprising, I suppose. Robert's picture was on a wall, along with some other men. We're trying to see if Siegfried may have been responsible for other killings over the years. Could be a cold case cleanup." Tony smiled at the thought. Even though his tenure to date had been brief, none of the cases meant anything personal to him. He put his envelope onto Thomas's desk and withdrew the war time photo carefully for the three others to see.

Vito felt the need to flesh out the picture of Siegfried. "I think the guy is a complete wacko. We tried his neighbours; no one knows anything about him, and he has never talked with any of them. His living quarters would make a priest's residence look like a lavish bordello. He has other war pictures on his wall that would not make it into Home and Garden, or any other publication. What's that stress disorder thing? He's got a double dose, I'd say."

"No ambiguity there," commented Thomas. "Wonder if he'll tell us who was pulling his wires, if it was indeed this minister over in Victoria. I assume he is being held in Surrey Remand now?"

"Yes." Tony answered.

Thomas continued looking at the photo. "A murder of commandos—that's what they should be called. The crows got screwed."

The three detectives looked at each other, wondering if Thomas was losing his mind.

Thomas continued, "Let me know about the long guns. Some older files will also be checked?"

Vito said. "I've talked to a couple of other detectives about it. They're pulling the old case notes out, comparing them with the pictures we pulled off Siggy's wall."

"Keep the notes coming to me. I need to keep the judge apprised, so he doesn't go and do something stupid like releasing Siggy on bail. And we'll leave this Diamond guy for now. I need to consider how to attack him first." Thomas finished this part of the meeting. "Now, the Two Tigers. Where do we stand?"

Finn spoke, eyes glittering slightly. "I found a lad who's very good with computers in the cyber-crime section down in the basement, name of Rory. I wonder if those people ever see daylight—seemed rather mole-like to me. Anyway, when I mentioned what the assignment would entail, his initial enthusiasm quickly evaporated. Not very keen on getting killed or tortured so early in his career, apparently. I told him he'd be protected and that his resume would be wildly more attractive after he was done, but he wasn't buying what I was selling. It seems news of Manny has gotten around."

"That's a shame. What happened to people's sense of adventure? Maybe we should offer a bonus. Money usually works," Thomas mused. "Let's move onto those teenagers."

"I have talked to the tactical people, so as soon as we get a confirmed location, we'll mount a raid to free them. Your guy inside didn't know where they are yet?" Tony looked at Thomas.

"Sounds like they have partitions within the gang. This Manny isn't totally stupid. So no, he doesn't know where the new brothel has been set up. I told him to find out, as quickly as he can."

The detectives looked at each other. Nobody seemed to have anymore topics, so Thomas ended the meeting by talking about a subject that had lain the background, Robert Lui.

"I think I need to meet with Robert." He was looking at Tony.

"I can set a meeting. Not in here, I assume."

Thomas nodded.

"There is a cafe on Main Street. When?"

"This afternoon, if possible."

"I'll call him." With that, the three got up, stretched, then proceeded out the office door, Tony nodding at Norma as he passed by and kept going, leaving the floor, bound for Cafe Paulo, knowing he wouldn't make it to the later cafe meeting without an interim coffee. The two others returned to their desks.

Rodney Fister got up and went over to Finn Black's desk and stood over him, staring down. "What was that about?"

Finn looked up at Rodney. "Thomas is thinking of giving us all commendations for our work. We were just discussing when an appropriate time would work for us." Then he smiled slightly, which was all it took to send Rodney over the edge. He lunged at Finn, his hands going for the neck, as if he was going to strangle him right in front of fellow officers. As soon as his hands were around Rick's neck, he stopped and backed up, realizing the blatant loss of control. Finn backed his chair up slightly, making a silent vow never to smile at Rodney again.

Vito walked over to the two, having missed most of the brief encounter. "You two alright?"

"Rodney just stumbled. We're fine, right Rodney?" Finn answered. Vito studied both men, dubious.

"Yeah, fine." Was the sullen reply by a red-faced Rodney as he walked back to his office. Finn sat back, shaking his head at the idiocy of it all.

Robert had returned from getting some exercise and was settling in to do some more research when his land line rang. It was Dan Prudence, "Hi Robert. Since you answered, I take it you are still alive?"

"It feels like I'm still alive. Is this why you called?"

"I was talking with my president, and we feel you should stop your research. We'll pay you the agreed amount, regardless."

Robert was silent. This was a smooth way out. If he was smart, he'd take it, but Robert was more stubborn than smart. "What about your forty-five million? I believe you said if there was criminality involved, you might be able to retrieve the money, or am I wrong?"

"You're correct, but we haven't seen any evidence that bad things were involved."

"Trust me, there was. I'm not at liberty to tell you what as it's a police matter now, but some ugly things were happening at GreenSide, not just a bad energy system. So, if it's all the same to you, I think I'll see this through."

Silence reigned. Robert could almost hear Dan thinking, "Okay. I'll talk to my boss again and get back to you." Dan hung up. Robert put his phone down, almost immediately regretting his decision. Why could he never take the easy road? Was it a character flaw? Was he addicted to self-harm? His phone rang.

"Robert?"

"Tony?"

"Thomas wants to meet with you. Soonest, if that's okay. Apollo cafe?"

"I was just about to make coffee, so I'm in."

"See you in a half hour, then."

He decided to walk over to Main Street, so he left immediately, but not before putting his Beretta and holster on his ankle. Robert was suddenly feeling very popular, but he was unsure if it was a good thing or not. After a pleasant walk across the east side, he entered the Apollo. It was a nice enough place, but lacked the personality given his favourite cafe by Gilberto and Carmelita. He ordered an Americano and went to sit at a table by the rear wall, waiting. He was missing what he was starting to consider as the good old days. A short time later, Tony and Thomas walked through the door, scanning the patrons until their eyes settled on Robert. He waved, pointing to the cup already by his hand.

Thomas nodded at Robert as he sat. "How are you these days?"

"Alive, so there's that. Never knew a private investigator's life could be so busy, much of it not in a good way either."

"Interested in coming back to the VPD?"

Tony looked surprised. This was not what he thought the meeting was going to be about.

"Didn't feel I was very popular with the brass somehow." Robert was taken off guard as well.

"Yes, that's so. Just wanted to gauge your feelings on the subject should something change up top.

"These days, my feelings would be in the affirmative. Do you know what a pain it is to be chasing your paycheque? I'm continually having to justify my actions."

Thomas gave a slight smile, "Okay, good to know, now to business. This Chip Diamond character over in Victoria, what can you tell us?"

"Not much. I have an audio recording given to me by Farhad a year ago that paints him as a class A money launderer. I believe that two gang members were doing the talking. But they didn't use his name directly, so I don't know what use it is. He was in Gaming and Enforcement at the time, and it was Edward Su who was using him. Perhaps a deal could be made with Edward to nail Chip to the wall."

Thomas thought about this as he looked at his coffee cup. "Yeah, he'd be motivated, that's certain. He wasn't involved in any of the violence, was he?"

"Not directly, but he facilitated the kidnapping of my son," Robert answered. "And I get the feeling that he may have indirectly ordered up the shot at me that I believe Siegfried took."

"We visited Siegfried's place yesterday, including his living quarters." Tony spoke. "Your picture was on his wall."

"Was there a heart drawn around it?"

"Funny. There were a few others, some who are familiar to some of the older guys, so we are hoping some cold cases might get solved. Looks like Siegfried was used by several people to settle scores or remove problems."

"Guess that is what I had become, a problem." Robert said slowly. "Siegfried could be another way to get to Chip; but if I had to guess, don't think Siggy is the deal-making kind of guy."

Thomas nodded as he glanced out over the cafe. "It sure would be nice to bag Manny somehow when this gets wrapped up. I'm just not sure what evidence our guy inside has on Manny, or how it would stand up in a court case. We are pretty sure he is behind the violence on the kids."

"I've found something else." Robert smiled thinly.

"Why am I not surprised that there is more?" Thomas looked back at Robert.

"Do you know Nile Gecko?"

"The councillor?"

"The same. He is a silent partner in the firm that is supplying hydrogen to GreenSide."

"That sounds a tad slimy."

"Wait, there's more."

"What, are you selling toaster ovens? Are we getting a free knife?"

"I found out that the price charged for said hydrogen is outrageous, the contract is essentially unbreakable, and the mayor signed the contract personally."

Thomas and Tony stared at Robert, Thomas shaking his head as if his worst fears had been confirmed, the city was being run by morons and cheats. "Do you have any good news to share?"

Robert smiled at the optimism. "Not really. Anyone want another one?" pointing to his cup.

Both Thomas and Tony had had their fill, so Robert walked over to the barista and ordered a short black. He watched her long slim arms work the machine. No markings to be seen, unlike many baristas. A crisp white bandana covered her neck, as if she was preparing to rob a bank. She smiled at Robert as she drew the shot. Robert couldn't help himself. "So, do you come here often?"

The barista burst out laughing. "I don't know if corn and coffee go together."

"Of course they do. How come no tattoos?"

"I have them. In other places."

"Oh." This sounded interesting. "I've been looking for a second home."

"I'm not sure whether this qualifies as a home."

"It'll do. I used to be a regular at Cafe Paulo, but because of complications, can't attend there these days."

"Get thrown out?" She laughed uncertainly.

"Nothing so dramatic, just the wrong locale at present." Robert winked as he accepted the coffee and retreated to the window table.

"Making time with the help?" Tony had been studying the exchange.

"Maybe. She's kind of pretty, no? So how is Tony doing?"

"Good. Be better if you were back with us, I believe."

"Yes, you keep saying that. I'm almost starting to believe it."

"We should get going. Good to see you, Robert. Keep in touch with Tony please." Thomas stood up and with a quick wave, he and Tony left. Robert watched through the window as they got into their unmarked sedan, unsure now how he felt about the possibility of returning to his former place of employment. He took his time with this cup, reflecting on dodging Siegfried a second time, then, with a nod to the barista as he passed by the bar, he left for home.

CHAPTER 19

B obbi Atwall had been puzzling how to trail Paneet without getting caught. He was certain that Paneet had been following him in his spare hours, determined to expose Bobbi as the traitor in their midst. It was slightly ironic, as Bobbi had done nothing wrong to date. He was merely planning to become the person Paneet had suspected him to be all along. Eventually, he hit on a solution. The only trouble was that it involved his sister, Safa. A couple of the older gang members knew about Bobbi's sister, but Paneet was unaware of her, coming later to the party.

Bobbi asked Safa over to his central Surrey condo one evening to discuss his plan. Safa had stayed away from the other gang members, especially after a date had gone wrong a year earlier. Not only was she motivated to help Bobbi get out of the gang, but she had demonstrated toughness herself in dealings with gangsters.

"So, Bobbi, what's going on?" Safa settled on Bobbi's couch as he handed her a cup of tea. She was looking west at the setting sun. Bobbi's place was well positioned, high up in a twenty-two-storey building with a view west all the way to Vancouver Island.

He opened. "I'm making my play to get out of the gang, Safa."

She smiled at this display of determination. "Great, Bobbi. And how are you going to do it?"

"Wrong question Safa. How are we going to do it? That's the question."

"Oh no, I'm not going on another date. Forget it."

"Relax Safa. I wouldn't ask you to do that. This involves following someone discreetly as a one-time thing. I just need to know where Paneet goes." Bobbi was reluctant to say anything more. The less his sister knew, the better.

"Who is Paneet?"

"One of the newer guys. He has it in for me, so I really can't be caught tailing him. He doesn't know you, so it should be fine. You don't have to be anywhere near him. This will be a car thing, and it will probably be at night."

"Okay, I guess. For you, I'll do it. But you must promise me to get out of this gang, okay?"

"I am trying, Safa, but it is not as easy as you might guess."

With that, Bobbi went into his kitchen and returned with a plate of sweet cakes, feeling relieved, at least for the moment. He then had a moment of enlightenment. He went into his bedroom and, going to his chest of drawers, he pulled out one of the guns that he had supposedly disposed of. It was a smaller gun, a Walther PPK. He brought it back to show Safa. Manny had been reluctant to part with it, as it was a special gun.

"This is for just in case, Safa. If you might need a gun, this is in my top drawer. It is loaded. Four bullets left in it, I believe. It's the one used by James Bond!"

"Where did you get it?" She was fascinated, not repelled at all. She took it carefully, feeling the weight of it. It felt comfortable in her hand.

"I was supposed to get rid of it after it had been used, but I thought I'd hang onto it." He didn't want to tell her what it had been used for. He showed her the safety features, then left the room and returned with the silencer, showing her how to screw it onto the barrel.

"Can I take it with me?"

"Don't think that is wise, Safa. Mom or Dad may find it. You have my key. You can always get in here if there is trouble. There is a second gun and silencer in my drawer as well." Bobbi was surprised at how easily Saffa had warmed to the idea of using a gun.

Safa smiled at being able to join the special club of gun owners in Surrey. Perhaps some practice might be in order. She'd look up local gun clubs tomorrow or ask her brother if the search came up empty.

Very early the next morning, before anyone else in his family was awake, Nile Gecko settled into the den in his westside home, door closed, and dialled the number of Oslo's city hall on his land line. His assistant had finally furnished him with the information he had asked about, so he was going fishing with it. When the call finally connected, he asked to be patched through to Kristian Axness. After some back and forth, establishing that Nile wasn't some huckster looking to make Kristian's day difficult, and that he was who he said he was, he was connected.

"Hello? Is this Nile?"

"Yes. How are you doing, Kristian?"

"Excellent. I have been expecting a call from you. What has taken you so long?"

"Oh, you know, city business, things like that. So, Kristian, remember our discussion several weeks ago as I was driving you back to your hotel in Vancouver?"

"Of course, like yesterday."

"Do you have any memorabilia of that night at the club that I could have?"

"You mean a picture. You North Americans sure go the long way around when you talk. Yes, I have some pictures, but they aren't inexpensive."

"Well, maybe we can make a deal. You send me a picture, and I won't let your wife and kids know what you get up to at your club."

There was silence for a moment, then Kristian cleared his throat. "Hmm, sounds suspiciously like extortion. You should know, Nile, that only works if I actually have a wife and children, but I don't, so the price just went up. You want a photo? It will be two hundred thousand Krone. E-transfer the money and I will send a photo." The line went dead.

Shit. Nile was confused. That didn't go as expected. He needed to have a little chat with his assistant. He opened his laptop to find out how many Canadian dollars he would have to part with. A couple of seconds later, he realized he would be about thirty thousand dollars poorer. He also needed to figure out a method of letting Mayor Dunbar know about his life options without revealing himself. Politics was getting complicated. First, he needed the picture. He vowed to make a call back to Ken Jalla later in the day to see how Sun Energy would feel about contributing to the picture fund; after all, it would serve all their interests.

At Two Tigers later that same morning, a meeting was underway discussing various drug issues, mostly problems with other smaller gangs trying to horn in on the action. After Ho Li-Fan had been tasked with the dispatching of a particular thorn in the Tiger's side, talk turned to Paneet and his up and running brothel. Bobbi watched as the discussion ended up with Manny directing Paneet to pick up two more workers and take them down to the brothel. The only thing Bobbi learned was that it was now in Yaletown, in downtown Vancouver. This narrowed things down somewhat, but he was going to need his sister's help to pinpoint the exact building. To add to the difficulty, Paneet was told to use a brown dented panel van to carry the merchandise. Paneet's car would have been easier to follow. He usually sported around in a scarlet red Mercedes that a blind person could pick out from miles off. All Bobbi needed was to find out where and when Paneet was picking up his human cargo.

He went up to Manny after the meeting ended. "Hey Manny, if I am really your second in command, then I should know a bit more about the sex side, no? To keep tabs on things."

Manny stared back at Bobbi. Bobbi was suddenly uncertain. Maybe he shouldn't have raised the issue.

"Yeah, you are correct. I'll tell Paneet."

Bobbi expelled a breath.

After Tony finally received some results from the forensic team, Thomas Harrow convened a meeting of the GreenSide group, but this time chose to do it at Cafe Paulo. He didn't need pesky staff asking impolite questions in-house. The four officers walked up to the cafe at different times, eventually filling seats in a rear corner. Coffees and a plate of pastries took up most of the table-top, leaving little room for elbows and case notes. Gilberto was both impressed and pleased that the police were using his cafe to conduct business, not least because they paid their way, unlike others lounging in their seats, studying laptops or phones, and not buying coffee.

"So, what can you tell us, Tony?" Thomas opened.

"We have a match between a Blaser R93 scoped rifle pulled from Siegfried's place and the bullet recovered from Robert's vest from a year ago. The rifle has a few prints on it that match Siegfried's. Circumstantial, but solid evidence. It won't hurt in a courtroom."

"Good news. I'll let the prosecutor know." Thomas smiled. "What else?"

"One of the cold cases might be solved as well. Same rifle, matching a bullet pulled from a victim six years ago. This guy was a Vietnamese gangster who was mixed up in drugs, twenty-one years old. Nice to see that ex-forces people are able to find meaningful employment."

"Pretty cold, Tony." Thomas scolded.

"I guess." Tony looked vaguely chastened.

Thomas then filled Vito and Finn in on the latest Robert research, which included both Chip Diamond and Nile Gecko. "Both these guys appear to be dirty, but if we build a case against them, it has to done quietly and carefully. Both these guys have some standing in the community, and powerful friends, I wouldn't doubt."

Tony had more to add. "I almost forgot. We are looking at Siegfried's phones. His landline answering machine has nothing on it, but we're checking records through the phone company. We also checked Siegfried's cell record, and bingo, a number in Victoria—this time Municipal Affairs and Housing, where Chip gets a paycheque these days."

Finn felt compelled to add. "That Rodney Fister is going to blow the whistle on us for working on this case. I can feel it coming."

"I will handle Rodney. Just don't do anything stupid. And please don't bait him." Thomas responded. Finn smiled as he recalled his last attempt at humour with Rodney.

Gilberto walked over to the officer's table. "Any re-fills, gentlemen? On the house!" Gilberto's public relations skills were on full display. Thomas smiled as he waved no.

Finn wasn't far off in his assessment. Rodney had noticed the other detectives leaving the office, one by one, and followed them after the last one had departed. He didn't have far to go after seeing Vito slip through the door of Cafe Paulo. He crossed the street to take a long view, and sure enough, he spotted four VPD officers sitting farther in the rear. Satisfied, not that he knew what the group was talking about, he wandered back to the station, keeping his eyes open for Steve Christie. It was enough for Rodney to throw some nails into the gears if he could find them working on the GreenSide case.

Nile visited his local cafe for a coffee before making his way to city hall, where he called Ken Jalla about a contribution to his picture fund.

"Screw off, Nile. Your lever, you pull it. I'm not being part of your sorry little extortion deal." Ken replied. "Next time you call, I want some good news, not feeble excuses."

That went about as expected, Nile thought. He went onto the website of his bank to move some money around in anticipation of adding to Norway's gross domestic product, then finished his coffee and drove over to city hall. When he walked onto the floor where his office was, there was no sign of his assistant, so he went to his desk, sat down, and sighed before transferring the agreed sum by e-transfer to Kristian Axness. He didn't expect an immediate reply because of the time difference with Oslo, so he started reviewing files for an upcoming council meeting.

After an hour of reading, his email pinged. He looked at the reply from Kristian Axness. There were two picture files attached, so he moved them to his Sun Energy folder. He paused, making sure his office door was closed, then opened the first file. It depicted a young half naked schoolgirl going down on Kirby Brown. No ambiguity at all. Curious as to the contents of the second file, he opened it and choked. He was looking at a picture of himself, leering at the naked rear ends of the schoolgirls as they were leaning over, depositing their purses on the side tables. Shit. So much for trying to extort Kristian. Now he was on the receiving end of it. The picture of himself was well done, taken from a difficult angle, yet clearly incriminating. Kristian was no amateur at this.

Nile had been trying to come up with a method to let the mayor know about his options, but now he was in a muddle, considering what trouble he might be in himself. The more he thought about it, the worse off he knew he was. He had just paid thirty thousand dollars for something essentially worthless to him, unless he didn't care whether Stanley knew it was Nile who was blackmailing him. And it might very well come to that, he realized, after some more thought. He also wondered how much heft Stanley actually carried as far as getting invoices paid.

Nile wanted more coffee, so he left his office, noticing on the way that his assistant was back at her desk. He went up to her, intent on giving her a reaming out for the shoddy research work on Kristian.

"Not happy with the information I received from you about Kristian Axness." His brows were knitted together. His assistant hadn't seen Nile this angry before.

"In what way, Nile?"

"The fact that he has no family. No wife, no kids. Where did you get your information, anyway?" He was yelling now.

Looking at Nile as though she was confronting a drunk, "Well Nile, I got it from his personal assistant. Why would you think differently?" Her voice raised slightly in reply.

"Because that is what he told me." Even as he said this, he realized it was as lame as it sounded. Kristian had screwed him, and it hadn't even been very difficult to do. He looked down at the floor, then turned and walked away, no hint of an apology on offer.

Mamie had received the excited email that Chopper had sent in haste. She was not impressed, nor was she worried. She printed it off, befitting someone from an earlier generation who still distrusted the electronic system, and marched up to the third floor again.

She walked over to the mayor's aide, who watched Mamie approach. "I am in receipt of this email from a very rude lawyer who is trying to represent Sun Energy. He has all the manners of a rabid racoon. It seems they are not happy about the non-payment of the last hydrogen invoice." The proffered piece of paper was taken and studied.

After a moment, the response came, "I wonder how successful Chopper is with an approach such as this? Certainly wouldn't want him as a guest at my summer tea parties." She looked at it further, then said, "I'll let the mayor see this before taking it to the lawyers up top, thanks."

Mamie gave the briefest of smiles before departing for the main floor, confident that her work on this file was complete, with the city lawyers now handling negotiations.

Over in Surrey, Bobbi lucked out. Paneet asked Bobbi to accompany him on his trip to pick up the two new workers for the brothel. They were to leave after lunch the next day, returning later to Surrey. Bobbi called his sister and told her the plan of action. She was not happy. She had a course at the local polytechnic university campus around the same time. Bobbi pleaded his case, asking her to be near the Two Tigers club when they returned. He had no idea where they were travelling to for the pickup, but he was uncertain whether Paneet would want him along when he went downtown. It sounded like his question to Manny was successful.

"What's it worth to you, Bobbi?" Safa asked.

"Whatever your heart desires."

"You can't afford that, big brother, but I will think up something, don't worry. You will owe me a lot after this task."

Bobbi smiled to himself. Good, things were dropping into place, "Thanks little sister, you are magnificent."

Robert had spent the day at home, trying to conduct more research into Fern Developments and Bamboo Construction. He had heard that construction had re-commenced at the GreenSide site. Apparently, an alternative energy system for the project was being quickly designed and would be built as an extra to the contract. No other bids asked for or accepted. From what Robert had learned, that sounded about right. No doubt, someone would be lining their pockets over this. The mayor had taken a fair amount of public heat in the media over the hydrogen debacle, but he was fighting back, as per what an adept politician would do. Naturally, lawyers were lurking, threats of lawsuits abounded. The city's lawyers were girding their loins, getting ready for strife.

Robert wondered if Bernard was keen for more action. He wanted to know about the ownership structure of Fern and Bamboo, and Bernard seemed to have the Victoria government connection that could shed light on this.

He called him. "Bernard?"

"Robert, I have been missing you. I need more things to write about."

"You can always make things up, like the people in your profession seem to do."

"That's low, Robert."

"I know. Can you find out the ownership for Fern Developments and Bamboo Construction?"

"In return? You mentioned the killings in Burnaby. Anything to report?"

"Sadly, no. The RCMP seem to be getting nowhere on that file, but when something breaks, I will let you in, don't worry. I take care of people that help me. I have something else that you will be the first to report on, when the time is right. It involves Victoria."

"Most mysterious. Should we do lunch soon?"

"Let me know what you find out, and I'll buy, don't worry." With that resolved, he started to consider dinner options for his children. After a look through his fridge, he settled on Chinese; steamed whitefish, pot stickers and junior *gai lan*, with rice.

As he was prepping the food, his mother called, still concerned about what she had heard on the news concerning the night of action at Robert's townhouse. Robert soothed her as best he could, but the worry in her voice was obvious. He told her that the person arrested was not getting out of custody—no reasons given, but it was all he had now. It seemed to calm her.

CHAPTER 20

At half past two, Bobbi got into the dented van, nodding at Paneet, who was in the navigator's seat. Safa was sitting in her rented car, a good half block away, watching the van. The rental was Bobbi's idea; a way to reduce risk in case Paneet caught sight of the car. Bobbi guessed that he was driving because Paneet wanted to send him a message. He didn't care. It all served his ultimate goal. As he drove past Safa, he gave her the barest of nods. Bobbi had instructed her to stay put until he was kicked out of the van, which was what he suspected would happen when they returned from their journey.

"Where are we going?" Bobbi asked.

"Langley." Not exactly a fountain of directions, but Bobbi headed south to Highway 10, which would take them east into the heart of Langley. At the junction where he turned east onto the highway, Bobbi glanced over to his left, looking at the judicial complex where Edward Su was spending his days. Farther along was the Surrey Provincial Courthouse, which gang members such as Bobbi and Paneet hoped to avoid. Bobbi smiled as they passed by. Paneet noticed, "Why are you grinning?"

"Because we're out here, not in there." A simple observation that few gangsters had the opportunity to be reminded of. Most of them assumed being 'in there' applied to other people, unlucky people, never themselves, until one day it didn't.

"I've got my eye on you." Paneet started in. "You're up to something, I know it." Bobbi looked over at him, expressionless.

Bobbi had the courage to not say anything. He just shook his head, not being unduly troubled. All his transgressions had yet to happen. "So, where are we going?"

Paneet was not impressed at being ignored. "I'll tell you when we get there."

"What an asshole." It was as good a comeback as Bobbi could think up. At that, Paneet reached over and smacked the steering wheel, angry at the disrespect. The van veered slightly as Bobbi tried to straight-arm Paneet away from him. He brought the van back under control, gripping the steering wheel much more tightly.

"You trying to kill us?"

It was Paneet's turn to ignore Bobbi. The remainder of the journey passing in sullen silence.

After driving through Cloverdale, with its feed stores and saddlery shops scattered in amongst the usual suburban retail menagerie, they crested a hill, then descended into a land of shopping malls and car dealerships. Bobbi assumed they would make a straight run, but Paneet pointed right with his hand at an intersection, directing him to the old village centre of Langley. After driving through this quaint piece of local history, Bobbi went on for another kilometre before being directed right again, past a copse of cottonwood trees and a left on a muddied track into what looked like an unkempt farm property.

There was a single-storey home in less than pristine condition, with enough debris scattered around it to indicate that the owners weren't totally on top of their maintenance schedule. A dog was barking at the visitors; foam coming out of its mouth, straining at a chain that could have anchored a good-sized boat, and bolted to the house wall. Bobbi wasn't up on his dog breeds, but if he had to guess, Pit Bull would spring to mind. He drove a good fifty metres past the dog before feeling safe enough to stop. In Bobbi's mind, this place had all the classic markings of a successful drug operation; except to his knowledge, it wasn't. It was something much uglier. They both got out of the van, Bobbi not keen on heading towards the house.

"Follow me. I've got something for you to do." Paneet headed behind the house towards a large weather-beaten woodshed with a sagging roof. Mud was everywhere. Bobbi could hear some snorting and scuffling going on behind the shed that could only come from animals. They rounded the corner and Paneet went over to the wall and grabbed a shovel. "Dig a hole and bury that." He pointed to a pale green footlocker.

Bobbi stared at Paneet. "What's in the box?"

"None of your business. Just bury it. I'll be back in a little while." He turned and went back around the corner. Bobbi followed him but stayed behind the shed, watching as Paneet got back into the van, then drove off under some hanging cottonwood branches. There must have been another trail, invisible to a newcomer like Bobbi. He looked back at three enormous pigs grunting in a small pen, chewing at something in the muck and weeds beside the chain link fencing. Bobbi shrugged and walked over to an open area away from where he imagined tree roots might be and started to dig. The soil was clay that had been saturated by days of rain, so, while the going was heavy, it didn't take long to dig a hole slightly larger than the box.

He went back over to the box. As he leaned over, a stench hit his nostrils. He stood and backed up a step. There was a lock on the box. Screw it. He wanted to know what he was doing. He gave the lock a good whack with the shovel. It popped off. He held his breath as he opened the lid. A shimmering mass of maggots were moving over the remains of what looked like a young man missing his legs. He had been dismembered, and his entire belly also looked to be absent. Bobbi almost retched as he looked away. Not that he needed any further excuses to leave Two Tigers, but this just added to the list, maybe moving to the top. He bent over and grabbed the leather handle on the end of the box, dragging it over to the hole, and shoved it in. He piled mud on top and tamped it down, all the while shaking his head.

As he stared at the pigs, he realized what they were gnawing on and fighting over. It looked like a leg, a human leg. He swore, then turned and went to the front of the shed to await the return of Paneet. He looked across at the dog, who had stopped barking, but kept his eyes on Bobbi the whole time. Bobbi smiled, which didn't seem to please the animal in the least. It strained at its leash.

After a while, with still no sign of Paneet and giving the dog a wide berth, he walked over to a front window to see what was inside the house. He peered into the darkness, looking at the remnants of a life lived at least three decades earlier. It didn't appear that anyone had been in the room for some time. He slipped around the back of the house, where he grabbed an old galvanized washtub to get himself high enough to see into what he assumed to be a bedroom. Ancient powder blue curtains were half open, but beyond them he could see evidence of more recent activity. A table with a couple of chairs occupied the room, no sign of a bed. This looked more like what the dog signified. A scale sat on the table, along with some empty plastic bags, evidence of industrious activity to fulfill the never-ending needs of a drug dependant population. He stepped off the tub and started back around the front when he heard the van approaching.

Paneet drove slowly along the rutted track, and as he got close to Bobbi, who was stepping forward, gunned the van so it shot by Bobbi, just missing his toes. About fifty metres on, Paneet stopped, having had his laughs. He got out, still laughing, and gestured for Bobbi to catch up and drive.

After Bobbi got the van into gear, he looked over at Paneet. "You are one piece of work, you know that?"

Paneet just smiled back at Bobbi.

"Who takes care of the animals?"

"Why do you want to know? You want the job?" Paneet smiled at the vision of Bobbi being eaten by the dog as he tried to feed it a doggie snack.

"Fuck off." Bobbi was now sorry that he had even opened his mouth. "Where are we going?"

"Back to the club. That's where you get out. Did you bury the box like I said?"

"Yes." He was back on a paved road now. The ride was quieter, so he could hear some thuds from the rear of the van. He didn't say anything further, thinking about who was in the rear of the van. Twenty-five minutes later, they pulled up to the club, where Bobbi stopped and got out. He looked down the street. Safa was waiting in her car, frowning. As Bobbi made his way to the door of the club, Paneet slid past him, on his way to Vancouver, giving him the finger as he went by. Bobbi grinned at Paneet, knowing his time was drawing to a close. Ten seconds later, Safa drove by. Bobbi nodded slightly at her and prayed that this would work out.

Safa had been told by Bobbi that Yaletown was the likely destination, so it made her job easier. She would only be concerned with getting close to the van when it was in Yaletown, on the north side of False Creek. She relaxed and settled into the drive to Vancouver. It was late afternoon, but the light was good, and she was travelling against the rush hour flow, so the job was relatively simple. She kept several cars back of the van and relaxed into the pace of the drive, considering what she wanted from her brother. A holiday would be nice. She knew he had oodles of money, so maybe Hawaii or Mexico in November, when a break from the rain was needed.

Paneet turned off the highway onto Knight Street, which bridged the Fraser River. The problem became trucks, Knight being the main truck route north to the Port of Vancouver. The container semis were slow, large, and hard to see around. At one point, Safa actually passed the van after losing sight of it. She zipped into the right lane and slowed, keeping an eye on her mirrors. The last thing she needed was for the van to turn off the road when it was behind her. She slowed enough that the line of traffic behind eventually passed her, including the van. She knew enough about Vancouver to guess the route Paneet might take, and sure enough, he turned left at Broadway. He'd likely turn onto

Cambie and north over the bridge to his downtown destination. In doing so, he would pass the front door of the police offices where the detectives were puzzling about their lack of progress on the GreenSide affair.

Light was fading as the van did exactly what Safa had anticipated. After crossing the Cambie Bridge, Paneet promptly took a left at Mainland Street, arriving in the midst of the food and bar scene called Yaletown. The original uses for the buildings had undergone changes the last two decades as Vancouver grew. What had started as a railroad terminus, with lumber processing and cooperages, changed to clothing warehousing. Railroad workers had lived in the area, so wooden houses and boarding rooms dotted the area. After Expo 86, most of the warehouse buildings had been renovated; some, several times over, into restaurants, condominiums, office spaces, bars, and boutiques. Single-family houses had all but disappeared, replaced by residential towers. It was one of the trendiest neighbourhoods in downtown, now that industry had been shown the door.

Halfway down the second block, the van pulled into a spare stall. The street parking on Mainland was diagonal, against a wall of concrete loading docks, extremely unusual for any large city. Safa slowed, then passed the van, looking for any spare stall up ahead.

Paneet had noticed Safa's car while they had been driving down Cambie, being aware of the dangers of what he was doing. When he turned onto Mainland, and the car made the same move, he guessed he was being followed. After parking, he watched his mirror, waiting for Safa to pass by. As she did, he relaxed slightly, not willing to believe that a woman would be tailing him. He kept watching as she travelled several stalls farther before pulling in. When she finally got out of her car, he watched. She was good-looking. Safa turned and walked in the opposite direction, so Paneet put the affair out of his mind, needing to concentrate on getting his two workers into their new lodgings with the least fuss. Not that he really needed to worry after the example that had been made of one of their compatriots.

Safa went farther before crossing the street and walking into the entry alcove of a small grocery store. She turned and peered around the corner at the van. After Paneet had taken his guests out of the van's rear and up the steps of the loading dock area, Safa carefully moved back down to note the address of the building. This done, she felt a sense of relief at accomplishing something for her brother. She walked west and, instead of getting into her car; kept going, deciding to celebrate by dining at one of the trendy restaurants along the street. She rarely travelled into downtown Vancouver, so this would be a well-deserved treat. As she slowly walked by a few cafes, reading the menus posted by their front doors, she settled on a small French-style bistro. Despite its name, it featured the type of Parisian cooking not normally found in Surrey, so she went in and was shown a small table by the front window.

After perusing the menu, she settled on a starter of octopus and pickled pears, with steak frites to follow. She smiled to herself as she pulled out her phone to call her brother.

"Bobbi."

"Hey sis. Are you okay? How did it go?"

"3155 Mainland. It is on the loading dock side of the street."

"Okay, great work. You're on your way home, correct?"

"Not exactly. I'm eating a meal at a very nice French bistro, Cafe Lyon."

"But not in Yaletown, right?"

Suddenly, the shine went off the meal. "Yes actually. I'm on Mainland. Bad idea?"

Bobbi felt ill. Paneet was stupid, but not totally brain dead. "I think you should eat and get out of there as soon as you can."

Now Safa was getting miffed at Bobbi. He just couldn't stop treating her like a little girl. She'd enjoy her meal, no matter what kind of cold water Bobbi was tossing around. She was just about to end the call when she saw Paneet walking along the sidewalk, looking into windows as he strode, "Shit, it's Paneet. Got to go Bobbi."

A metamorphosis then took place. Her face went from frantic to calm in a second. She knew Paneet didn't know who she was, and she was very good at putting gangsters in their place if needed. It helped that Paneet was not any larger than she was. She looked down at her starter and picked away at the delicious octopus.

Sure enough, Paneet came through the door, smiled at the hostess, then came over to Safa's table. "Are you following me?" No longer smiling.

Safa slowly looked up from her meal, studying her foe. "If I was following you, wouldn't I be behind you? Who are you anyway?" Shaking her head, as if having to deal with a simple-minded child, she signalled to the hostess, who came over to her table, "I have no idea who this man is, but he is pestering me. Can you ask him to leave me alone?"

"Please stop bothering our customers and leave." The hostess mustered all her determination.

Paneet was confused. Maybe he had got it all wrong, but the girl looked like she could be from the Punjab. He was undecided, until the bartender, who was much larger than Paneet, started walking his way. This decided things for him, so, with a sneer at Safa, he left. As he walked back to his van, he passed by Safa's car and took a picture of it, then noticed the rental sticker. He thought about waiting to follow her when she finished eating, but didn't have the patience, so he got into his van for the long ride home to Surrey.

Safa watched Paneet's retreating back as she continued eating. A few moments later, the van passed by the window. Safa studiously avoided watching it but was relieved.

Paneet looked at the restaurant window as he drove by, but the girl wasn't paying any attention to the street. Maybe his paranoia was all that was happening. After all, what he had been doing was dangerous.

Safa relaxed slightly, trying to enjoy the rest of her first course. She called Bobbi back, knowing he would be worrying. "Hi Bobbi, he's gone. I saw him drive away."

"Did he see you?"

"He actually came into the cafe to accuse me of following him. I told him to get lost, and he left. He looked confused. Maybe he saw my car, I don't know."

"I think he must have. Otherwise, why would he have approached you? When you return the car to the rental place, make sure they don't give your information out to anyone." Bobbi started to fret. This had been a stupid idea from the start. Now he may have put his sister in danger. However, he supposed that nothing else could be done except to let loose the police hounds.

When Bobbi arrived home at his condo, he called Thomas. "It's Bobbi. 3155 Mainland Street. Paneet just dropped a couple of more kids down there. My sister tailed them into town. And I know where they keep the kids in Langley. I was there today, and it is ugly, Thomas."

"We are set to go. We will take Mainland tomorrow night and call you about Langley when this is completed. Thanks Bobbi. Be careful."

"Okay, I guess." He looked down at his phone. He needed a drink. He texted his sister, asking her to let him know when she had arrived home.

That evening, Thomas worked on his raid plan after the alert from Bobbi earlier in the day. The team would be comprised of his three detectives, and a heavily armed tactical squad supplemented by several uniformed officers. None of the top floor brass were aware of what was about to happen. Thomas knew that this put him in a dangerous position, but he was past being political. He would do his job even though it would be a very public action, Yaletown being a hotbed of drinking and eating every night of the week. If he had to guess, it sounded as though the brothel was above one of the restaurants on Mainland. Building plans would need to be obtained from city hall first thing next morning. If all went to plan, the raid would happen the next night. After some deliberation, Thomas called it a day to get some rest. Tomorrow would be interesting. Langley would be a different challenge. Any raid on that location would directly implicate Bobbi, so some consideration would be needed before any action happened.

CHAPTER 21

First thing the next morning, Thomas tasked Tony with getting the information from city hall on the Yaletown property. Tony called planning, and after a few attempts by staff at diverting his attention, he finally got connected to the correct department.

"Hi, it's Detective Tony Bortolo, Vancouver Police Department. We need the building plans for 3155 Mainland Street, right away, and a list of current tenants as well."

"We'll need written authorization from the building owner first before anything can be released."

Tony laughed, "No you don't. This is a police action, we're not renovating the place. Let me talk to your supervisor."

Tony waited patiently while he could hear staff scurrying around. "Sherman here. How can I be of assistance?"

"Well, Sherman, we need building plans and a tenant list. Your underling has the info. We need it now, for a police action."

There was silence on the other end, then. "We are not supposed...."

Tony cut him off. "Let's assume you like your job and want to keep it. Here is my email address. Forward the information, please." He ended the call after giving Sherman his address. That done, self satisfied with his newfound bravado, he left the floor to head up the street for coffee before the day got busy. After ordering a macchiato, Tony sat and called his mentor.

"Robert, we are going after the brothel tonight."

"That was quick. You obviously have it located, right?"

"Well, almost. We have the building in Yaletown, but we're trying to narrow down exactly where it is inside. We'll rip the whole building apart if we have to."

"That's the spirit." Robert wished he could be part of the action. "This should put a dent in the Two Tigers. Might even make them do something stupid if they react quickly."

"Here's hoping. I'll let you know tomorrow how it goes, Robert."

"Best of luck tonight."

As Tony sipped his coffee, he was checking his cell, waiting on city hall. He supposed it would take some time to dig out the appropriate plans, but he wasn't going to give them any more than an hour before he'd go higher up the food chain to get what he wanted. Ten minutes later, he headed back to the station, ready for a meeting with Thomas.

Finn Black and Vito Cotoni had been tasked with reconnaissance of the building and were wandering around Yaletown. There were no laneways in Yaletown, unlike the remainder of downtown, so the building in question also fronted onto Hamilton Street to the northwest. Due to the slope of the land heading down to False

Creek, the Hamilton side was a full level above the Mainland side. Shops and a small cafe took up space on the Hamilton side. The Mainland frontage included a large furniture store selling petite modern things sized to fit in small Vancouver apartments. Restaurants took up space in both adjacent buildings, so there would be no hiding the raid from the public. Access to the building lobby was not secure, so they entered and looked at each floor after taking a picture of the directory in the lobby. They checked out both exit stairs, then went up top to see if the roof could be accessed. It was locked. Satisfied, they returned to the Hamilton Street level and entered one of the cafes.

"Sure would be good to narrow down the choices in here. I hope Tony has some success." Vito said. He watched as a pair of men ambled slowly along the pavement just outside of the cafe; they were thin and semi-transparent, their dirt encrusted pants ill-fitting, stopping well short of their clumsy looking work boots. Checkered shirts were framed with suspenders. Their faces were dark, as though they had spent years in the sun. Both wore floppy grey caps, the type a newsboy might wear decades ago, and one was carrying an old-fashioned lunch bucket. The hands were rough, those of manual workers. His partner had an axe resting on his shoulder. Vito looked back at Finn, wondering if he was seeing the same thing. "Did you see those guys?"

"What? It's a nice area. I don't get down here very often." Finn mused as he also studied the sidewalk life, however, not seeing what Vito was looking at.

"Do you believe in spirits?" When Finn declined to answer, Vito continued the original line of thought, "I think it's nice if you don't live around here. I've heard that the twenty-four-hour light and noise can be draining, unless you like that kind of thing and don't waste time sleeping." His head swivelled back to the street, but the two men were nowhere to be seen.

"You mean, like a real big city."

"I suppose, although not really that big, actually...." Vito's remark petered out as their attention focused on a pair of young, fashionably dressed women walking by the window.

"As I said, I like it down here." Finn drained his coffee without taking his eyes off the women. "Let's go. Things to do."

Once back at Cambie Street, Vito and Finn went looking for Thomas. Norma pointed at Thomas's office door, so they both went in and reported their findings.

"It would be good to narrow down the options inside. Hope Tony comes up with the tenant list. It is a big building, six floors. We can dismiss the two lowest floors, but that still leaves quite a few possibilities." Finn opened.

"We checked the stairs, and the roof is locked off, but the stairs exit at both the Mainland level and Hamilton, a storey up," Vito added.

"I think this time we will take control of any kids we find. Not keen on repeating our mistakes, so we'll need a place to keep them. Ambulances as well, just in case." Thomas continued, "The top floor doesn't know about this action yet. I have had a discussion with the tactical squad leader, so hopefully, this goes smoothly." Left unsaid was the reason for not informing the brass, which both detectives noted silently. "If we are wrong, and there are no underage kids in there, then I will be the goat. We'll meet this afternoon up a floor with the tactical squad to iron out the plan. Anyone seen Tony yet?"

A minute later Tony's head appeared at the doorway, studying his cellphone as he walked slowly into the room, so intent that he bumped into Thomas's desk before he halted. "Got the building plans, but no tenant list. I have to call the building owner for that information. I'll go to my computer and get Norma to print out the plans." With that, he left the room without even looking up at who was present. The other three officers present shook their heads in unison.

"Let's continue this at the tactics meeting this afternoon," Thomas concluded.

Up the street at city hall, George Ascot had been handed the copy of the email that Mamie had printed a day earlier. He studied it quickly, not surprised at the content of the message, but was less than impressed with the way it was written. He sat, thinking about his next move. Once Sun Energy responded in the manner he predicted, he assumed he would then let the mayor dangle in the wind—the victim of his own incompetence. But the tone of the lawyer's message set his teeth on edge. He realized that even though someone had apparently done an end around to get the contract signed off, the city's lawyers would need to be very active on this file. He needed some intelligence on this Chopper person before making a move, so he asked his assistant to find out what he could about the firm, its lawyers, and who at city hall had been dealing with Sun Energy. After learning that it was Mamie from accounts, he decided to have a short meeting to get her perspective. George was very thorough before he acted on any matter, and Mamie had a reputation around city hall.

It was early afternoon when, one by one, the detectives wandered up a floor to a large meeting room for the pre-raid meeting. There were twelve people in the room; a few uniforms, five from the tactical squad, and the four detectives.

Thomas led off. "Thanks for your attendance. This action should not be violent, but we need to prepare as though it will be. We believe that teenagers are involved in a brothel, against their will, otherwise, we wouldn't be wasting our time. The Two Tigers are behind this set-up, so we are expecting repercussions once the action is complete. I also would expect someone from the gang to be on site, maybe more than one. The location on Mainland Street is very public with restaurants on either side of the building in question, so conduct yourselves accordingly. I want stair exits covered at the Mainland and Hamilton Street levels. Hamilton is one level up from Mainland. Tony here will show you the building plans, which we can only hope are current, but I would not depend on them. They were obtained from city planning today." Thomas's look spoke of someone who wouldn't trust anything that came from the city.

Tony brought the plans up to the screen at the front of the room, scrolled through all the levels, then returned to the third-floor plan. "I have a list of tenants in the building, but only one tenant recently leased space on this level."

"How recent?" Thomas asked.

"Three weeks ago."

"Okay. This is our target."

"How can you be certain?" The head of the tactical squad asked.

"Because the same brothel was recently put out of business when GreenSide exploded. This is their new home."

The tactical members looked at each other. This was news to them.

"We will hold all the clients we find on the premises for the night, enough to cause some embarrassment, we hope, but we won't be able to hold them after that. The real intent is to free the kids. If there are any gang members on the premises, then we'll arrest and hold them, probably on weapons offences, as they're likely to be armed. Some of these kids will probably be the same ones who were kidnapped after we took control of them last time. The murders of the two group home leaders are connected."

Thomas addressed the uniformed officers present. "I'd like you to control any of the public that gets the idea that they should get a close up look at what is unfolding. You know they love filming anything they can on their phones, so use your discretion. I think we will exit at the Hamilton Street level, then we'll be away from the restaurants on Mainland. Hamilton is where we'll have the trucks and ambulances waiting. Any questions?"

No one seemed to have any, so they agreed to meet back at the station eight-thirty that evening.

The action went without any major incidents, except for one surprise. The four uniforms keeping watch at the Mainland side of the building on the loading dock apprehended an elderly customer who was trying to slip out the back way after the action had started. It was warm enough that diners were sitting in the outdoor terrace areas of the adjacent restaurants, so the officers could not escape notice as they lolled by the rear wall waiting for whatever was to take place. The elderly gentleman had been in the washroom when the police had burst into the suite, and had somehow made his way to one of the exit stairs un-noticed, that was, until he exited onto the loading dock into the arms of the attending officers. He protested his innocence, using the working late line, but the officers had heard it all before. He was led by one of the officers down the street and around to the Hamilton side, to the waiting police vans. One or two diners pulled up their cellphones to record what was happening on the off chance that some police brutality would be on display.

The sole possibility of violence in the action was quickly dealt with by the tactical squad member, who was second through the suite door. A Two Tiger employee was manning a table just inside the door and started reaching for his pistol, but quickly thought better of it, raising his hands as high as they would go.

Vito was the man to find the waiting surprise. The detectives were entering the small side rooms one by one, gathering up the customers and the workers. Vito entered a room by himself, and was face to face with Steve Christie, who was putting his pants on, about to fall over in his haste. Vito was speechless for a moment, then gathered his wits and, sticking his head outside the door, beckoned for Thomas to come over. Thomas entered, and his mouth dropped open. Steve and Thomas stared at each other for about ten seconds, then Thomas recovered. "Sex with a minor. Not what a superintendent should be up to, I would say." Then he had a thought. "Get your clothes on."

The young boy caught with Steve was watching the three officers, fear in his eyes. "I'm going to take this lad out to the street." Vito said, then gently grabbed the youngster by the shoulder, got him dressed, and led him out of the room. Whatever deal was going to happen in that room, he had no stomach to hear it play out.

Steve slowed down his dressing. The two officers looked at each other warily, like a mongoose and a viper, each waiting for the other to make a move.

Steve cracked first. "So, what do you want?"

"I'm going to think about it, don't worry. You better finish dressing and come out after I leave the room. Or you can stay and slip out the back way later if there is a stair out. Your choice. We'll leave someone at the suite door to secure the scene overnight." With that, Thomas left the room, gently closing the door behind him. He went looking for Vito. On Hamilton Street, the boys and girls were being loaded onto two small buses after being checked out. The customers were shepherded into police vans for a trip across the bridge, where they would spend the night in a cell. The boys and girls were being sent to two safe houses in Vancouver, each with a female officer and nurse on board. Thomas would notify social welfare in the morning about the situation, but not where the children were being kept.

"Vito, take a walk with me," Thomas yelled as he turned and walked up Hamilton. Vito hesitated, then followed Thomas, catching up.

"What happened in there?" Vito started.

"You saw it. A superintendent of police was caught with his pants down, literally. And with a minor. I am going to extract what I can from this situation, then we'll file charges. I believe that the GreenSide case will be back on the front burner shortly. And there's something else I want."

Vito was grinning, relieved that his boss hadn't turned against his principals. "I can tell the others?"

"Just Finn and Tony, no one else for now."

"Yes sir."

"Let's get out of here. I want a watch put on the two safe houses. Those officers are not to know who is in the houses, understood?"

"Yes. I'll get that organized right away."

"Let's meet back at the station for the post operation meeting." With that, they parted, and the operation wound down; the vehicles left, and Hamilton Street slowly returned to its normal evening activities.

Back at Cambie Street, a late meeting was convened in Thomas's office. The head of the tactical squad was thanked and sent on his way, so it was only the four detectives who remained from the action taken earlier.

Thomas led off. "I would like those kids interviewed as soon as possible. Tony, you mentioned none of them spoke English?"

"That was last time. There were some new faces tonight. Finding out who we need as interpreters would be a start."

"Agreed. However, the more people who know where these kids are, the leakier the ship will become. Finn, could you look into this tomorrow? We have a larger problem. If we are going to do the right thing and return the kids to where they came from, we'll probably never see them again. Certainly not for a court case, which will take months and months to get underway."

Vito had told the other two about Steve Christie on the drive back to Cambie, so all three were waiting expectantly for Thomas to say something.

"I assume that Vito has told you about the disgusting find at the raid. I mean, it was all disgusting, but this topped it." There was nodding of heads, but no one uttered a word. "Amongst other things, I believe I will use this to bring Robert back to the VPD. And the GreenSide investigation will be back full force."

Tony grinned, and the two others were smiling. "So, something good did come out of this shitty mess after all!"

"I want a watch kept on the two houses, round the clock, starting tonight. Let's meet tomorrow late morning. Go home and get some sleep." With that, Thomas ended the short meeting, suddenly exhausted from the tension of the day.

Chapter 22

The next morning, Tony woke feeling better than he had in months. He didn't need to be at the station until late morning, so he took his time getting ready, heading directly to Cafe Paulo before work. After the customary greeting extravaganza with Gilberto, he took his coffee to a table and called Robert. He decided he would just be sharing information. If Thomas had warned him not to talk to Robert, he would have complied.

"Hello? Tony?"

"Yup. Guess where I am."

"Can't guess, my coffee hasn't dripped out yet."

"Cafe Paulo. As I am talking, Gilberto is attaching a name plate to a chair. I believe it says Robert Lui."

"What are you trying to say, Tony?" Robert asked. "In your twisted way...."

"That you will be getting a job offer shortly from one Thomas Harrow."

"You are kidding me. What happened?"

"Someone high up in the chain of command got caught with their pants down, literally."

"That visual is not helping the start of my day. Who was it?"

"Don't think I am at liberty to say, but it's not a good situation."

"Well, if I am being brought back, then it can only be one of two people, McKnight or Christie. I wouldn't want to see either of them with the pants around their ankles," Robert responded.

"Now you are making my coffee taste funny. Just thought I'd let you know. We broke up the brothel last night. I have a feeling that the Two Tigers will be prowling for trouble."

"Brothel? Hmm, I didn't think Thomas would stoop to extortion."

"Extortion? Gentle persuasion is what he has in mind, I believe," Tony responded, as he twirled his cup gently.

"Well, whatever. You just made my day, Tony. I will wait for the real thing, but my first order of business will be to exit my current employment scenario."

"Is that what you call it? A scenario?"

"Feels like it more and more every day. Got to go—my coffee is ready. I'm looking into Fern and Bamboo today. I'll let you know what I find out. Ciao Tony."

Tony looked over at Gilberto behind his machine but thought better of telling him what might happen. Better not queer the deal before it gets done. He eventually rose, nodded at Gilberto, and went out into the morning sunshine.

In Surrey, Paneet was waiting for the usual morning phone call from his man in Yaletown. He required a daily briefing on money totals and any potential trouble brewing, just in case Manny was in the mood to ask questions. The brothel guy always had been punctual, probably afraid to do anything else. It was ten-thirty, a half hour after the usual update, so Paneet called him. On the other end, the cell was sitting on Finn Black's desk, ringing. It finally went to voicemail.

"Where are you? You're half an hour late. Better call me or you are screwed." Paneet was temporarily satisfied with his threatening bluster and returned to his cup of tea, not worried yet.

Finn contemplated the cellphone, wondering how he could get into it, not knowing the pass code. He'd take it downstairs to the geniuses in the basement. Then he paused. If he had just answered the call when it came in, he might get into the phone and all its information. Talk about geniuses. He was exhibiting characteristics of a class A idiot. With that brilliant insight, he decided to wait for another call by staring at the phone.

Thomas got into his office after ten and sat behind his desk, looking up at puffy clouds outside his window while he evaluated his next move. Not knowing what Steve might do next, he acted while he had the advantage. He called the top floor admin assistant. "Hello Ranit, would you mind asking Steve to come down to my office?"

Ranit was baffled. "Isn't it supposed to be the other way around? As in, you come up here?"

"Not anymore, Ranit. Tell him right away. Thanks." He hung up, smiling to himself as he contemplated getting his pound of flesh.

Something sounded off kilter to Ranit. She was pretty sure she knew how the chain of command worked in the police world, but she shrugged her shoulders, went over to Steve's door, and knocked sharply.

"Come in." The reply croaked through the door. Ranit walked in and recoiled slightly. Steve did not appear to be in top condition; eyes bloodshot, tie carelessly knotted, hair askew.

"Thomas from downstairs requested your appearance in his office rather urgently."

Instead of replying, Steve exhaled, got up, and slowly walked past Ranit out the door. What the heck was going on? Ranit grew more puzzled by the minute.

Steve eventually ended up on Thomas's floor and headed over to Norma's desk. "Is Thomas in?" Already knowing the answer.

Norma nodded her head at the open door, forgoing the spoken word.

Steve went into the office, sitting in the chair pointed out by Thomas, leaving the door ajar. Both men stared at each other. Thomas fired his first shot. "I am hiring another detective. You can let McKnight know. His name is Robert Lui. And I don't expect any issues with the hire. In fact, I want a raise in pay for him."

Steve's eyes fired briefly, then not. He remained silent.

"That's it, Steve." Then he rubbed it in a little more. "Oh wait, one other thing; GreenSide, which we never stopped working on, is front burner again. Thanks." With that, Thomas looked down at the paperwork on his desk, not caring what Steve did.

After a moment, Steve got up and silently left. With that, Thomas filled out the forms with the particulars of Robert's rehiring and stepping outside his office, asked Norma to print and file them, then send the offer letter to Robert. Naturally, as Norma read over the employment forms, she could not help smiling to herself as she contemplated life at the office with Robert back.

Thomas was not smiling as he pondered what trouble Steve could make for him. So far, only a few people knew about last evening. He was going to need to report to Deputy Chief McKnight soon, or maybe.... He stood up and paced in front of his window, checking on the frothing clouds, areas of blue playing hide and seek, then decided. "Norma," he called, "can you find out if the Chief Constable is available? Tell them it's important."

A few moments later, Norma peaked around his door frame. "He will be able to meet with you after one-thirty today."

"Okay. Please confirm that I'll attend." Thomas then prepared for his GreenSide team.

Well after eleven, three detectives entered Thomas's office one by one. Things had changed; Tony was now looking where he was going, and Finn was intently studying the phone in his hand, not paying attention.

"What'cha looking for Finn?" Thomas wondering if some teenage virus had infected his troops.

Finn bumped into a chair. "Waiting for this phone to ring."

"Usually, you have more chance if you don't look at it. Got a date coming up?" Vito asked.

"This is the phone we took off the concierge at the brothel. Waiting for a ring so I can get into it. It rang this morning, but I was too stupid to answer it."

Tony nodded slowly, looking at Vito and Thomas as he rolled his eyes. "We understand completely Finn."

Thomas started. "Two items on the agenda this morning. Number one is those kids. I've reconsidered and don't think we should do any interviews just yet, even though I really want to. They have been through a lot, and likely wouldn't talk to us, anyway. They need to get a hint of a normal life back for them first, however that is accomplished. I assume they have counsellors working with them. Finn, you should check on that and please line up the correct interpreters. The second item is Steve, which I will deal with somehow. I'm meeting with Caleb Woo after lunch. Going right to the top on this one."

Vito asked, "Anything I can do?"

"Contact the Burnaby RCMP. Find out where they are in the case. Tony, you can see if Robert has learned anything more."

"Is he really coming back?"

"Offer letter is going out. He seemed to be favourable to the idea a few days ago. We'll know soon." Just then, there was a beeping from the table.

Finn looked up, grinning as he picked up the cell and answered, "*Han.... Ji.*"

"Who the hell is this?" Paneet fired back in English.

"Vancouver Police Department, jackass."

Paneet quickly hung up and studied his phone for a moment as it dawned on him why his man in Yaletown hadn't called in.

Back at the meeting, Thomas asked, "*Han Ji*? What is that? Mandarin?"

Finn was busy with the phone now that it was open to him, looking at the contacts and recent calls in and out. "It's yes in Punjabi. I added the *Ji* as a sign of respect."

The others started laughing. "You realize we're dealing with thugs, correct?" Thomas asked. Finn ignored them and started to write items down in a small notepad he carried with him. Thomas shook his head, pointing to the door, signalling the end of the meeting. "Finn, you should probably take that down to the basement while it is open. They will handle it now." Finn looked up briefly and nodded, eyes shining at his small success. He rose and walked slowly out the door, making his way to the elevator, still looking down at the cellphone, everyone giving him a wide berth.

CHAPTER 23

In east Vancouver, Robert's email program made its annoying sound as Norma's message arrived on his laptop. He looked over from where he was eating some cereal, taking a late breakfast. Norma. She was persistent, he had to give Norma her due. He inched over and opened the message. An employment offer! Excellent. He didn't read any further for the time being, savouring the feeling of being wanted again, luxuriating in it, knowing that after he accepted, it would be all downhill after this day. Except for Norma. As he thought about her, he knew he was not above making the same mistake twice. In fact, he might be looking forward to it. Surely, he was wiser after what had transpired with Camille. Surely, he thought.

It sounded like Tony's phone call earlier that morning had been spot on. Dependable Tony. Something bad must have happened for Thomas to gain the upper hand and want him back. He supposed he'd have to tell Dan Prudence soon that he was returning to the fold. Then there was Bernard to consider. Once he was back on the force, he would be severely limited in what he could relay to Bernard. And he felt he still owed him, for the information, and the arm.

Robert returned to his research after the cereal was finished. Fern and Bamboo were linked in ways that were un-natural. He had learned that some larger developers had their own construction divisions as a way of controlling the final product; supposedly improving quality, but the real goal was to drive down and control costs, enhancing profit. This relationship was different. There seemed to be similar directors on both boards. Once again, he was shut out of the ownership roster. He was going to need Bernard's information, but this time, he felt a story was owed in return. He also started to delve into the poster boys for each company; Bob April, CEO of Fern and Alexis Tile, President of Bamboo.

He then found a story from a business news feed about nine months old, telling of a labour dispute with a subcontractor working on a project for Bamboo. The company, a ceramic tile supplier and installer, missed receiving a couple of payments due to them, so they did what subcontractors do, filed a lien against the site. This legal move was intended to protect the company's rights in a dispute and ideally, get them the money owed to them. The reason a story had been written at all in an otherwise unremarkable event was that the lien was then discharged, apparently by the company that placed it in the first place, Shiny Ceramics. Robert was scratching his head, wondering if there was more to the story, so he looked up Shiny Ceramics.

Around the time of the lien issue, a foreman for Shiny Ceramics had ended up in hospital, severely beaten by an unknown assailant. Then three weeks later, the owner of the company was found dead in south Surrey at the side of a road—shot twice in the head. The company had subsequently ceased operations. The RCMP had no suspects and no charges had been laid. They had issued the standard appeal for the public to call in with any tips, to no apparent avail. To Robert's eyes, this had the hallmark of a Two Tigers action, all violence, no subtlety. He called Bernard and let out some old news as a way to ask for more intelligence.

"Hello?"

"Robert here. I have some information, so listen carefully. Do you remember a couple of weeks ago, two people getting murdered in group homes in Burnaby?"

Bernard was fully attentive, hardly believing that this was happening; his inside source was spilling some beans. "Yes, I remember."

"The kids who were taken that night from the homes had just been liberated by the VPD from a brothel located in the Green-Side building that half fell down during the explosion. And they were all underage."

Bernard's mind was exploding; there seemed to be two or three stories here. "There was a brothel in GreenSide?"

"Yes."

"But that was a new project."

"Exactly. You will have to do your own digging from here on in. But I still need what you can find out about Bamboo Construction and Fern Developments. I need the ownership of both companies, please."

"Okay, I should get on that."

"One other thing, I am rejoining the VPD shortly."

"Wow. I don't know whether that's a good or bad thing for me."

"You will figure it out, you're smart. I'll call you for lunch soon. And oh yeah, Bernard? Be careful." He ended the call, smiling to himself. He could be a real bastard.

In Surrey, Bobbi had heard the news about the raid in Yaletown. He was the only member of the Two Tigers who regularly followed the news; the rest of them couldn't be bothered, assuming nothing of importance would be missed by their cellphones. He wondered when Manny would find out and explode.

Paneet was, at that moment, calling Manny with his report on what he thought happened to the brothel, along with his suspicions about Bobbi's role in the story. As expected, Manny unleashed a string of curses, then he was silent for a good thirty seconds. Paneet found this unnerving, as it was contrary to form.

"We are having a meeting this afternoon at three. I want Bobbi there and a couple of the others. Find out what happened. I want a report from you." Manny finally breaking his silence.

Paneet was both smiling and perplexed. Happy because maybe Bobbi would be exposed, and concerned that he really had no way of finding out what had happened in Yaletown. That wouldn't go down well with Manny. It didn't take long before he had an answer. He'd use Bobbi. Bobbi had demonstrated a big mouth in the past, boasting about keeping up with current affairs, so he would get him to do the work, and just maybe, Bobbi would dig his own grave into the bargain.

Paneet called Bobbi, "Hi. Manny wants a report on the brothel problem in Yaletown. This afternoon. There is a meeting, three o'clock, at the club."

"What problem? You're in charge of the brothel. Why aren't you doing it?"

"Manny told me that he wants you to do it."

"Okay, see you later." Something didn't sound right. Manny had never requested a report before on anything. If this was the way things were veering, they all might as well go and work for a real company where reports were a way of life.

Bobbi decided to check, so he swallowed and made a call. "Manny, it's Bobbi here. You want a report from me this afternoon?" He kept things generic.

"On what? Don't be an idiot. If I wanted something from you, you'd know it. Stop wasting my time." The call ended. That was clear, Paneet was up to something. Suddenly, Bobbi was looking forward to the afternoon meeting.

Robert relaxed at home for the rest of the morning, contemplating his new future, then called to see if Tony would meet him at Cafe Paulo for a late lunch. Tony agreed, so Robert headed over to Cambie Street. By the time Robert arrived, Tony was already sitting at a corner table with a big grin on his face, a steaming mug by his hands. There were only a couple of other customers, the lunch rush having abated, so Robert went to the counter and ordered a couple of paninis and coffee from Carmelita.

"You may be seeing more of me soon." Robert smiled at her, then turned to where Tony was sitting, evidently happy as he waited for Robert.

"Hey Tony. Looks like I am returning to the fold."

"Excellent, however, I'm not sure now whether you will get that name on a chair here. I have risen in Gilberto's rankings to where I might be ahead of you in that department."

"How so?"

"We are now conducting the occasional work meeting here. Gilberto appreciates the extra business and Thomas seems to be rather taken with the place."

"Well played Tony, well played." Seems that he had competition. He hadn't exactly created a monster, but his own pre-eminence at Cafe Paulo seemed in jeopardy. That's what happens when one goes missing for a while.

"So, have you found anything else?" Tony asked.

"Not really. I wanted to meet for lunch, don't need an ulterior reason, do I?"

"Well, usually something is up with you."

"Yes, you're correct. I think that Two Tigers have their claws into Bamboo Construction. I should have the owners list soon. Also, Fern and Bamboo seem to have a very cozy relationship. Are you going to tell me who got uncovered the other night?"

Carmelita then brought their food over to the table. "I think I'll let Thomas tell you that one. He's meeting with Caleb this afternoon." Tony smiled at Carmelita.

"Mmm...." Any reply was garbled as Robert bit into his prosciutto panino.

Meanwhile, Thomas was making the walk up to the top floor to meet with the Chief Constable. His poor political skills required that he'd keep his talking to a minimum and stick to the facts. After a wait of twenty minutes, he was ushered into Caleb Woo's grand office by Ranit. Caleb was sitting on a small settee in front of his desk, some papers scattered across a low table. He gestured to a club chair opposite him.

"So, how is Thomas today?" Caleb asked as Thomas settled into the leather seat.

Thomas smiled thinly. "Okay, I suppose."

"And how is your crew doing?"

"We are managing. I could use a couple of more detectives, but I am working on that."

"So, what are we meeting about?"

"You heard about the brothel we broke up last night?"

"Yes. A bit unusual for the VPD to be doing actions like that, and especially with detectives. And I don't think anyone up here was warned about it."

Sounded like Caleb was paying attention. "I agree, but we received some intelligence that those kids that were taken from the group homes the night of the murders might be there. Turned out to be correct. But that's not why I am here, Caleb."

Thomas noticed Caleb's brow furling, probably caused by the use of his first name.

"In one of the rooms a senior member of this force was discovered in the midst of a sexual act with a minor. It was Steve Christie." There, he had said it. He waited for a reaction, an explosion, anything.

Caleb remained silent, then, "I didn't hear anything about it in the news. I take it that they didn't find out... yet," he added.

"Only a few detectives know about this so far. I gave him the option of leaving by the rear door." Thomas waited.

"Anything else?"

"Yes. The day that the kids were rescued the first time from GreenSide, they were taken to two group homes in Burnaby. As you know, inside of thirty-six hours, those two den mothers were dead, and the kids taken. Even we couldn't find the location of where they were being kept, but someone found out pretty quickly. That's it."

Caleb remained stone-faced; his thoughts impossible to discern by Thomas.

"Who are the detectives who knew about this?"

This was the question Thomas feared would be asked. As he searched for the resolve to answer, Caleb spoke again, as if he were inside Thomas's mind.

"I suppose you want to know why I asked that question."

Thomas remained silent, waiting.

"Being thorough."

This hardly put his mind at rest, but he supposed he had no other option than to answer, "Detectives Bortolo, Black, and Cotoni."

Caleb nodded. "Leave this with me." He then looked down at the papers on the coffee table signalling the meeting's end. Thomas got up and after looking at Caleb, who did not return the favour, left the office, nodding at Ranit as he walked by her to the stairs. Somehow, the sharing of this information didn't make him feel any better. It filled him with dread.

At the club the Two Tigers called home, six people were in Manny's meeting room, waiting for Manny to enter. Ho Li-Fan was present, as well as three other minor gang members. Paneet sat at the far end of the table, smirking at Bobbi as he contemplated what Manny would do to him. Bobbi remained stoic. The door finally opened; the entire entry taken up by Manny's bulk. He hadn't sat down before he looked at Paneet and asked, "So what happened?" as he moved to the head of the table.

Paneet responded without thinking, not that any of the gang members present wasted much time on this task, anyway. "Bobbi has a report for you."

"I don't recall asking Bobbi for a report. I asked you, so start talking."

Suddenly, Paneet's stomach didn't feel quite one hundred percent. He looked up from the table at Bobbi, who smirked briefly at Paneet before turning away. He had been screwed by Bobbi. When he should have been marshalling his thoughts into a cogent presentation to Manny, all he could think of was revenge.

"I'm waiting." Paneet realized Manny was on the verge of losing his temper.

Since Paneet had no idea what happened, he started fabricating as best he could. "The Vancouver Police busted the place. I lost my man in there."

"What happened to him?" This was a new side of Manny that no one in the room was aware of. It spoke of concern for a gang member, perhaps.

"He was arrested. Hasn't got out yet."

"What happened to our workers?"

"They got put into group homes again." The lying was going pretty good, he thought.

"How did the police find out about the place? I'm tired of this. You get the kids back this time."

"I think I was followed when I took the last batch of kids downtown." He was pleading mitigating circumstances.

"What makes you say that?"

"This girl was following me—I'm sure of it. Does Bobbi have a girlfriend? The girl was Punjabi."

"What does Bobbi have to do with your fuck-up?"

Paneet remained silent, staring at Bobbi. Manny looked at Bobbi, head tilted slightly.

"If I have a girlfriend, point her out to me." Bobbi did his best to look un-ruffled.

Then one of the junior gangsters tried to be helpful. "Doesn't Bobbi have a sister?" Bobbi suddenly felt chilled. The danger to his sister became reality.

"Yeah, I have a sister. Would you like to date her Paneet? Remember Maccha? He was the last one to take her out. That didn't work out so well for him."

Manny was watching this back and forth, appearing puzzled by the interplay. Paneet was silent, finding it hard to believe that Bobbi was this confident in the meeting. Maybe he was totally wrong. He couldn't decide. He looked at Manny.

"So, you'll clean it up. Good. This meeting is over." With that, Manny left. He hadn't even sat down.

Paneet, however, did not look happy. Bobbi had come out as a shining success, and he now had to find those kids and retrieve them — a task he really didn't know if he could accomplish. But Bobbi had a sister, something he hadn't known about. Bobbi left the room quickly. All Paneet had to do now was to find out what this sister looked like, then nail Bobbi to the wall if his suspicions proved out.

CHAPTER 24

The first Monday in June saw Robert arrive at Cambie Street promptly at eight. As he made his slow way towards Thomas's office, several officers and administrative staff with whom he had previously worked congratulated him on his return to the fold. The exception was Rodney Fister. He watched the scene unfold, but didn't add anything, not even a smile.

Thomas looked up at Robert as he entered his domain. "Good to see you again. Don't sit down, better get yourself down to personnel to finish the paperwork. Then we need to see where we are on this GreenSide mess, meeting at nine-thirty. There is a desk beside Tony you can have in the interim." When Robert walked out of Thomas's office, he was staring directly at Norma, who had just arrived.

She grinned up at Robert. "Hi Robert. Welcome back." That was it. The smile told the rest of the story. He had been determined to remain neutral, but cracked and grinned, all but sealing his destiny.

"You look different." Robert stared at the tangerine framed glasses sitting atop Norma's pert nose. "Raises the intelligence level of the whole department."

Thomas had left his office and stopped to witness the tiny drama, already having some mild regret at his hiring practices. He knew exactly what the smiles portended. Trouble in the office at some point in the future. As Robert slid by Tony's desk, he whispered. "Meet you at the cafe in fifteen after I'm done downstairs."

After watching the small show, Rodney Fister had decided enough was enough. He headed to the stairs and up to the top floor, determined to tell Steve Christie what was going on, like a child ratting out a wayward brother. Once he made it up to Ranit's desk, he was disappointed. Apparently, Steve was on leave, return uncertain. Ranit asked if David McKnight would do, but Rodney just cast his eyes at the floor without responding and returned to the stairwell, wondering why his world had changed so much, and why he seemed unable to do anything about it.

At Cafe Paulo, Robert was the toast of the day, certainly for the morning at any rate. Gilberto would not let him pay for his coffee and Tony marvelled at the attention Robert garnered just by showing up. Didn't someone say a job was ninety percent about appearing? The extra ten percent was if you actually accomplished something, and ten percent more if it was halfway decent.

"Not sure if they hired you to come here and drink coffee, just saying is all." The pair were sitting by the window after the initial ruckus had died out.

"Cut me some slack Tony, I've only been working for an hour."

"Half of it spent here, though."

"I suppose." He squinted at Tony, wondering if he was going to be a new burden, or some kind of watchdog for Thomas. "So, what's the word on Siggy? Staying put?"

"Seems that the ballistics evidence on his rifle is enough for bail to be denied."

Robert relaxed ever so slightly at this news and smiled. "Maybe he and Edward can get a game of pinocle going in remand. What news on Manny?"

"It seems that it is going to depend on the guy Thomas has on the inside. I believe his name is Bobbi Atwall. We can't build any kind of serious case unless we get some inside dope. But we don't know what Bobbi can bring to the table yet. He talked about a place in Langley, but...."

"You still seeing that girl? What's her name?"

"Chiara, yes. Surprising. I didn't think it would last given where she hailed from, but there you go."

"You Italians and your north-south thing." Robert shook his head, looking out the window.

"I don't think Rodney is super happy about your return."

"I got that impression as well. Can't please everyone. I'm happy to be back, even if he isn't. By the way, what is he doing in my office?" Then he changed topics. "Didn't you say you were starting to have the odd case meeting here? Suppose we should get back to the station."

"Yes. Don't know if it will continue, though." They swallowed the remainder of their coffees and, waving hands at Gilberto and Carmelita, headed back to the office.

Thomas convened the meeting in his office once the wayward detectives had returned. This time, the room was full, with Vito and Finn joining.

Thomas started, "This will be my last meeting with you four."

The detectives looked at each other, uncertainty in their eyes.

"Robert will take over this case moving forward. I have other business to attend to, as you no doubt know. I'm sure your four minds will be more than enough to solve the problems with GreenSide. Perhaps Robert could summarize what we know and don't know."

Robert was not prepared for this, but he could think on his feet, so he tried to organize what he had learned into a cogent presentation.

"Leaving the site review and the brothel angle to you three, I'll start with what I learned the last several weeks. There are five lenders to the condo project. The two largest, being the bank and the insurance company, are clean, so far as I can tell. As for your stock portfolios, I'm issuing a 'Do Not Buy' warning for Fern Development and Bamboo Construction. Possibly linked to Two Tigers, so are guilty by association until proven otherwise, but proof of a criminal variety will be difficult to come by. I am still working on the ownership rosters of each company."

Everyone remained silent, so Robert continued. "I have found that Councillor Nile Gecko is a silent partner in the company supplying hydrogen to GreenSide for an ungodly amount of money. This may not be overtly criminal, but definitely slimy. Safe to say that city hall doesn't know about this arrangement. I haven't found if Sun Energy, the hydrogen supplier, has links to the Two Tigers as yet. I've also learned that Chip Diamond, an assistant deputy minister over in the Housing branch of the provincial government, used to help the Wide Bay Boys launder drug money at casinos. He seems to be linked to the GreenSide project by helping it get launched, and may very well know about all the criminal activities that seem to emanate from it. I understand that there are a few incriminating records of phone calls to Siggy, relative to trying to end my stay here on Earth." He looked at Tony, who nodded.

"There is one more thing. I have been liaising with a reporter for the CBC. He has a connection in Victoria that has helped me in finding out details of these companies. If charges fail to stick to some of these politicians, then the published stories should be enough to get them turfed permanently from office."

Robert looked over at Thomas, who was staring back at him, so a clarification was in order. "And no, I didn't tell him anything about your investigations." Conveniently forgetting what he had told Bernard about the brothel and subsequent murders. Thomas seemed mollified, so Robert ended his dissertation, looking at the other detectives.

Tony started with the VPD discoveries. "The study of the hydrogen service room at GreenSide doesn't indicate any criminality. The explosion looks like an accident. Site techs said that it appeared that the backup tank exploded first, then the other one joined in, so I did more digging and found out that the backup tank had never been pressure tested. Seems like negligence at a minimum. The set-up in the tower third floor was a brothel, populated by teenagers in the main, who seem to have been trafficked into the country. There are so many crimes here that I am starting to lose count. I think if we leaned on the guy who we picked up during the raid, we might get charges laid. Thankfully, he hasn't been released yet, but his lawyer is working hard on it. I think someone should explain what his outlook might be once Manny gets his hands on him. Maybe he'll agree that remand sounds better health-wise."

He stopped to marshal his thoughts. "The RCMP have gotten nowhere with the Burnaby murders, so maybe it will be up to us to solve them. Then there is the night of the raid." With this, he looked over at Thomas, eyebrows raised. Thomas nodded briefly.

"Steve Christie was caught in the act with a minor, witnessed by Vito here. Lucky Vito." In other circumstances, a joke might have been told at this point, but no one was smiling. This was both serious and dangerous.

Thomas spoke, "I informed the Chief Constable about the matter, but have heard nothing back from him. I understand that Steve is on paid leave. I will go visit a prosecutor this afternoon about laying charges. I don't like where that leaves me, but this crap isn't going to stand. If Caleb doesn't like it, tough."

The others nodded slightly at this display of fortitude, thankful it wasn't them who had to butt heads with the top brass, but more importantly, that there would hopefully be no cover-up that they'd be replaying to themselves for the rest of their careers.

CHAPTER 25

In the lawyers' fiefdom at city hall, the lawyer, George Ascot, continued his planning on how to deal with the hydrogen mess foisted upon the city by its politicians. He'd met with Mamie the previous Friday, not learning a great deal, other than that she was less than one hundred percent impressed with the city's financial dealings. That accomplished, he had his staff do some research on Chopper's firm, establishing that their court record was fifty-fifty at best. So, despite the display of bluster by Chopper, George felt the city was on firm ground as he waited for the predicted lawsuit to be launched. However, this feeling of confidence failed to consider the wild card in the entire mess, His Worship, Mayor Stanley Dunbar.

At Chopper's firm, the lawsuit was ready, so he called Ken Jalla at Sun Energy before the trigger was pulled. "Ken, Chopper here. We are ready, just waiting for your say-so before we go down this rabbit-hole." He waited expectantly, noting silence on the other end.

"Hold on for now. I am going to make a call first. I'll let you know."

Chopper had heard this story before, clients getting cold feet as reality started to dawn on them. It was okay. He'd still be sending Sun Energy a hefty invoice, partly juiced up because of his less than satisfactory exchange with Mamie. He disliked coming out on the wrong end of conversations, and she wasn't even a lawyer. That's what nettled him most.

After he finished with Chopper, Ken Jalla called Nile. "Nile, it's come time to earn your money. I want the city to pay those energy invoices. Does the mayor think he's still at school, that everything he does can be shrugged off like it's not real, with no consequences?"

"I don't know what the mayor is thinking, frankly."

"Not what you told me a few months ago. If you can't do this, I think you can consider yourself out of the company, and maybe I'll have a word with Manny about you."

Now Nile was worried. He had heard stories about Manny, but had always assumed that he wasn't directly connected to any of the GreenSide business. Suddenly, what the mayor thought about Nile was not such a large hurdle. "Okay. I'll send something to Stanley that should do the trick." He terminated the call. He was back at his westside cafe, enjoying the morning. Was enjoying the morning, before that unpleasant call.

He pushed his latte to one side and composed a message to His Worship, **'Believe you should have that energy invoice paid before the rest of the Eco Party finds out what you get up to on your journeys.'** He then added the incriminating picture of that evening in Club Otta. He waited, then sent it to an internet address that he had used as a cut-out previously. That the address was linked to the Eco Party was of little concern to him—bunch of green idiots was his kindest assessment of the party. When he arrived at city hall, he would access it, forward onto the mayor, and wait for the fireworks to start.

In the heart of Surrey, when Paneet should have been working on how to get the kids back and his brothel up and running again, he was instead puzzling how to find out what Bobbi's sister looked like. In effect, he was putting all his money on this one move, hoping that he would be out of this mess and Bobbi would wear the problem instead of him. Bobbi had not been wrong when he had assumed Paneet had been following him at times; however, nothing had ever come from these excursions, so Paneet was perplexed.

Perhaps a radical move was needed here, such as holding Bobbi at gunpoint until his sister showed up to rescue him. He would expose his sister as the spy and embarrass Bobbi at the same time. The more he thought of it, the more he liked the idea. No need for the other gang members to know about this until the sister had been exposed, so he would do the deed at his condo, then haul the two in front of Manny for his moment of triumph. He didn't even contemplate any other ideas; in this respect aping Manny, violence being the problem-solver for all issues. He'd do it tomorrow evening. Then he would be golden, maybe even taking over the coveted number two role in the gang, raising both his pay and prestige.

By the end of his first day back at the VPD, Robert was tired but satisfied. His thoughts turned to dinner. Surely such an auspicious day called for a celebration of sorts. He decided to cook chops on the barbeque with a grilled Caesar salad as a side. He texted his kids to let them know what to expect, then, yelling his goodbyes, made his way to the local market. While shopping, he realized he hadn't formally resigned from being the private detective. He'd fix this oversight tomorrow.

After parking at home and making his way into the kitchen with a bag of groceries, he noticed a new addition to the counter display. It was a sculpture, that much he knew, fabricated out of metal. It wasn't Giacometti, but it wasn't bad. He was no art connoisseur, but he knew what he liked in this world. He yelled for Robin to come down and explain.

Robin bounced into the room, grinning. "What do you think?"

"I thought you were taking a welding course. This looks like an art project."

"Oops."

"I like it. Your sister see it?"

"Not home yet. I think she is bringing Rose for dinner. At least, I hope so."

Robert looked at Robin with a slight grin. His son had finally spit out what had been on his mind for a couple of years. "Don't worry, I won't say anything."

Robin looked relieved. Robert washed his hands and started prepping the fennel rub for the pork chops. He had Robin do some garlic chopping for the salad dressing and arranged all the ingredients needed for the feast. Next was a glass of his favourite Japanese whisky. As he worked, he considered how he would prevent some backsliding now that his former work routine was back. Finding time to get some runs in might be the most difficult thing to achieve. Or maybe cutting back on his drinking. That might be the most difficult. He pushed these things out of his mind. Time to celebrate, not dwell on potential problems. And he definitely didn't want to think about GreenSide.

As he was chopping the romaine heads into halves for the grill, two girls came through the front door, giggling at something. "Hey Dad, can Rose stay for dinner?"

"As long as she likes fine dining, of course." He always picked up extra when he shopped, in case of the unexpected, so they were not short of food.

It was Rose who commented on the sculpture, not Sophie, making not just Robin's day but possibly his entire year. A hint of a smile lay on his lips during the whole meal. It was one of the most animated home dinners Robert could remember in the past year and seemed like an omen of the summer to come. He could hope, at least. The past winter was a weight of memories and emotions he wanted to put in a box and bury somewhere. Isn't that how police officers dealt with bad things, ignore the problems, miss the psych appointments, and add a little alcohol to help smooth things out? And now he was an officer again. Only sunny days lay ahead, or so he prayed.

The next morning, in city hall, Stanley Dunbar stared at a most disturbing message with an accompanying picture on his computer screen. He was flustered. He knew one thing, however; he didn't want anyone seeing the picture. Who was doing this to him, someone at Sun Energy? How did they get this picture? It must be Axness—he had been taking shots at him while he was visiting Vancouver; jealous of the whole hydrogen idea, especially the fact that Stanley was the one who got it up and running. Practically a world first.

He called his assistant into his office. "Change of plans. I need you to get that hydrogen invoice paid. As soon as possible, please." Then he thought of something else, almost letting her see the message, stopping himself just in time. He wanted to find out where the message came from but didn't know how to go about it. "That's all, thanks."

The assistant left the mayor's office, shaking her head. She sat for a few seconds, then called Mamie on the phone.

Mamie listened, then said, "I'll get right on that." What she hadn't said was, 'I'll pay that as soon as possible' or any other affirmative reply. What she meant by her answer was that she would talk to George Ascot before she did anything of the kind. She agreed on one thing, however, when the assistant brought it up: the mayor seemed to be coming un-hinged. Mamie made a call up to the lawyer's kingdom and was put on hold. While waiting, she looked across at her bookkeeper, winking at her.

Finally, George came on the line, "What's up Mamie?"

"Just received a call from the mayor's office, reversing their decision."

There was silence, then, "What decision?" He sounded impatient.

Mamie did not like people who were in a hurry, so she took her time, finally answering, "About paying that hydrogen invoice, of course. They want me to pay it now." More silence while George processed this new direction from His Worship.

"Please don't pay it. I'll find out what's going on." Mamie smiled as she hung up the receiver. It was nice to have legal help on your side when dealing with the mayor and his band of crazies.

Meanwhile, Stanley examined the email that he had received. He clicked on the sender, but all it displayed was that it seemed to come from his own political party. How could Kristian access this server? Was he in league with someone here in Vancouver? The only common thread was Nile Gecko, who had been in the club that evening. Was he the one behind this? Why would he do this, if it was him?

He was contemplating giving Nile a call to see if he could explain things when his assistant entered the room. She reminded him of an impending visit by the local mission society coming to talk to Mayor Dunbar about the ongoing homeless problem in the city. Stanley's mind instantly reset into mayor mode, leaving his inexplicable issues for later in the day, confident that he had at least dealt with the most serious part of his problem.

CHAPTER 26

Late Tuesday afternoon at the club, Paneet beckoned Bobbi closer. "How'd you like to come over to my place for a drink? Maybe I've been wrong about you. We could consider a reset."

Bobbi wasn't stupid. He was probably brighter than most of the gang combined, and he wasn't buying this sudden turn of heart by Paneet. However, he was interested in what Paneet was up to exactly. "Sounds good. Today?"

"Sure, let's get going in a few minutes."

The weather had turned cloudy and threatening rain, not unusual for early June in the Lower Mainland. Like Bobbi, Paneet lived in one of the newer residential towers that had been sprouting up all over central Surrey, and it was only a five-minute drive from the Two Tigers club. Bobbi followed Paneet and pulled over to park on the street once Paneet had disappeared into his parking garage. Bobbi got out and leisurely walked over to the front of the lobby, waiting for Paneet to let him in, spots of rain falling. Once they were in the elevator, Paneet stayed silent, the 'let's make friends' attitude missing in action suddenly. Bobbi said nothing, waiting for whatever was to happen.

They entered Paneet's suite, which featured much the same view that Bobbi enjoyed from his condo. "Have a seat, Bobbi. I'll mix you a cocktail. What do you like?"

"How about a Rob Roy?" knowing Paneet wouldn't have a clue. Bobbi had heard about the drink but never tasted one.

"How about asking for something I can make. What the hell is a Rob Roy?"

"Beer will be fine, then." Bobbi could discern a couple of muttered curses as Paneet rummaged in his fridge, finally bringing out a beer. Then he watched as Paneet opened the freezer compartment and pulled out a gun.

"Here is your beer, asshole."

Bobbi stared at Paneet. "So, no reset then? Just a lousy beer?"

"I want you to call your sister and get her to come over here. Tell her that your life depends on it."

Bobbi watched as Paneet cocked the gun, then shifted it to his left hand. "Too cold for you, dork?" Paneet was obviously less comfortable with the gun out of his right hand.

"Call her, or it's all over for you."

Bobbi wasn't too concerned. You'd have to be pretty brain-fogged to kill someone in your own apartment with no silencer on the gun. On the other hand, Paneet had demonstrated plenty of stupidity in the past, so he pulled out his cellphone and called his sister.

"Hey Safa, it's Bobbi. I'm at Paneet's condo. He is standing here, pointing a gun at my face. He wants to meet you. Think you could come on over? And could you stop by my place on the way over to get my other cell, the quiet one? Thanks." He broke the connection before Paneet could start asking questions. He looked up. "What is your address? I'll text her the location."

Paneet looked confused as he reeled off his address. "What's this about another cell?"

"This one is almost dead. I keep a second one at home." Then Bobbi had a thought. "Aren't you going to have a drink as well while we wait?" He smiled.

To Bobbi, Paneet's befuddlement seemed to increase. He returned to the kitchen to make himself a rum and coke, but did so facing Bobbi across the island. The chance to jump Paneet and grab his gun seemed gone. He could only hope his sister could come through.

Safa was alarmed. Her brother being held at gunpoint? Bloody gangs. This is where his choices in life had gotten him. But she would help her brother. She was certain that his reference to his second cell, which he didn't have, was to the gun he had shown her how to use. It also sounded as though she should bring the silencer. She considered her wardrobe, and settled on adding a trench coat where she could comfortably hide the pistol. She yelled to her mom that she had to go out for a while, then left the house to go rescue Bobbi. Rain had settled in for the evening, so the coat was perfect for what she had in mind.

She didn't hurry; Bobbi had sounded relatively calm and, knowing that haste usually made mistakes, she took her time driving south to the centre of Surrey. She had been to the gun range all of one time to test out firing a pistol. She hoped what she had learned in the two hours she had been there would be enough this day.

At Bobbi's condo, Safa found the Walther, silencer still attached from the demonstration Bobbi had done for her. She decided to leave the safety on until she had arrived at her destination. She noticed the second gun in the drawer, but wasn't sure what make it was, deciding one gun should be plenty. She looked at the address Bobbi had texted her and realized she could easily walk to Paneet's building from Bobbi's place. Deciding to put the gun in the top inside pocket, it nestled against her left breast, feeling very comfortable. Maybe she could become a secret agent after this was over.

As she walked slowly, she considered what lay ahead. Who knew what might happen? Safa may have looked cool, but anxiety was building. She went to the lobby and pressed the enter phone number. After she was let inside, she looked at the elevator, then walked up to the tenth floor, not needing her face on the cab security camera. She reached the tenth floor, took the gun out, and flipped the safety off before slipping it back into her coat. She leaned against the wall for a moment to catch her breath. Finally, screwing up her courage, she went to Paneet's door and knocked.

Paneet opened the door. "Aha! I was right all along. You guys are going to regret screwing with me." He grinned as he said this and grabbed her arm, pulled her inside, and closed the door. He kept his gun trained on Safa until they were in the living room. He motioned her to sit beside Bobbi, so she did as she was ordered. She didn't sit right beside him, but a couple of feet away on the sofa. They were both facing the kitchen.

"You guys are going to be dog meat after Manny finishes with you." He smiled broadly at the success of his idea.

Bobbi lifted his hands palms up, still playing it cool. "Yup, looks like you got us Paneet. How about one more beer before we leave?"

Paneet was sufficiently full of himself that he acquiesced, still smiling as he turned to head to the kitchen. Safa reached in her coat and in one motion drew the pistol and aimed at Paneet's back with both hands securely on the grip.

"Hey, jackass."

As Paneet turned, he realized he had not only underestimated Safa but also suddenly lost control. He raised his gun just as Safa fired. The bullet hit him squarely in his upper chest, ripping through one of his lungs. He looked shocked. When Safa's second shot hit him as he was spinning, the vacant look suggested he wasn't surprised anymore. As Paneet hit the floor, Bobbi couldn't believe what had just happened. He stood up, looking down at Paneet's inert body, his gun laying on the floor beside him like a metal atoll in a growing tide of blood.

"We should get out of here, Safa." He looked at his sister. She had dropped the Walther and was trembling. He hugged Safa for a long moment, then bent down to pick up the gun. "Did you touch anything?"

"No, I don't think so." Bobbi looked around, grabbed the beer bottle, putting it into Safa's coat side pocket. "Let's go." They sidestepped Paneet, the dark pool expanding around his body, and exited the suite, not touching the door handle with their hands.

"Let's take the stairs. No cameras in there." Safa grabbed Bobbi's hand and headed for the exit stair. They descended quickly and left through a door directly to the outside, heading for Bobbi's car.

They got in. "Let's go to my place, Safa. I'll make some tea."

"Okay. Did I just kill someone, Bobbi?" Bobbi looked over at his sister. Tears were streaming down her face. "I thought I was tough." Sara bowed her head, sobbing audibly now.

"Thanks for saving me, sister. I can't believe what just happened. I am so sorry I involved you. Can't believe how stupid I am some days." He grabbed her shoulder, then started the car and put it in gear, driving the short distance to his tower. After they got into Bobbi's home and he put on the water, they sat in his living room, looking at each other. "You can never tell another living soul what you just did. Understand?"

"Okay."

"I'm serious.... never. I guess my picture will be on the video in the elevator going up to Paneet's suite. Nothing to be done about that, I suppose, but you should be in the clear. Don't expect they'll find him for a few days."

"But they'll arrest you, eventually?"

"Probably, but they aren't very swift from what I've seen, and I have some cards to play." He poured some more tea. "Give me the gun. It's going in the river, along with the beer bottle." After a bit of further thought, he added. "I've changed my mind about the other gun. You should take it with you. Once the police come for me, they'll search my place, I'm sure." They settled in for some more drinking, but soon changed from tea to something more fortifying and memory erasing.

Bobbi then started talking about what he had seen in Langley at the farm. Safa listened intently, slowly going numb from the alcohol and the stories of what the gang could do to teenagers. Safa wasn't sure that she wanted to know all this, but the horror of it took the edge off her guilt at what she had just done.

"Bobbi, you really need to get away from these people."

Bobbi nodded but remained silent.

The next morning, after Robert settled into his temporary desk back at Cambie Street, he made the overdue call to Dan Prudence. "Hello Dan, it is Robert. As you can probably see from your call display, I'm back with the VPD. I want to thank you for hiring me a few months back. It was a tricky time in my life, but I hope I provided some value to your company. No need to make the last payment, and like I said, I'll keep you apprised of the criminal case regarding GreenSide as it progresses."

"Thanks Robert. You were a most unusual investigator. My boss insists on paying you out, so keep me informed if you can, and best of luck."

"Same to you Dan." He hung up, thinking there were many worse ways to make a dollar. He looked around the partition, but Tony was so far missing in action. He looked back at his computer screen, and there it was, the not unexpected message from Norma, **'Would you like to come for dinner this Friday at my place?'** So, he bit, **'I'd be delighted to.'** He was already looking forward to whatever was on offer that evening.

His social life figured out, he reset to the tasks at hand. Now that he was in charge of the GreenSide mess, he needed a plan of action. The other three detectives were counting on him to provide direction. So far, he hadn't been saddled with any other cases, but he knew that wouldn't last, so he needed to get the GreenSide house in order quickly. Manny became target number one, so he needed to milk every last drop of intelligence from Thomas before the case became a distant memory for him.

Several feet away, Thomas Harrow was in his office looking at the view on offer while he considered the events that led up to his hiring of Robert Lui. He felt much more confident about his team with the experience Robert brought back to the force. He could now attend to his other duties with a calmer mind, knowing things were in hand, at least on the GreenSide case.

His mind drifted to the mess that Steve had gotten himself into, and while he could never prove it, he was sure that this thought precipitated the next event. His phone rang. "Thomas? Ranit here. The Chief Constable would like a word with you this morning, if it is convenient."

"Right away?"

"Actually, yes."

"Be up shortly." This was ominous. He had carried through with his intentions to talk with a prosecutor about filing charges against Steve the previous afternoon. Maybe it was blowback time. He sighed and proceeded up to the top floor. This time, Caleb was sitting behind his desk, all business. He gestured to one of the side chairs in front of him, not a hint of a greeting on offer.

"Do you think this is the wild west, that you can do what you want without letting us know what you are up to?"

As an opening salvo, this wasn't bad. About as Thomas expected. "What exactly are you referring to?"

"I have heard that you have spoken to the prosecutor about Steve without letting me know first."

"I recall coming up here a few days ago. I hadn't heard anything since, so I acted. Sex with a minor by a senior officer is not small potatoes, and accessory to two murders may very well be added to the charge list."

"Two murders?"

"We think Steve has been providing information to the Two Tigers but can't prove it as yet."

"Why would he do that?"

"We don't know. Maybe Manny has something on him? Maybe he is getting free sex. It is a very powerful motivator for all kinds of bad behaviour, as we are all aware."

Caleb remained silent for a few moments. "I suppose we could fire you."

Thomas wasn't particularly surprised at this threat but felt compelled to at least fight back. "Why is Steve being so protected? David seems to treat him like gold."

"I think we're done for today. You can go." Caleb turned his attention to whatever was on his desk, ignoring Thomas. Thomas rose, shrugged to himself, and left the office, nodding at Ranit as he passed by her. He had talked far more than he had intended, but really, what choice did he have? He could not read Caleb. What was the word? Inscrutable, yeah, that described Caleb.

Robert had noticed Thomas leaving, then returning to his office a half hour later wearing a grim look, so he decided now was a good time as any to ask him about any remaining information. He walked over to Thomas's office and rapped on the door frame, peering in at Thomas. "Interested in a coffee while you tell me what you know about GreenSide?"

"That'd be nice after the meeting I just had. Let's go." As the pair walked by Norma's desk, Thomas couldn't help seeing the smallest of grins on Norma's face. Well, whatever was to come, at least some of the staff seemed happy. Small mercies, he figured.

After the two detectives settled into their seats at the window table, Robert started the questions. "Tony says you have someone on the inside of the Two Tigers who is helping us?"

"Bobbi Atwall, yes."

"The guy who was in Steveston a year ago?"

"The same. He gave us info on the new brothel location and says that there is a place in Langley that they use. He wants out of the gang and may testify for us. That's still a bit iffy, I'd say."

Robert shook his head slightly, just as Carmelita brought their coffees over. Robert looked back at Gilberto, who was grinning. This was a new uptick in service; usually the patrons were required to fetch their own coffees once they were set, steaming, on the marble counter. This just firmed up his decision that, going forward, he'd continue holding some of his case meetings at Cafe Paulo.

"I think it is time I talked to Mr. Atwal, so if you'd give me his cell number....?"

"Okay, but get hold of him in the evening. He's kind of busy during the day being a gangster. Don't think he'd appreciate his pals knowing he's talking to the police."

"Also think it's time to file charges against Mr. Diamond as well, given the evidence of his ambition to end my life?"

"You can assemble it and go see the prosecutor yourself. And on another file, we'd really like to find out who told the Two Tigers where those kids were being held. If it was Steve, I don't like our chances of finding out. There's obviously a big difference between sex charges and first-degree murder, but perhaps some kind of deal could be brokered?" Thomas finished, then added, "Upstairs seems to be protective of Steve. Maybe I am dreaming this up, but on the other hand, I was just threatened with being fired."

"Well, if they threatened you, then you must be safe. If they were really going to do it, I'd think they'd just pull the plug, don't you?"

"Probably correct." Thomas touched his coffee cup, twirling it around as he sorted through the machinations of the Chief Constable.

At the Two Tigers club, Manny was working up a rage. It had been a few days since he had tasked Paneet with getting the brothel up again and wanted to know that his wishes had been followed. Trouble was, no one had seen Paneet, and he wasn't answering his cell. He tried Bobbi, no answer. It was as if they had both taken off to Hawaii, or somewhere farther. What was the point of having gang members if they were too stupid to answer their phones?

Manny went to the lounge in his club to find someone to do his bidding. Ho Li-Fan was sitting at a table stuffing some takeout Singapore Fried Noodles into his mouth. He looked up at Manny.

"I want you to find Paneet for me. Try his home first, *capiche*?" Li-Fan had finally picked up some English to add to his arsenal of imperfect languages, but it was difficult to know what, if anything, he understood when he was being talked to. Li-Fan nodded and went back to his noodles. The failure to jump immediately into action didn't sit well.

"Now! Not tomorrow." Manny clarified the time frame by yelling.

"Need sustenance, then go."

Sustenance? Had he heard correctly? Shaking his head, Manny turned and went back to his office, where he texted Paneet's address to Li-Fan, then returned to his money-counting.

Chapter 27

B y mid-week, Ken Jalla had not received a confirmation from Nile that the outstanding hydrogen invoice was being paid, so he got his people to talk to city hall people to find out what was what. Sun Energy also received a large invoice from Chopper's firm, and Ken hadn't even given the go-ahead to launch the lawsuit.

Ken's comptroller got back to him. "They are not paying the invoice."

"Did they give a reason?"

"No."

"Shit. I'm going to wring Nile's neck." He looked down at his cell and fooled around until Manny's info came up. He sent a message, **'We need to talk about Nile Gecko.'** That done, he thought about lunch.

In Surrey, Manny received the text from Ken and shook his head. What did these people think he was, a personal valet to make their messes go away? He ignored the request, mainly because it had no money attached to it.

Ho Li-Fan broke into Paneet's suite after failing to rouse any kind of answer on the entry-phone for the building. He possessed some lock-picking tools and the knowledge to use them, so in he went, after midnight. He didn't think to use the stairs, as he was merely conducting a search, not expecting bodies. As he worked on Paneet's suite door, something didn't smell right. Apartment halls are pressurized as a matter of normal design to keep cooking smells from wafting about, but even this couldn't stop what had been developing for the last two days. When he finally opened the door, the stench of decay starting its job hit him in the face.

He didn't go in; staring at the body starting to expand on the floor next to the kitchen island, he covered his nose and mouth and vacated the premises immediately. He didn't even bother to close the door. He wore gloves as a matter of course, so prints weren't a problem, but his face on the elevator camera would be, eventually. Looked to him like Paneet had been shot, his body laying in the midst of a dark stain.

When he arrived at the Two Tigers the next morning, he went to Manny's office and looked in. Manny didn't say anything, but his bushy eyebrows raised in question.

"Paneet dead." Then, feeling maybe more explanation might be welcome, he elaborated, "Shot."

"Really. Where?" For once Manny wasn't swearing but appeared to be thinking.

"His place." Li-Fan wouldn't win any awards for comprehensive reporting.

"Find Bobbi for me then, and make sure he is alive." Manny felt that perhaps he hadn't been specific enough when he had sent Li-Fan out the first time to find Paneet. Manny wondered who had killed Paneet, and more importantly, why.

Over at Paneet's residence, it hadn't taken long for the first neighbour on Paneet's floor to walk by the open door the morning after Li-Chow's visit. She looked in and start shrieking. Emergency Services were eventually called by another neighbour and the police showed up to calm people down and process the scene. As soon as Paneet's identity was confirmed, the Surrey Police informed the gang task force. They in turn called Thomas in Vancouver, who responded that, in future, they could contact Robert Lui directly, who would be handling the gang related file. This was news to the task force. Last thing they knew was that Lui had been put on irretrievable waivers.

Robert was still at his temporary bullpen desk, wondering if temporary was the new VPD word for permanent. As he was contemplating making the call to Bobbi that same evening, he received the news from the Surrey Police, who had some preliminary intelligence about the Paneet killing. All Thomas had told him was that Paneet had been found dead in his condo, a gun laying by his side, apparently un-fired. Robert knew little about Paneet, other than that he had been Robin's jailor during his kidnapping, and even this had only been pieced together recently. Robert wasn't shedding any tears over this departure but was interested to learn about video showing Paneet alive, taken from his building's elevator camera, with a fellow gangster by the name of Bobbi Atwall.

Robert felt this news unnecessarily complicated his GreenSide case. Barring some shift in evidence, Bobbi was suspect number one in Paneet's killing. Of equal interest was the elevator video from last night showing the missing in action Ho Li-Fan, the same man who had blown off his bail money and disappeared six months earlier. It seemed to Robert that perhaps Mr. Ho was working with the Two Tigers.

Robert figured Thomas had already checked out of the case, so he peered around the divider and beckoned Tony closer. "You know that guy Thomas had on the inside at Two Tigers?"

"Yeah, Bobbi somebody."

"Looks like he will be suspect number one in a new murder case. One of his gang-mates was found dead this morning. And I was going to call him this evening. Craps is all I can say."

"Surrey will pick him up?"

"I guess." Robert was staring down at the floor. "I have to call them and explain what is going on, then wait and see what happens. I may have to take a trip to Surrey."

Tony nodded.

At the police offices in Surrey, a couple of officers were preparing to go take Bobbi into custody for questioning. They had been advised that the VPD were extremely interested in Bobbi and had requested to be kept up to date with progress, so with this complication in mind, they started their journey north to the centre of

Surrey. Bobbi's home address wasn't hard to find, so they checked it first. A couple of cars were sent, but as it turned out, Bobbi was extremely cooperative and was apprehended with no issue at all. He almost seemed to be pleased about being taken in.

As Bobbi was standing beside the parked cruiser on the street while an officer finished searching him, Ho Li-Fan pulled up in his car halfway down the block, interested in what he was witnessing. Looked like Manny was going to be disappointed. Too bad. Manny didn't generate any fear in Li-Fan. He had dealt with plenty worse back in Hong Kong where he hailed from. He slid down in his seat until only his eyes were above the dashboard. Sure that a warrant was out for his arrest, he didn't need the police spotting him. The cruiser eventually pulled away. Li-Fan's stomach told him to go find some noodles and beef for lunch, Manny forgotten for the moment.

That afternoon, Robert was at his desk ruminating about all the malfeasance that GreenSide had generated. The more he thought about Nile Gecko and his relationship to the hydrogen, the angrier he got. He was going to do something about it this evening—enough coddling. He wasn't sure that any laws had been broken, but he knew crap when he smelled it.

Robert was cleaning up his desk, getting ready to leave for the day, when a call came through telling him about the arrest of Bobbi Atwall by the Surrey Police. He arranged to attend the next morning in Surrey to ask some questions of the prisoner. That done, he headed out into the sunshine, home to prepare a dinner featuring wontons, soup, and greens—a simple meal.

With both children present and the meal served; Robert dipped a wonton with his chopsticks into a small bowl containing soy, hot sauce, vinegar, and shaved ginger, then broached the subject of his date the following evening.

"I've been invited over to Norma's place for dinner tomorrow evening." He started with just the facts.

Robin was first in. "Who is Norma?"

"Well Robin," he fixed his son with a look that suggested everything was going to be just ducky, "she works as an admin assistant down at the station. She is Dutch." He threw in her heritage to make the brief explanation even more plausible.

Sophie decided to add her perspective. "But you just started your new job. Do you even know this person?"

"Well Sophie, she has been there for a few years, and I have worked with her before, so yes, I would say that I know her." Not in the biblical sense, he thought to himself, at least not yet. He smiled at Sophie, waiting for the next round.

"Do you like her?"

At last, a sensible question. "Yes Sophie, I would say that I like her. But she isn't moving in here or anything. I'm just going for dinner. I'll order in some pizzas for you two if you are worried what you're going to eat tomorrow."

Sophie looked over at Robin. "I may be out with Rose, I don't know."

"I'll get a couple in here anyway. Robin won't mind if there is extra."

"You could always bring her over here for pizza." Robin countered with an extremely audacious gambit.

Sophie had long suspected her brother had eyes for Rose. This was just more evidence to back up her theory. The complication was that she also had eyes for Rose. She just didn't know how to broach the subject with her, or even if she should try.

"We'll see." Sophie said.

The television had been on in the adjacent area, tuned to the local people's network news, CBC. Topics included the usual melange of locals whining about not receiving their due entitlements or respect, along with some international news dropped in for viewers with broader horizons, when Robert heard something about GreenSide. He twisted his body around to the screen, and if it wasn't Bernard Lily standing there, doing the story. Some still shots of the remains of the tower were included as he spoke about the den of evil that had been running out of GreenSide. The City of Vancouver didn't appear very competent, and had refused to comment on the story, caught off guard, Robert guessed. There was no mention of the two murders, so Robert assumed Bernard was still working on that story. Looked like he'd been correct when he wondered if Bernard might not be angling for a news presenter position.

Robert gave Bernard a call to unleash more news, but he only received a busy signal, so he left a message.

Half an hour later, "Hi Robert. Did you see me?"

"Indeed I did. Looking quite dashing. Where was the scarf? Unfortunately, this is not why I called. I am letting you know that you could go with that hydrogen story, but maybe leave out the mayor's signature on the contract. I don't want this rebounding back to me."

Bernard was grinning to himself. This was turning out to be one of the best days of his short professional life. "Robert? I'm still working on those companies you asked about." He needed to keep his source happy.

"Okay, good. I seem to be back where I was a year ago, chasing gang members around. I'll be in touch." With that taken care of, he looked around the room. His kids had disappeared, but the dishes and bowls remained. With a sigh, he started clearing the table, but only after pouring himself a small glass of an Irish whisky.

The next morning, Robert headed south to Surrey for a heart to heart with Bobbi Atwal. He was being held by the police next to the large remand complex that Robert had visited only a couple of weeks earlier to see Edward Su. He didn't muck around with the parkade this time, parking on the street a few blocks away. He headed to the police building and, once inside, asked to see the officer in charge of the Bobbi Atwal case. After fifteen minutes sitting in the dour lobby, an officer came up to him, "I understand you want to talk to Bobbi Atwal?"

"Yes. He's kind of integral to a couple of cases we have ongoing." He wasn't going to say much else until he knew which way the winds were blowing.

"Wait here and I'll get him into a room for you."

When Robert finally entered the room, he wondered why the upgrade. His conversation with Edward had been in a closet. Nevertheless, he assumed the room still had the standard recording equipment. He nodded at Bobbi and asked the officer who was present as a precaution to leave. "I'll be okay."

Robert sat down opposite Bobbi. "Do you want anything?"

"I'm good. You are looking fine. What has it been, a year?" Bobbi was trying to reverse the roles.

"I'll ask the questions, if you don't mind." Robert countered. "So, someone named Paneet is dead. Did you do it?" Cutting to the chase.

"No."

"Kind of what I'd thought you'd say. Do you know who did?"

Bobbi remained silent.

"I'll take that as a yes, then. Let's change the subject. Did you know about the brothel in Yaletown?"

"Not really. Manny likes to keep divisions separate. Paneet was the one in charge. Now he is gone."

"Gone indeed. Was it retribution for his screw up?"

Again silence, then. "I don't think so."

"Since you brought up Manny, we would really like to put him away for all the mayhem he has unleashed. How can you help us?"

Bobbi knew this day would come, so he was prepared. "If I testify for you, I am not interested in doing time for anything. Although I can't think of too many people who would do anything for Manny once he is put away. He commands fear, not respect. I can show you the Langley site where the trafficked kids are processed and at least one was killed. I know where the body is. Since I am his second in command, I also know a few numbers that will help you access things."

"Not bad. What about the violence? The murders. One was a police officer."

"I never directly saw him murder anyone, but I know it happened. He would kill without a second thought. He is a pig."

"A rather large pig, I understand."

"Yes." Bobbi was silent for a full minute. "I may need another favour."

"What?"

"Can't say for now, but please keep it in mind."

"Mysterious." It was Robert's turn to be silent. Then, "When are you ready to do this?"

"Soon as I get out of here."

"Well, there may be charges filed against you for Paneet's murder. I'll talk to some people and be in touch." With that, Robert went to the door and signalled that he was done. An officer escorted him back out to the lobby to collect his things. There was no sign of the first officer, so Robert left, ready to head back to Vancouver.

That officer was busy doing other things, including taking the recording of the conversation between Robert and Bobbi to his desk, where he made a duplicate before submitting the original to the sergeant for filing. Then he put the copy in his pocket for eventual delivery to Manny Dhillon.

Robert returned to the office just after four on Friday and nod-ded at Norma as he passed her desk, then turned and stepped back to her. "What time? Think I also need an address."

"Seven okay? I'll text you my place. It's in Yaletown on the south edge close to the water just west of Davie Street."

"Great, I am so hungry." What he was hungry for was left unsaid.

"Me too, Robert." She looked up at him, a small grin pulling her lips.

One or two officers were looking at them, so Robert headed for his desk to finish some of the paperwork that seemed to crop up every day. He glanced at the small pile but decided that his concentration was not on focus. Instead, he wrote up a few notes about his discussions with Bobbi. He texted his children to let them know he would bring them their dinner pizzas before departing for his date, then left for home.

Once home after his pizza detour, he showered, dressed, and put on some cologne for the occasion. This was immediately noticed by the three teenagers lounging in the family room. Rose and Sophie had decided to eat in this evening. Robin looked happy.

"Smells like a real date, Dad." Robin started with the obvious.

"Indeed. Don't burn the house down while I'm gone and don't wait up." With that piece of parental advice dispensed, he headed out the front door to wait for his cab. He knew parking in Yaletown was an experience best avoided, no matter the situation.

After the cab had deposited Robert on Marinaside Crescent, he looked around. He wondered how an admin assistant working for the police could afford the neighbourhood, but maybe she was renting, like himself. He looked at the address again on his phone. It appeared to be one of the terraced buildings fronting the creek. Pretty nice digs. After he was buzzed into the lobby, he went to the eighth floor, then up to Norma's door and took a big breath before knocking.

Norma opened the door, eyes sparkling. The first thing Robert noticed was her scent. It was momentarily disorienting. He blinked a couple of times, then realized that it must be the same perfume his wife had worn. She was wearing jeans, a light-yellow blouse, and nothing on her feet. The second thing he noticed was more basic. Norma seemed to have forgotten her bra, her breasts pushing against the blouse.

"Norma. You look great! Nice place, is it yours?" He slipped out of his shoes and followed her into the living room.

"Yes, Robert, believe it or not. I was left some money by an aunt back in Holland, so I invested it in real estate. Not bad, eh?"

Robert went to the window and was staring down at a rather ritzy looking marina adjacent to the building, nary a scow or beater boat in evidence. A steady stream of people were walking, riding, and running on the seawall. "Smart move."

"Would you like a drink?"

"That would be nice. Whisky?"

"Coming up. Scotch okay? I'm drinking wine."

"Sure. A little ice would be fine" He noticed that the dinner table had been set, but cooking odours were mysteriously absent.

She poured his drink, adding a small cube. "Here you are Robert. So happy you could come over. Cheers!" They both took a long sip, grinning at each other.

"Would you like a tour?"

"As long as the price is affordable."

"I think you can afford the price. This is the living room, in case you hadn't guessed. Please take note of all directions from the tour guide and don't lag behind."

Robert took another large swig of his scotch and followed Norma into what seemed to be her bedroom. He went up to the window and looked out. "Seems to be the same view, Norma, just saying. What kind of tour is this?"

Norma came up behind him, her left hand rubbed against his rear, and wrapping her right arm around his body, her hand reached for his crotch. Robert had been partially aroused at the sight of Norma's breasts. She now finished the job. Norma whispered in his ear. "This tour has been terminated due to foreseen circumstances. And no, there will not be any refunds, despite your evident extreme interest in how the tour ends."

"Utmost interest." He responded thickly.

An hour later, the two intertwined on the bed, both dripping in sweat, Robert commented, "You know, there was a dinner invitation in amongst all this somewhere. I think I'm hungry. Want me to make some eggs for us?"

"You cook?"

He smiled. "Perhaps. I may make some noise looking for things, but relax, I'll get something together." As he left the room, he looked back at Norma. They both had the same contented looks on their faces. A moment later, he returned and put his jeans on.

"Don't want to burn anything important." He headed back to the kitchen.

Eventually, after sharing an omelette Robert had whipped together, they picked up where they left off and wore each other out, falling into a deep sleep. Shortly after five, as the sun was about to make its appearance, Robert woke, looked over and kissed Norma, "I should get back home, before my kids wake."

"Okay, Robert." She mumbled, barely moving.

"Thanks Norma. You throw a great dinner party. I'll call you later this weekend. I think I'm still hungry." Norma was able to open one eye and watched Robert's rear as he left the room, then sank back into a coma.

CHAPTER 28

M anny had been filled in by Ho Li-Fan as to why he hadn't produced Bobbi as instructed, so Manny contacted his police insider for some intelligence on the matter. The tape from the police didn't get to Manny until late Monday morning at his club. After listening to the disturbing contents, Manny was at first astonished at the betrayal of his number two man. Then he started throwing items off his desk against the wall, an ashtray barely missing the head of one of his men who had the temerity to open his office door to see what was happening. After some energy was expended, Manny calmed down a bit. It sounded like Bobbi had killed Paneet. Paneet was dead, and Bobbi had been arrested, so it seemed logical to Manny. There was also the issue of Robert Lui. He started planning how to deal with both troublemakers. Forgotten was his last response about Robert, that no good came out of targeting police officers.

After the weekend, Nile Gecko visited accounts on the main floor of city hall. Upon questioning one of the accounts people, he was directed over to Mamie's desk.

"Mamie?"

"Yes. Who are you?" She knew who it was, but enjoyed the discomfort she could induce in others she thought deserving of it.

"I am Councillor Nile Gecko."

"Well, pleased to meet you, Mr. Gecko." She was all pert and sparkly on a Monday morning.

"I'm here to confirm that an energy invoice has been paid with respect to GreenSide."

"Yes. I can confirm that we paid the April invoice. Is there anything else?"

"I was referring to the May invoice."

"Perhaps you should be more explicit when you ask questions, then." With that, Mamie looked down at the papers in front of her, the discussion at an end as far as she was concerned.

Nile was perplexed, not used to being addressed in this fashion, but remained silent. He was unaware of Mamie's reputation.

Eventually Mamie looked up, "You're still here. Is there something else you need?" The pertness suddenly missing in action.

"The May hydrogen invoice. Has it been paid?" Nile's voice was rising.

"No." Further elaboration was missing.

"Can I ask why not?"

"Of course." Mamie was by now certain that Nile had slept through any course in logic that he might have taken.

Nile reset himself, one final step from losing his temper, "Why hasn't the May invoice been paid?" This came out rather loudly. Several staff looked over at Mamie.

"You are a rude one, aren't you? How did you ever get elected? I don't know why the invoice wasn't paid. Ask the city lawyers upstairs. They are the ones running this file now."

This wasn't good. Nile didn't know what to do, but he suspected he had lost what little control of the situation he ever had. He turned and slowly walked away as Mamie's assistant was grinning over at her, guessing Mamie had put another showboat in his place.

Apparently, Nile's threat to the mayor hadn't produced the expected results. He was now clueless about what to do next. It would be other events that would decide this for him, and they weren't long in coming. During the day, fallout from the Friday news piece about the brothel running out of GreenSide was front and centre for all the local news organizations. Pressure was mounting on the mayor to cancel the project outright after what had been allowed to happen, not to mention the original explosion that exposed the whole mess. Interviews had been requested of Fern Developments and Bamboo Construction, but no one had stepped up to answer media questions so far. Dan Prudence had been following the fallout and convened a meeting of the senior people at BC Coastal Insurance to plan their moves. This kind of reaction would sink the project whether the mayor wanted to continue or not.

That evening, the CBC television broadcast at six ran a piece about the energy contract for GreenSide. They painted a picture of Nile that was unflattering in the extreme. It seemed that Nile Gecko was in the job as councillor to enrich himself, about what many people assumed of their politicians. It was just depressing for the public to have it explained to them by Bernard Lily on the evening news. When asked for comment before the piece ran, Nile was sufficiently flummoxed to provide a no comment, something he regretted.

As for Bernard, he was a rising star at the CBC, not only coming up with scoops no one else could find, but then also presenting them on the live news program. It was only natural that his head gained a couple of sizes. He felt that it wouldn't be too much longer before he would be asked to move to Ottawa to cover the seat of national power.

After the evening news aired, it didn't take long for the other Eco councillors to call or email Nile, expressing their disgust at his perfidy, as if they were all saints themselves. His evening was turning into shit. Then Stanley Dunbar called. At least he had the sense to ask if the story was true before launching his tirade, unlike the other councillors who seemed to take news reports at face value.

"What kind of friend are you?" Stanley started in.

Friend? How did the mayor get the idea that Nile was his friend? "Hey, I don't know where they got that story from. I'm going to sue those people."

"So, the story is a lie?"

"I'm going to make those people wish they never heard of television."

"What do you know about a picture I received by email?"

"What are you babbling about, Stanley?"

"A picture. From Oslo." As if this explained everything.

"Again, don't know what you are talking about. Are we about done? Have to go. Got another call coming in." Nile did his best to sound impatient as he hung up. He decided not to answer any further calls for the rest of the evening.

Stanley looked down at his phone, confused. What the hell was going on? The news program had aired on the CBC. He knew enough about them to know that they didn't do fly-by-night stories, their stuff usually being meticulously researched. And that picture of him was tied to paying the invoice. At least the picture had not come out publicly, so far, that was. He was calling Oslo tomorrow to get to the bottom of this. This decided, he poured himself a large scotch to smooth his nerves.

Over in Surrey, Manny Dhillon was planning his revenge on Bobbi and his move against Robert Lui. He called in a couple of his more ruthless men to help him map out the tactics. His plan for Bobbi was straightforward. He'd offer his man at the police cash to kill Bobbi in the lock-up. His plan for Robert would be more complicated because he wanted some questions answered before the killing. First things first, though. Eliminate Bobbi, then go after Robert. He'd call his inside man Monday evening, get things moving. He had some ideas about what should be done to Bobbi, but he'd leave the details to his man so Bobbi wouldn't be blabbing the Two Tiger's secrets to all and sundry.

Robert showed up to work Monday morning with a spring in his step. He had indeed talked to Norma on Sunday afternoon, and he could say with confidence to himself that he was eager to continue. They agreed they should keep it professional in the office, but a lot less so outside. He was sitting at his desk looking at a pile of paper when he heard Tony slide into his cubicle.

Robert looked around the divider. "Hey, let's go to our other office." Tony nodded, so they left the floor and made their way up to Cafe Paulo. Robert didn't waste any time on pleasantries as they sat by their favourite window. "I'm going to get Bobbi sprung today, hopefully. Going to need Thomas's heft on this one, seeing as how it is a potential murder charge. I'm going to go see him after we're done here."

"So, Bobbi is rolling over?"

"Don't think there is much to roll here. He's been trying to get out for a while. He said he didn't kill Paneet, and I think I believe him, but I also think he knows who did the deed. There is more to the story, I'm sure."

"Did you go out with Norma on the weekend?"

"What's that got to do with the case?"

"Not much." He remained looking at Robert square in the eye as he waited, a glimmer of a smile developing.

"Okay. Yes, I did."

"And?"

"It went well. That's all I'll say for now."

"Apparently you haven't learned from your past."

"Apparently, but we'll see how it goes."

Tony laughed. "We going to get Bobbi down here, then?"

Robert slapped the table with his hand, making the coffee cups jump. "That's brilliant, Tony. The Surrey Police aren't going to be very happy about releasing Bobbi, but if they realize he will still be in custody and charged, they will probably crack. Let's get back to the office and put the wheels in motion. This new office is proving to be indispensable." With that, they got up and Robert roared a loud goodbye to Gilberto as they passed by the counter and out into the summer air.

Once back on their floor, Robert went by Norma, gave her what he hoped was a professional look, then pointed to Thomas's door. She nodded, then quickly looked down at her desk.

Robert rapped on Thomas's doorframe as he looked in. Thomas looked up and beckoned Robert in. "What's up?"

"I interviewed Bobbi last Friday. He is ready to testify for us, but I'd like to get him brought here, today if possible. I assume Surrey have filed charges, but I'll check. Can you use your pull?"

"Yes, I should be able to use the connections from my time running the gang unit. I'll make a call. Anything else?"

"No. That would be more than plenty." Robert returned to his desk and picked through the list of unfinished issues related to GreenSide. One item caught his attention; the lack of progress made with the kids who had been rescued from the brothel and had been stuck serving time at safe houses.

Again, he leaned over to look at Tony. "Did anyone interview those kids yet?"

"Oh yeah. I don't think so. Guess we should get on that."

"I assume they are all still accounted for?"

"As far as I know. I'll get Vito to head over there, try for some statements, or at least to see how they are faring."

Satisfied, Robert returned to the list. The next item apparently not completed was the arrest of Chip Diamond over in Victoria. He would attend to this himself as it felt personal; Chip trying to have him killed. Robert was unsure what kind of solid case would stand up based on a couple of phone recordings, but he was going to try his best. Just having the police show up and arrest an assistant deputy minister would be worth the effort. He'd make sure it was done on a workday for maximum embarrassment. This decided, he spent the rest of the day preparing the paperwork for the arrest.

Mid-afternoon he received an email from one Norma van Kleet requesting his presence at a dinner on the north side of False Creek this Friday evening. He responded immediately, whatever he had been working on, shunted to the back of his head. **'I'd love to attend. See you Friday, if not before. Will there be another tour?'** He was already fretting about how long the next four days would take to pass: at a guess, probably eight days.

One other item stood out, the charges against Steve Christie. He read through the summary. Apparently, Steve had been charged, then released on bail. It appeared he was suspended, but it wasn't clear if he was still being paid or not. If Robert had to guess, he was sure Steve would still be getting money into his account regular as clockwork. You'd have to be a serial mass murderer with body parts sprinkled all over the city to rate being suspended without pay. With that depressing thought, he packed up and left for the day, puzzling as he drove home as to what he would cobble together for dinner.

While Robert was winding up his workday, an officer in Surrey had received directions from a superior to transfer a prisoner by the name of Bobbi Atwal to Cambie Street in Vancouver. He talked to the sheriff's service, who were the ones normally shuttling prisoners around the Lower Mainland and arranged for it to happen immediately. One less prisoner in the Surrey lock-up was a blessing, as far as this officer was concerned.

As he walked in the back door of his townhouse, Robert was momentarily disoriented by the smell of something cooking. What the heck was going on? His daughter had her back to him, doing something at the stove, while his son looked up as he was tipping some beans. He grinned at his dad.

"Have I entered an Outer Limits episode?"

"What's that, Pops?" Robin asked.

"An old television program that dealt with bizarre and strange events. Am I actually witnessing my dream come true? My children making a dinner?"

"What would you like to drink, Pops?"

Robert feigned a stagger, as if he didn't know what hit him. Then he recovered, smiling back at his son. "A glass of white would be sublime."

"Sublime? It comes from a box." Robin pulled a half glass of wine from the box in the fridge for his father. "Here you go."

Robert raised his glass to his children. "So, what are we eating?"

Sophie answered, "We have chicken thighs roasting in the oven along with smushed potatoes, and we're blanching some beans that will have a vinaigrette added." She was beaming. Robert knew darn well that the chances of this culinary episode repeating itself were very slim, so he was determined to enjoy it as much as possible, repairing to the sitting area adjacent to the kitchen and proceeded to watch the scene unfold.

Meanwhile, over in Surrey that evening, Manny's man in the police received his orders. For a sum of twenty thousand dollars, he was to make Bobbi Atwall dead, and Manny did not care how it was done. The officer was both pleased and anxious, puzzling how he would make this happen while keeping his fingerprints away from murdering someone in a lock-up.

This dilemma was solved for him early the next morning after arriving at work and enquiring about the status of Bobbi. He learned Bobbi had been transferred the previous evening into Vancouver at the request of the VPD. Now all he had to do was to tell Manny the bad news. Maybe he'd go get some coffee while he thought this over. After much deliberation and some considerable fretting, he decided to let Manny know that evening after he had arrived home from work. No need to rush with bad news.

Robert spent the morning talking with the Victoria Police Department regarding the apprehension of Chip Diamond. Victoria was at first not that keen on making a big display of the arrest, but after Robert told them the charges and that it was a tad personal, they relented and planned the arrest during a lunch event that Robert had learned was taking place on Thursday at the Ministry of Housing. This confirmed, Robert decided that maybe some extra attention to the event wouldn't be out of order, so he texted the bare details to Bernard Lily at the CBC.

He then switched his attention to Bobbi who had spent Monday night in the Cambie Street lock-up. He felt that things were running so smoothly, he headed up to his favourite Broadway noodle house, where he ate enough lunch for two people. Sufficiently sated, he returned and asked for Bobbi to be placed into an interview room. As Robert entered the room, Bobbi looked up and gave the smallest of smiles.

"So how is Bobbi?"

"Good. I spent a restful night. Well, as good as it gets in this place." Bobbi added. "Happy to not be in the Surrey lock-up. Never know what might happen in there."

"Thought we might take a trip out to Langley if that is alright by you."

Bobbi considered this. "I don't know who exactly might be on the property. It seemed to be largely abandoned the one time I was there."

"Maybe we'll call it a reconnoitre mission then, go in quietly and get the lay of the land. Just the two of us, tomorrow. It's probably best if you spend one more night in here."

"I suppose."

"We will leave around ten. And I'll have a word with prosecution about what charges they are thinking about and if bail is needed."

"See you then, Robert."

With this accomplished, Robert's next thought was naturally coffee. He returned to his floor, but with Tony mysteriously absent, and Norma out of bounds, he signalled to Vito, who smiled and got up to join him.

"I feel like I've been invited into some exclusive club." Vito said, as the pair made their way up to Cafe Paulo.

Robert looked sideways at Vito. "You have." Then he laughed, "You realize you can come here on your own, don't you?"

"Still has that special feeling." They entered, ordered some Americanos, and went to sit by the window while the coffee was being made.

"I'm going to make the trip to Langley tomorrow. Taking Bobbi. I think I'd like you to follow along, but lay back a bit, as an insurance policy. We're not going to raid it until I've done this reconnoitre. Bobbi wasn't exactly a fountain of information about the place. He'd only been there once, with Paneet." Robert looked back to the counter and nodded to Vito, who was confused about what was happening. "The coffee is ready, Vito."

Vito got up quickly and went to fetch the cups, returning with a sheepish look, "Guess my club membership might be in jeopardy already."

Robert nodded. "It's not as easy as it appears." He sipped at his mug, instantly feeling better. "We'll leave here after nine tomorrow. You should draw some extra arms, just in case." With that taken care of, they relaxed and enjoyed their drinks, surveying people walking by the window.

CHAPTER 29

Manny had been expecting a call from his man inside the Surrey Police. He got the call alright, Tuesday evening, but the contents were not to his liking. He swore a blue streak, then slammed his phone onto the table. Then he puzzled how to get at Bobbi with Robert in possession of him in Vancouver. After some time at this, he made no progress owing to the lack of confidants he could discuss things like this with. Nobody in the Two Tigers dared to be friendly with him, so Manny was an island, a large island, but alone, nevertheless. He remained in a foul mood the rest of the week, his fellow gang members giving him a wide berth.

Wednesday morning saw Robert get Bobbi out of his cell and made him arrange for bail. The prosecutors reluctantly agreed that Robert could let Bobbi return to his apartment after the Langley trip, but on several conditions. Bobbi didn't have a problem with these, so they got into the VPD car and headed east to the farm in Langley. Vito followed in a second ghost car at a respectful distance. After the short jaunt through old Langley, Robert followed Bobbi's directions, driving slowly up the dirt track, then stopped well short of the farmhouse. There weren't any other vehicles present.

They exited the car and crept towards the old structure through the underbrush. Robert had his gun in hand, ready for the unexpected. Bobbi had told him about the dog, but the silence indicated Fido was absent. Bobbi showed Robert the front and rear of the house from the exterior, including the room where drugs were parcelled up. As far as Bobbi could discern, nothing seemed to have changed from his first visit. He showed Robert where he had buried the footlocker; the fresh dirt evidence of Bobbi's work, but they left it alone for now, Robert wanting forensics to handle it.

Then they took a walk up the semi-hidden trail that Paneet had disappeared on several days earlier. A hundred metres on, they came upon a decidedly down at the heels recreational vehicle sitting in a clearing. The large vehicle had flat tires, and what little paint left on the rusted body suggested an indigo exterior when it had been younger. Remnants of a brand adorned the rear corner, but deciphering the name was impossible. Vito was out of his car, still back near the farmhouse, his head swivelling around, looking for anything out of place.

The pair approached the RV slowly, not sure what to expect. Nobody seemed to be around, the woods silent except for a few singing birds. The underbrush surrounding the clearing was thick, overgrown from years of apparent neglect. Robert went up to the door, grabbed a handkerchief, and rather boldly tried it. It opened outward with a tired squeak. Robert peered into a dark interior. A smell of old socks wafted by his head.

"Anyone there?" Silence.

"Seems like no one is around." Robert backed up, declining to enter, figuring the forensics team would prefer an un-mucked up scene. He looked around, but there didn't seem to be anything further to see. Robert picked the phone out of his hip pocket and asked Vito to walk down the trail to the clearing. He explained to Bobbi what Vito was doing there.

"Suppose this is where they kept the kids before transporting them downtown. Wouldn't it be nice to catch them bringing in a new group?" Robert looked at Vito, who had joined the two others.

"Guess so, but with no brothel to send them to, maybe the pipeline has gone cold." Vito answered.

"You're assuming they only had the one, Vito."

"Good point."

"Got any cameras we could leave to monitor the place?"

"Think so. I'll check my car." Vito walked back the way he had come, returning a few moments later with a small camera, which they tethered to a tree trunk off to the side. Robert stood, staring back at the motor home. He thought he saw a small group of teens running through the trees. They were thin, vapid wisps, with a dog running after them. He shook his head, then looked again. There was nothing.

"Either of you have kids?"

"Not that I know about," Vito responded. Bobbi shook his head.

"Well, I do, and they are the same age as the kids under the control of the Two Tigers. I am going to break these guys if it is the last thing I accomplish." Robert's eyes were shining, just a glimpse of moisture in evidence. Vito didn't know Robert very well, but he knew one thing: he had never in his career seen an officer shed tears under any circumstances.

"Let's get out of here. We'll give it a few days, then come back to see if there have been visitors, before turning the place over to forensics." Robert started back to the cars with the other two following, still keeping their eyes wide open. Their eyes may have been open, but they ironically missed a critical item. The Two Tigers had their own camera tacked to a tree, back from the farmhouse, but with its eye on it. Some leaves waved occasionally in front of it, rendering it well hidden. The camera was a standalone type, needing to be visited in person to see what it contained, so Manny would remain ignorant of the visitors for a short time.

Robert retraced his route to Vancouver, dropping Bobbi at his condo before finishing his journey. Once back on his floor at Cambie Street, he beckoned Tony to a small room and filled him in on what he and Vito had done in Langley.

"I think we'll head back Monday with some backup to see what we have. Maybe you could notify Surrey, give them some warning."

"Okay. Tactical squad?"

"Don't think so. It seemed deserted. More like gathering evidence. I need to eat something. Want to go up the street?"

Tony smiled. "Thought you'd never ask."

As they walked by Robert's old office, he shook his head. "Don't suppose anything will dislodge Rodney from there."

Tony smiled. "I believe you are correct."

After they settled into their chairs, Robert explained in detail what he had found out about Bamboo Construction and Fern Development, and what he was waiting for from Bernard. He then texted a short reminder to prod Bernard into action.

"Anything from those kids?"

"They are pretty damaged, is what the people looking after them say."

"How about that goof who got picked up in the raid?"

"Doesn't appear to be too cooperative. Probably scared of Manny."

"But still being held?"

"Yes. Charges pending, running a bawdy house and a weapons charge. He'll make bail soon."

"Small potatoes. Manny is the one we want; put away, or dead, I don't much care. Dead would be a favour to the world."

Tony smiled. "Don't think that kind of talk is the VPD party line somehow."

"Suppose. Time to get going. Check the news tomorrow, Tony. Big doings in Victoria around lunch time!"

"Chip?"

"The same." With that, they returned to the office and the endless paper and computer work needed to document their cases.

Other than the splashy arrest of Chip Diamond, who seemed more than miffed at the whole episode, and which was also captured by television cameras courtesy of one Bernard Lily, little happened of any interest in Robert's world on Thursday. He still hadn't heard from Bernard about the companies, so he concentrated on what he would make for dinner for his children. The next day being Friday and date night with Norma, Robert would be absent from Inverness Street. Eventually, he decided on a chicken parmesan-like dish, so he left early to pick up some groceries and headed home to start on the prep work.

After yelling at his kids that he was home, he decided to switch from rice to potatoes as the side dish, realizing that there'd be no sauce for the rice to soak up, and added roasted carrots to round out the affair. Robert set up the dipping trays for the chicken, which included flour, eggs, and breadcrumbs, then set to pounding the breasts flat, imagining they were Manny's head. He got a bit carried away and had to give his head a shake. He stopped, then poured more wine to help him calm down.

Dinner turned into a relaxed affair. No further questions about Norma. Robert explained away the menu as being a different part of the chicken compared to Monday's choice by his children. Both the kids were going to be out Friday evening, so Robert was spared dinner plans for the two. He was eagerly anticipating the next evening and waved both children away. They retreated up the stairs to their rooms and electronic social lives, relieved that their dad seemed happy.

Chapter 30

E arly Friday morning saw one of Manny's less important foot soldiers make a trip to the farmhouse in Langley to change out the SD card in the on-site camera. He found it hard to believe how cheap Manny could be. For some extra money, they could have had a direct feed to their club in Surrey by installing a better camera, but no, that would be spending money needlessly. In the end, he did what he was asked to do, and also took a quick look around the site. He neglected to see the police camera set up by Vito.

Back in Surrey, he slipped the card into his computer, quickly realizing that it contained things Manny would be interested in. He grabbed his laptop and went to Manny's office. "Hey Manny, I found Bobbi!"

Manny immediately looked up. "Where?"

"At the farm, look at this." He then played the clip from the card showing Bobbi, Robert, and Vito wandering around the property. The gangster didn't recognize the other two, but Manny knew that one of them was Robert.

"When was this?"

"It's from Wednesday, just after noon."

This was exactly what Manny had been trying to prevent—Bobbi spilling all the Two Tiger's secrets. He was working up a rage again. "Take someone and go to Bobbi's place. If he is there, grab him and take him to the farmhouse. Let me know when you have succeeded."

Manny's man noted the word 'when' instead of 'if'. Sounded like failure would be frowned upon. What a shitty day this was turning out to be. He nodded, grabbed his laptop, and left the room. He then stowed the computer, took his gun, and went into the lounge to grab two men, not wanting to take chances with this abduction. One of the men was Ho Li-Fan, who was familiar with where Bobbi lived.

Bobbi relaxed in his living room, happy to be out of holding cells, when a sharp knock sounded on his entry door. He was puzzled, not having buzzed anyone into the building. He went up to the peephole and recoiled, immediately feeling ill. Outside his door were three members of the Two Tigers, and it didn't look like a friendly drop-in to Bobbi. He knew he was screwed, with no other way out of the apartment. Out of the few remaining options available to him, he called his sister.

Fortunately, she picked up the call as he heard the gang members working on his door lock.

"Safa. Listen carefully, I am about to be taken by the Two Tigers. My guess is that they'll take me back to the farmhouse in Langley—it's the only other place they have. I am going to text you a map of where it is. I have to go. Love you, sis."

Safa hadn't even been able to say a word before the connection was severed. A couple of seconds later, a map showing the farmhouse location arrived on her phone. This sounded several degrees more dangerous than her previous rescue of Bobbi. Why couldn't he stay out of trouble? It was obvious what was going to happen to Bobbi if she didn't act. He sounded afraid this time. She wondered if she should call the police, but then put that thought to the back of her mind. If Bobbi thought the police should be called, he could have done that. She was at school, and needed to get home to fetch the second pistol that Bobbi had let her keep before she went anywhere near that farm.

In Vancouver, Robert was having extreme difficulty concentrating on his work, and after several hours of non-productive work, decided to call it an early day. He walked by Norma's desk. "I'm heading home, then I'll be right over. Okay by you?"

Norma smiled back at Robert. "I'll leave early as well. Come as soon as you can."

Robert walked back by Tony's desk, waving his hand. "See you Monday."

Tony shook his head, certain what was going on. He waved back, then returned to his report.

Before Robert headed out into traffic, heading home to change before his date, he decided to pre-order a cab. He didn't want any mucking about when he was ready to head to Yaletown. He was unaware that most of the cab companies in the Lower Mainland were run out of Surrey, but wouldn't have thought anything of it, even if he knew.

Forty-five minutes later, he was outside his townhouse waiting by the curb, looking and smelling date ready. A bright red cab pulled up. He stepped over, opened the rear door, and was greeted by the barrel of a large gun pointed at his mid-section. "Get in, Robert."

He complied slowly, cursing inwardly. He was completely unarmed. This was the result of his brain being at the mercy of his balls. How could he be so stupid?

"Marinaside Crescent please." He had to at least try.

The driver laughed. "Don't think so. I believe your friend wants us to go to Langley to meet someone named Manny."

This wasn't good. He didn't fancy being killed on that god-forsaken property. The only thing he had with him was his cell, which he expected would be taken once they arrived at the farm. He was thinking furiously, but nothing was working. Could he jump out of the car at an intersection?

As if the man beside him could read his thoughts, he produced a set of handcuffs and manacled Robert's left hand to the partition ostensibly installed for the safety of the driver. Robert didn't say a word.

The man with the gun didn't say much either, but what he said was chilling enough. "I think Manny wants to have some fun with you and Bobbi. What did those Iroquois used to call it? Caressing? Yeah, I think that's what Manny wants to do with you two."

A trip from Vancouver to Langley is interminable at the best of times, but when all you can think about is how you are going to be tortured, then probably killed, the journey stretches out, then is over, all too quickly.

The taxi pulled onto the dirt track, stopping in front of the decrepit house. A pit bull started barking, frothing as it strained at the chain holding it to the corner of the building. Robert looked at his watch. It was five-thirty. This wasn't how his Friday evening was supposed to go. He was unshackled, then marched into the house through the front door by the driver and was confronted by a scene of blood.

Bobbi was taped to a dining chair in the middle of the room. He didn't look topnotch. One of his fingers was laying on the floor, blood dripping slowly from his left hand, his face bruised and bloody. One eye was closed, but with the other one he acknowledged the arrival of Robert to the party. His pants were also stained, the urine and blood scents mixing together. As Manny looked over at Robert, a gruesome grin creased his face. Ho Li-Fan stood up from the couch he had been lounging on. Manny nodded at him to get Robert securely fastened to another chair, his phone and wallet taken. Manny then told both taxi men to get lost. Robert thought about Sophie and Robin, hoping he had given them enough to survive this life. He automatically curled his fingers into fists, knowing where Manny would strike first.

Manny smiled his gruesome smirk at Robert, then asked his questions, cuffing Robert in the head a few times when answers weren't quick enough coming. None of the questions made any sense to Robert. After a rather savage slap to the head, Robert's fists relaxed of their own volition.

"Good." Manny grabbed one of Robert's pinkies and bent it back until it snapped. Robert blacked out momentarily. The pain was blinding. He shook his head and swore, but it didn't help much. As far as he could determine, Manny wanted to focus on causing as much pain as he could.

Robert looked over at Bobbi, who seemed to be enjoying the reprieve offered by Robert's abuse. He looked back up at Manny as he selected the next finger to work on. He chose the next in line, snapping his ring finger slowly. Robert passed out again, then slowly came to, hearing the dog outside starting its incessant barking. This went on for about fifteen seconds, then stopped. Manny paused, looking over at the curtained window, confused about what was happening outside. He hand-signalled Li-Fan to go investigate.

The front door opened. Safa entered the room, took one look, raised her silenced pistol with both hands and shot Ho Li-Fan smack in the middle of his chest, the bullet entering, then exiting his heart. He looked surprised as he fell back. Safa wasn't one to wait around. She swivelled slightly and fired again at Manny, both hands still on the grip. Manny presented a large target, so he was hard to miss. The calibre of her gun didn't carry a lot of stopping power, so Manny started coming toward Safa, even as the wound to his belly started to spurt blood. She fired again, a little higher up the mountain of Manny's torso. He didn't stop coming, so her last shot was at the head. This one tore through Manny's cheeks, as his head was slightly turned. The bullet took out several teeth, some of them ending up on the floor. He was only a metre away from Safa at this point. The last shot wasn't enough to kill, but Manny collapsed onto the floor with a tremendous thud. Her second shot had finally had some effect.

Safa looked at Bobbi and went over to him. "Is there anyone else?" It came out as a scream.

"Don't think so. Get Robert loose first, please." Bobbi tried to smile, but it didn't come off very well. Safa moved over to Robert and struggled to loosen his bonds. She looked around for a blade to cut the tape but didn't see one at first. Robert nodded at the table by the wall, where the knife used on Bobbi was sitting. She retrieved it and got to work. He got up slowly.

"Give me your gun." Safa handed it to him, then went over to Bobbi. "And you are?"

"My name is Safa, Bobbi's sister." The tears were starting.

"Do you have a cell? Can you call 911, please? Get an ambulance and some police." Robert then walked over to where Manny lay on his back, moaning and bleeding. He looked down and briefly struggled with the training that had been drilled into him from his days as a new officer, but it was only a brief fight. He pointed the pistol at Manny's head, having trouble holding it with only two fingers and a thumb in working condition. Manny looked up at him, fear finally in his eyes as he realized what was going to happen.

"You have been sinning for too long, Manny. Time to atone." Robert fired at Manny's forehead. A black hole appeared, leaking blood. Wanting to be sure, he fired again, but all he heard was an empty click.

Robert went over to Ho Li-Fan's body. It was laying in a growing pool of blood. Robert wasn't interested in CPR or anything along those lines. He wanted Li-Fan's weapon in case someone nasty returned before the police arrived. He then retrieved his cell off the table, fumbled briefly with it and made a call to Tony,

"Tony, sorry to bother you on a pleasant Friday evening, but do you think you could find Vito and come out to Langley—tell Vito it's the farmhouse?"

"What? What's happening Robert?"

"Got waylaid by Manny. He is dead, mostly thanks to Bobbi's sister. It's a mess here. Wouldn't mind some friendly faces. Surrey Police and ambulances are on their way."

"Geez Robert. Okay, we'll get out there as soon as possible. Hang on." Tony then called Vito, explaining what was needed, then felt the urge to call Thomas to let him know what little he had been told by Robert.

Robert crouched down, rocking on the balls of his feet, watching Safa trying to wrap Bobbi's damaged hand, crying in fits as she realized what she had done, and what she had accomplished. Robert started to think as he watched Safa, and what he concluded that maybe Safa had been the one to kill Paneet. Good on her. He wasn't going to mention it to anyone. He knew that his career was about to take a bump or two once the various agencies started their investigations into what had just happened. Then he heard the sirens.

Back in Vancouver, on Marinaside, Norma was concerned. It was past six-thirty and there was no sign of Robert. She tried his number, but it went to message. She went to her computer to see if he had a land line she could try. Sure enough, he did, but again, no one answered. Was this all a big mistake? She didn't know what to do, except wait.

An hour later, her phone rang. "Norma?"

"Robert, what happened? I've been trying to call. Where are you?" Her voice was an octave higher than usual.

"Langley. Work related. Bobbi and I are a little worse for wear, but on the plus side of things, Manny is dead. I called Tony, and he is bringing Vito out here. I was hijacked by a cab to Langley. Not exactly the way I envisioned Friday night. I'm really sorry, Norma."

"Who is Bobby? Are you okay?"

"Broken fingers, hurts like hell. We are going to be awhile here, giving statements, then probably the hospital. Two bodies, and maybe a dead dog. I believe we will be put through the wringer. Bobbi is a gang member who was helping us."

"I'm coming out there." Norma sounded right on the edge to Robert.

He tried to calm her. "I'm okay, Norma. Don't come all the way out here. Too many procedural things happening. I'll call you first thing tomorrow. Hopefully, they won't keep me in the local hospital."

"I guess, Robert, as long as you are okay. Please take care. Please?"

"Will do Norma. Have to go now. Tony and Vito just arrived."

Chapter 31

onday saw Robert Lui arrive at Cambie Street to a royal welcome. Word had quickly spread about the shoot-out in Langley, so most of the office staff had heard stories, some of them already getting inflated by the re-telling. Robert nodded at people as he made his way to his desk, hand well bandaged in testament to his war wounds. Another bandage on his forehead covered the injuries that Manny had inflicted on him, this being surrounded by ochre and purple skin. Robert would not be doing cover shots for Gentlemen's Quarterly this month.

A few officers came over to congratulate Robert. Robert noticed Rodney Fister coming to the door of his office, watching the small commotion, but he declined to join the festivities, turning and closing the door. Robert desperately wanted some coffee but thought he should talk with Thomas first. He peered around his partition at Tony, who had beaten him in.

"I'll talk to Thomas, then we can go to our other office."

Tony nodded.

Robert got up and went over to Norma. "Is the chief in?"

"Please proceed, Robert." She grinned.

He rapped on the door frame as he entered Thomas's office.

"Enter." Thomas looked up from his screen and nodded at a chair. His expression was hard to read. "Well, Robert, I'll say one thing for you. You are nothing if not consistent. Another shoot-out with dead gangsters, and a media extravaganza added. I would congratulate you, but I've heard that there is a young girl who deserves no small bit of credit." He was smiling now, so Robert relaxed slightly, not sure where Thomas had been heading with his oration.

"What has happened to Safa?" Robert asked.

"She was taken into custody but released on bail. There is an ongoing investigation, of course."

"What about Bobbi? He didn't look so good by the time his sister arrived."

"He will be okay. Lost some blood when his finger was severed, and the beating to his head was not minor, but apparently he will pull through, although he may have headaches for a decade or two. I believe a surgeon tried re-attach the finger, but the jury is still out on whether it will be successful. He's still in Surrey Memorial Hospital. Surrey has an officer watching him, just in case any of the Two Tigers get ideas. However, I think they may be done as a force without Manny."

"Agreed. I think more than a couple of them may send flowers to Safa, not threats. That is, until they realize that their source of income has evaporated."

"You are going to be put on desk duties for a while, until you have healed, and the investigations have wrapped up. That will take some time, I suspect."

"Okay, thanks." He got up, nodded to Thomas, and left to go grab Tony. His hand ached fiercely.

Over at city hall, Mayor Stanley Dunbar was having a bad day. Kristian professed ignorance when confronted with the compromising photo, and asked Stanley what he had been smoking, then hung up. The next thing Stanley knew, the picture had mysteriously arrived on the desktop of a reporter for the local newspaper. The resulting media furor, along with the story about Nile Gecko, guaranteed that the Eco Party was done as a force in Vancouver politics. And Stanley really had no idea how this had all happened.

Nile figured that if he was going down, then he'd take someone with him, hence the picture of Stanley sampling the pleasures of Oslo being sent to the local media. Most of his so-called friends and fellow Eco Party members had been shunning him since the hydrogen contract revelations. Revenge was what he wanted, even as he really did not know how this had all been revealed to the public, thus who was really responsible for his predicament. Somehow, the thought that perhaps he was the author of his own problems didn't enter his mind. Even his own family were giving him a wide berth.

As they walked up to Cafe Paulo, Robert was uncharacteristically silent. Tony wasn't sure what to make of this. Robert hadn't said much on Friday night either, once all the officers and techs had arrived on scene. They entered and Robert acknowledged the shout from Gilberto with a smile and a wave. After ordering, Robert led